PRAISE FOR

SATURDAY'S CHILD

"A skinned-knuckle crime story . . . a two-fisted read."
—*Booklist*, starred review

"British noir at its darkest and meanest . . . Banks handles plot
U-turns with the bravado of a NASCAR driver . . . Banks has
an ear for the vernacular as sharp as, but a shade or two bluer
than, that of George V. Higgins. Let the squeamish stick with
Tony Soprano; this is real tough stuff."
—*Kirkus Reviews*

"Tough and assured . . . Banks is updating the noir novel with
an utterly original sensibility."
—*Publishers Weekly*

"*Saturday's Child* is fascinating, fresh, and darkly funny. It will
be an exotic entertainment for American readers of hardboiled detective fiction."
—THOMAS PERRY, author of *Fidelity*

"Ray Banks mixes sharp humor with crackling dialogue in a
wild ride across the pond. *Saturday's Child* is a page-turner,
start to finish."
—CHARLIE STELLA, author of *Mafiya: A Novel of Crime*

"Fast, funny, and hard as nails, *Saturday's Child* proves to America what the UK already knows: There's a heart in the darkness of today's finest crime fiction, and Ray Banks will take you there. Buckle up."

— SEAN DOOLITTLE,
  author of the Barry-winning *The Cleanup*

"A savage hardboiled spanking, *Saturday's Child* will leave you begging for more. Banks is a talented storyteller and a gifted wordsmith. He's also demented in the best possible way. Keep sending the creamy goodness across the pond, Mr. Banks. We want more!"

— VICTOR GISCHLER,
  author of *Go-Go Girls of the Apocalypse*

"Banks wields language with a knife-fighter's precision, with much the same result. From the first words to the last, this book flashes brilliantly."

— DON WINSLOW, author of *The Dawn Patrol*

"*Saturday's Child* has to be one of the finest PI novels of the year. With crisp, seamless prose and laugh-out-loud observations, Banks gives us a whole new spin on the classic detective novel. Ray Banks and his hard-edged, cynical PI Cal Innes are true originals. Read *Saturday's Child* and you'll realize that the future of UK detective fiction is Ray Banks."

—JASON STARR, author of *Lights Out*

SATURDAY'S CHILD

ALSO BY RAY BANKS

The Big Blind

Sucker Punch

RAY BANKS
SATURDAY'S CHILD

MARINER BOOKS
Houghton Mifflin Harcourt
BOSTON / NEW YORK

First Mariner Books edition 2009

Copyright © 2006 by Ray Banks

www.hmhbooks.com

First published in Great Britain in 2006 by Polygon

Library of Congress Cataloging-in-Publication Data
Banks, Ray.
  Saturday's child / Ray Banks. — 1st U.S. ed.
    p. cm.
  1. Ex-convicts — England — Fiction. 2. Private
investigators — England — Fiction. I. Title.
PR6102.A65S28 2007
813'.6 — dc22   2007007456
ISBN 978-0-15-101322-7
ISBN 978-0-15-603457-9 (pbk.)

Printed in the United States of America

DOC 10 9 8 7 6 5 4 3 2

To Anastasia,

mad but magic, there is no lie in her fire.

PART ONE

The Saturday Boy

You will be taken to the prison reception.

Reception made me think of an airy room with a bubbly blonde behind a counter, all smiles and bright eyes. It was a room, that's where the similarity ended. Badly lit. It smelled vaguely of shit, and I couldn't place the source. I didn't mind. I'd get used to it.

Already conditioning myself.

You will be allowed to keep some things. These things will become your 'property'. You will be asked to sign a form saying that you have seen what is in your bag, and that it has been sealed in front of you.

They asked if I understood what was happening to me. I stared at the fat guy with the pockmarked skin behind the reception desk. I watched the way his face moved. His cheeks buckled around the sides of his mouth. Before he got a chance to ask me again, I nodded. I understood exactly what was happening to me. I leaned over to sign the form. My wrist ached as I pressed down on the pen. When I set it down, I noticed blue ink on the inside of my hand.

You may have a bath or a shower.

I'd already had one that morning. The skin on my face still felt tight, newly shaved.

You will be given a prison number and told where to sleep. You will be seen by a member of the prison health team. Please tell the health staff if you feel very down or panicky or if you can't cope with your feelings or worries. This will be treated as medically confidential.

I went through the examination without complaint. I was fine, I told the doctor. Absolutely fine. I wasn't panicking. I wasn't worried. Everything was fine. Because I'd told myself this was inevitable. At twenty, I'd resigned myself to Her Majesty's pleasure. I'd already gone through the bullshit accusations in my head a long time ago. I'd already spat at the police, kicked off with the duty sergeant, and it had got me this far with a cracked rib (healing) and not much else.

And, Christ, I didn't show it, but I was knotted up inside. Scared wasn't the word. Petrified. Terrified. Stone cold fucking dead on my feet frightened.

Sometimes it doesn't matter if you're innocent or not. Sometimes all that matters is how you do your time.

I had a maximum of five years to look forward to.

Thanks to Mo Tiernan.

ONE

Always get the client to come to the office. Rule number one. Get them to come to the office or they try to fuck you over. Especially when they're out of their heads.

But my client isn't a client. If he was a client, he wouldn't have followed me into the gents' toilets at a pub called The Denton. He wouldn't have that Parkinson's tremble. And his grin wouldn't be so fucking desperate.

'You got the wrong Innes, pal,' I say.

The skinny guy with a face like a rolled-up newspaper shakes his head side to side. He *has* got the wrong Innes. He's after my brother, Declan. The brother who's now out of the city, in rehab, and a shadow of the junkie he once was.

But try telling that to the quivering psycho in front of me.

'C'mon, I got nowt. Got coinage, but I'm good for it. You know I'm good for it.' When he opens his mouth, he shows bad teeth. A by-product of the methadone, his gums purple in places. His eyes are clouded up like marbles. That's the valium, the temazepam. He should be calm, the amount of sedative in his system, but something sharp looms over the haze. Because behind that stare, there's a million thoughts swirling into one unassailable notion: I'm holding out on him.

'I don't have anything, mate. I think there's been a misunderstanding.' Trying to be diplomatic when my arse is clenching in time to my heartbeat. I start to back away from him. I'm slow, but the movement's still too fast for him. I'm holding out, and he's not letting me go without a scuffle. A blade falls into his hand. Short, jagged, looks like a chib. I've seen them before. I had one of my own not so long ago.

I wish Paulo was here. He'd know how to handle this. He's been working the doors since Moses wore blue jeans. But he's not here, so I give in. Hands up, show him my palms. Nothing here, mate. Nothing up my sleeve, either. 'C'mon, put the knife away, eh?'

His right hand curls and flexes around the handle, smooth wood, like he's just jammed a blade into a piece of dowel.

'Put it away, man.' My voice hardens. 'Don't be a dickhead.'

He thinks it over and goes for the second option.

He's slow with it. One step forward, and I feel myself pull to the side. My right foot digs into his instep. I hold it there, twist hard and watch him lose his way. His foot stays where it is, but his body crashes through the cubicle door behind me.

There's a clatter as he goes head first into the toilet. The blade skitters from his hand towards me. I toe it towards the door to the gents as he tries to pull himself up, one hand on the toilet bowl. His head turns, one eye closed. Searching for the knife.

What now?

Subdue the bastard. Wash behind his ears. I slip into the cubicle with him, drop to my knees and get a firm grip on the back of his head. There's no hair to hang onto, but I squeeze my fingers tight against his skull. He feels it, squirms under me.

I push his face down sharply. It connects, but the muffled crack tells me it wasn't with water. Blood runs down the porcelain. His body goes into spasm. Tries to pull up, but the back of his head catches the toilet seat, jamming him in place.

He spits blood at the wall, screaming he's gonna kill me, just you fuckin' wait. The toilet seat rattles on its hinges.

I use my weight on his head, make sure his face goes under this time. His right arm flails. His back tenses up. Got to keep him under. Just enough so all the fight's drained out of him. But not too much. I don't want to kill him.

The smackhead's right arm shoots out, elbow catching me full in the cheek. The shock keeps my grip tight, but my head starts buzzing. I can taste blood in my mouth.

He bubbles with rage just under the surface, grabs air when he can. Keep him held down until my arm is soaking wet, the muscles in my shoulder twitching painfully.

Then he goes limp.

About thirty seconds pass before I realise I'm still holding him face down. My fingers loosen on his skull, my knees ready to push up.

His head flies back, roaring, and I'm on my feet. He coughs, gagging on day-old toilet water. His eyes are screwed shut and there's a piece of shit on his cheek. When he coughs, he sprays a mixture of piss and blood at me. I grab him under the arms and yank him out of the cubicle. My feet slip on the floor; his start kicking feebly.

We stumble through the door to the gents, out into the bar. He kicks his legs out at passing tables, rattling ashtrays, spilling pints.

One bloke grabs his glass, lager slopped into his lap, and yells at me to take it outside.

'Fuck d'you think I'm trying to do?'

When we hit the front double doors, I launch him through. He buckles on one knee, tumbles down three steps into the street. Rolls forward onto his stomach, gags again, then spews onto the road. I watch him from the door, shake the water from my arm. Try to massage the knot out of my shoulder.

He pulls himself to his hands and knees, spits the last of the vomit from his mouth and fixes me with a glare. He'll be back. But I won't see him coming.

Oh yeah, I'll look forward to that.

I watch him get to his feet and back off down the road. Fireworks scream through the sky, glowing orange, bonfires raging from Salford to Hulme. A rocket explodes and throws the smackhead's shadow three ways before he disappears. The smell of smoke in the air makes my eyes water. The stench from my jacket doesn't help matters.

In the distance, I can hear kids screaming. Writing their names in the air with sparklers and looting industrial estates for pallets to use as kindling. Hell on earth to commemorate a traitor.

It's enough to give a guy a thirst. I spit blood at the street and turn back towards the bar.

TWO

Settled in at a corner table, a pint of Stella in front of me. I managed to salvage a few cigarettes from a wet pack of Embassy and I've got one of them on the go. The rest are pulped, a stodgy mess of wet paper and tobacco. The cigarette tastes like toilet water, but I still smoke it.

My shoulder still hurts, but not as much as my mouth.

I should've known better than to meet the client here. He didn't tell me his name on the phone, but he had that urgent tone I took to mean he needed help. Course, at the time, I didn't know what kind of help he had in mind.

Sip my pint, wash the beer around my mouth. The bugger took a good swing at my tooth. I poke around with the tip of my tongue. One of the molars towards the back waggles in the gum. I poke too hard and it starts throbbing. Another drink to numb the pain.

If he'd been a client, I would've charged him extra to get that fixed. And normally he would've paid it. But then normal clients don't take a swing at me. They get me to snoop on their beloved wife or follow their kids to see what they do nights. That's what clients want, a personal spy who doesn't judge. But business is slow, almost dead. That's why I came here. I must be losing my mind.

A plump blonde with black roots leans over the bar, giving the landlord an unhealthy dose of cleavage. She grabs a clear drink and spots me looking at her. I look away, but it's too late. She wanders over, her legs crossing as she walks. She probably thinks it looks sexy. It just looks like she's pissed.

I drain half my pint as she slumps onto the seat next to me. She takes a moment to adjust her dress, a black number that probably looked good when she was twenty pounds lighter, but which now clings to her like shit on a blanket. She fumbles with a pack of menthols, puts one between her red lips and lights it with a pink disposable. A few puffs, then she sets the cigarette in my ashtray. The filter's scarlet where her lips touched it: her lipstick, or her gums are bleeding.

'My husband's a bastard,' she says. Shifts her position so I'm pinned in the corner. She takes a drink from her glass. The smell of gin is heavy on her breath when she speaks. 'He's playing around on me.'

I don't say anything.

'I know you,' she says.

'You know me.' Plenty people know me. Most of the time, I don't want to know them. But there you go; can't have it all. 'Who am I, then?'

'You work for Morris Tiernan.'

My tooth pricks at the gum. I cover it with my tongue for a second to kill the ache. Then I take a drink to get rid of the blood in my mouth. 'I don't work for him.'

Her eyebrows arch. 'I thought you did.'

'I was working, Tiernan got involved. Doesn't mean I work for him.'

'Oh, right.' She closes one eye. Trying to wink, but she looks like she's having a stroke. 'I understand.'

Somewhere in the pub, a jukebox wails out a country standard. Stand by your cheatin' man, even though he beats the shit out of you and the dog. I don't want to be here much longer. As long as it takes to finish this pint, then I'm off.

'He's a fucker,' she says. I follow her gaze to the landlord.

He's a stocky guy, shirtsleeves rolled up to the elbow revealing two muscular and hairy forearms. From here I can make out blue tattoos, faded over time.

'That him?' I say.

'That's him.'

The knot in his jaw, the way he looks at his customers. Yeah, the guy's a fucker. But it's got nothing to do with me.

'There's always marriage counselling,' I say.

'Too late for that.' She turns to me. The light catches her face, and she looks drunker than I thought. No different to the rest of the wannabe divorcees who've accosted me since I got out of prison. Heavy round the hips, sagging up top. Lines around the mouth like the first strikes of a chisel against rotting wood. A sultry look that may have worked at one time, but has grown sickly with overuse. These women, they must smell Strangeways on me like a cheap aftershave. The prospect of rough trade, or something far worse.

She looks me dead in the eyes, says, 'How much would something cost, d'you think?'

'Something?'

'Something to happen to him.'

'I don't follow,' I say. But it's pretty obvious what she's after. Sometimes it's just a case of making them say it.

'Course you do.'

I smile, but I don't mean it. I look back at the landlord. He's fiddling with the till. 'I don't think you've got the money, love.'

'I can get the money.'

'And that's not the kind of thing I do.'

'Then what do you do?' she says. She squints at me, smoke from her cigarette swirling up into her eyes.

'What's your name?'

'Brenda.'

'Well, Brenda, you shouldn't be asking strangers to do over your husband. It isn't nice. Now, I never met the guy, but he looks like a proper shithead. And I feel for you, I really do. But knocking him off isn't going to solve anything, no matter how much you've had to drink.'

'I'm not –'

'Yeah, you are. Tell you what, you sober up and you still feel the same way, you give me a call, alright? We'll look at some less drastic options that don't involve GBH.' I write my name and office number down on a beer mat, slide it across the table to her. 'Don't get yourself worked up for nowt. God knows I'm cheap enough, so you have a think about it and get back to me.'

I down the rest of my pint and get to my feet.

Brenda looks up at me. Her eyes are watery, her mouth twisted. 'You need to help me,' she says.

'And I will. Just give me a call, okay?'

She thinks about it, stares at the beer mat. Then she grinds out her cigarette. Her hand is trembling.

'You okay?' I say.

'Fuck off,' she says.

She lights another cigarette as I move away from the table. Staring at the glass in front of her. It's all fun and games when she's playing with the idea of killing her husband. But once morality kicks in, she's deflated. Daft cow. Telling me to fuck off. It's her right, but I don't have to like it.

I pass by the bar. Brenda's husband gives me the evil eye. I give him one straight back.

Time I left, anyway. The whole night's been a bust.

THREE

'Mo, fuck's the matter with you?' said Baz.

I looked up. He were in the middle of summat, but I'd not catched it. He were looking at us, his eyes wide like I were supposed to say summat. He were a fat fuckin' bastard, were Baz. Big shoulders and a belly like a fuckin' toddler hanging off him. Didn't help that he always had his T-shirt tucked right in his trackie bottoms.

'You what?' I said.

'I were telling you summat, Mo. Rossie, he went and fucked a brasser up Cheetham Hill.'

'Uh.'

'Sharone,' he said. 'You know Sharone?'

'She's a fuckin' crack whore. I seen her with fuckin' Columbo, man. He selled her fuckin' rocks.'

'Aye,' said Baz. 'And Rossie did it.'

'Fuck's sake. He wants to get himself to the clinic.'

'Call him Johnny Nob-Rot, man.'

'Fuck off.'

'G'an, call him Johnny Nob-Rot.'

'You call him Johnny Nob-Rot. I'll call him Rossie Skank-fucker.'

Baz lapped that up and the vallies kicked in. I smiled. Didn't laugh, mind. Because even with the vallies, I still didn't feel like it. Not after the news I just had. I downed the rest of me pint and pulled on Baz. 'C'mon.'

'I still got a half here.'

'Fuck it. I'm off.'

Which meant he were giving us a ride. Baz swallowed what he could and we went. I got Baz to drive us over to the Wheatsheaf. He started on with pissing and moaning, but when he clocked the look in my eyes, he said nowt. Baz might've been a big bloke, but he knew when I were serious as fuckin' cancer.

'I got to go and see Callum Innes tomorrow,' I said when we was in the car.

'You need snooping done, like?' said Baz.

'What d'you mean?'

'Way I hear it, he's a private eye.'

'You what?'

Baz cracked a grin. 'Aye, he's a private eye. Like a fuckin' detective an' that.'

'You're kidding.'

'You never heard then.'

'Nah, I just thought he were a jailbird.'

'He got out,' said Baz. 'Fucker thought he'd set up his own PI business.'

'Fuck does he think he is?'

'Straight, from what I hear.'

'How can he be straight working for a poof like Paulo Gray?'

Baz liked that one. He laughed and I stared out the window some more. A private detective. Wondered if me dad knew about that. Probs. Which were why I had to go and see him.

Fuckin' private detective. Shit. How did that happen? Weren't so long ago the lad were throwing up on himself 'cause he were so scared.

Baz turned up the music, but it were gonna take a lot more than a tune to keep this lad from churning.

We got to the Wheatsheaf. I left Baz in the bar, went through to the lounge and saw me dad. He were in his usual place, right up against the window. He had a pint of the black and he were smoking. His old mates all around the place. Little Frank were crooning out summat about a daft tart called Kathleen. The fuckin' Irish, man, get 'em drunk enough and they'll sing any old shite. Dad liked the bloke, but I knew for a fact Frank liked to cut off cats' heads and leave 'em in people's cars as a joke. Yeah, he were sick in the fuckin' head, you ask me. Lad should've been banged up a long time ago.

But that weren't what I'd come for. I went right up to me dad and stood in front of his table and said, 'I thought you said we was keeping this in the family.'

Dad looked up at us like I were shite. 'I'm not talking about this.'

'You said we was keeping this schtum.'

'We are.'

'So what's this about me going to see Innes?'

'You're going to see him.' Dad screwed his Rothmans into the ashtray and lit another one, sucked half of it down with one draw.

'How's that keeping it in the fuckin' family?' I said.

He pointed at me with his ciggie. 'Watch your fuckin' mouth, Mo. Sit down and show a bit of respect.'

I looked around. People was staring. I wanted to knock a hole in their fuckin' heads. But I didn't. I sat down, said: 'I thought I were taking care of this.'

'I never said that. That's not going to happen.'

'You promised.'

'I promised nowt. You go sniffing about with your scally mates in tow, you'll fuck it up.'

'Dad –'

'Don't "Dad" me, you little prick. Do as you're told. You go round there tomorrow and you tell Innes I want a word. That's all you do. You don't tell him nowt about this, you don't say a fuckin' word, else I'll knock you sideways, you hear me?'

Wanted to tell *him* to show a bit of respect. Felt my left eye twitch and sting. Shook it out. 'Dad, he's a fuckin' pisshead. You want someone you can trust, know what I mean?'

'Yeah,' he said. 'I want someone I can trust. So do as you're fuckin' told.'

I had plenty I wanted to say; it were boiled up in my head. But I had to swallow it back. I stood up, left the lounge bar and slammed the door as Little Frank went into another song about Galway Bay.

Baz saw us and went, 'Y'alright?'

'Nah, mate,' I said. 'I'm pretty fuckin' far from alright, know what I mean?'

'Uh,' he said.

'Get us a Kronie.'

Baz got the landlord over – a fat lad called Brian – and told him what I wanted.

'Get us a brandy, too,' I said. And walked away from the bar. Slumped behind a table and stuck me hand in me pocket, felt for a couple vallies. Head spinning, and it'd take too long for the beer and brandy to kick in. I needed a helping hand. I popped the vallies and chased them down with the brandy Baz brought over.

Dad were Dad, like. I weren't about to argue with him, even though I wanted to. He said jump, you fuckin' jumped even if you was family. Used to be, he'd brought me up like I was his only, even after me mam fucked off. But these days, there were summat worn, summat frayed at the edges. Like he were itching to knock me on me arse. And there were nowt worse than getting floored by your own father.

Dad might've been a soft touch with everyone else, but he had a fuckin' blue-veiner for making my life shite.

FOUR

My head rattles like *Stomp* in stereo and the Greggs sausage roll I'm trying to eat is burning the roof of my mouth off. I huff and puff, finally spit the pastry onto the road and let the rest of it follow suit out of the window. Watch it jump and splatter under the wheels of the car behind me. Tell myself it was rank anyway.

Round Salford, the morning sun is a disc of yellow in a sky of smoke. Some of last night's bonfires have yet to be extinguished. Now the place looks like a riot's just finished. Footage of Bosnia, Belfast, Baghdad and now North Manchester. The streets are dead; all that's left is the vibe of something exciting.

I drank at home after I left The Denton. It took the best part of a bottle of Vladivar to kill the pain in my cheek. A quick examination in the mirror told me that the smackhead had almost knocked the tooth out of my head. I wish he had. Right now it's hanging by a nerve, throbbing like a bastard. I'd go to the dentist, but I don't have the cash. And it's been that long since I had a check-up, my old dentist is probably pushing up the daisies. Fuck it, I'll soldier on.

I'm on my way to a morning spar with Paulo, so he'll probably do me a favour and knock the tooth out for me. He's good like that. The guy might be pushing fifty, but he's still got a nasty right hook and an uppercut that could floor an elephant.

At this time of the morning, it's a quick drive. But when I pull up outside the club, Paulo's waiting for me with a face like a smacked arse. I check my watch: I'm still half an hour early. I slow the car; wind down the window as he approaches. This can't be good.

'What's up?' I say.

Paulo leans in. 'You've got company.'

'A client?'

'I fuckin' hope not, Cal. And you want to get him out of there before I get back from the paper shop, else you're both on the street, you understand me?'

'Hang on a sec –'

'I want him out. No buts about it.'

Paulo pulls away from the car, points at me, then starts walking towards Regent Road. I park up and get out of the car, chew the inside of my cheek. Company means one of two things. Either a client's in there, or Detective Sergeant Donkin's decided to pop by to fuck me over. Neither of which have made Paulo this edgy before. In fact, not a lot makes Paulo edgy. He's famous round here for being cool as.

Which makes me jittery as fuck.

I push open the double doors to the club, feel a wave of heat across my face. My back starts to sweat. This place was a second home when I got out of Strangeways. Paulo was the guy who got me my parole, stood by me. He saw something in me I couldn't see in myself. Took me to one side, threw me in the club with the rest of the prison-fresh lads and watched us beat the shit out of each other until we'd had enough. I was twenty-two then, it's a couple years on now, and I've worked out plenty of aggression in that time. I might be too old to keep coming back, but Paulo's got plenty of work for me. It's part of my probation that I still attend this place. Two years down and six months to go, then I'm a free man. Until then, I have to pop in and see my PO every couple of weeks. It's hellish. That tiny wee office, sitting there while the skinny prick patronises the hell out of me. He doesn't give a shit, to be honest. The moment he saw me, he saw the crime. And he didn't want to see any further. Which was fair enough. Because when I first saw him, I saw a prick. And I didn't want to see any further.

Me and Paulo talked about setting up the agency, one-horse operation that it is, and it was a joke until people started coming to see me. I don't advertise, but word spreads round here, and most of my clients aren't the type who have the money for a professional outfit. Either that, or they just don't trust the pros. It's got to the point where Paulo's charging me rent on the office.

He's got a cheek. It's really nothing more than a broom cupboard with a desk and two chairs in it. Oh yeah, and a window with a fine view of the bins.

The door's open. I can make out movement in there. Someone gangly, moving about at random.

My stomach turns.

No wonder Paulo didn't want to stay around. It's not the kind of company any ex-con would want to keep, especially one who's straight as a die and intends to stay that way. I blame Brenda for mentioning the name last night. Morris Tiernan's ears must have been burning.

So he's sent his son round to have a word.

Morris Junior, called Mo to avoid confusion. He's a six-foot-four beanpole with all the charm of a liquid cough. Bad skin, worse attitude, shaved head, a natural born scally. When Manchester was mad for it, Mo had his plooky hands full dealing out of a pub opposite the Hacienda. He was minting it then, but had his dad's knack for staying out of any serious trouble. When a couple of kids on mountain bikes let loose with a converted air pistol at the club's bouncers, people knew it was Mo fucking about. One dead, three wounded, and not a single charge the Tiernans' way.

Then Tony Wilson called it a night. Some say he was pushed into it. Too many drugs, too many bad influences, and Madchester was fading fast. The last night the Hacienda was open, when Wilson spread his arms and told the clubbers to loot the place, Mo was first in line. Back then Mo was pilled up and hip. These days he just gets pilled up and fashion can get to fuck.

I make my way across the club floor. Mo doesn't pay social visits. I look around the club for anyone I don't know. It's unlike him to turn up on his own; he's normally got a couple of shellsuits hanging about the place with car aerials in their trackie bottoms. But I don't see anyone. It looks like an average morning.

Step into my office, and he turns at the squeak of the door. His pupils are pinpricks in a sea of blood vessels. This isn't an early morning for him; it's a late night. He holds a bottle of Yop in one hand. When he sees me, he takes a swig, leaves froth on his top lip. It makes him look like a rabid dog.

'Y'alright, Mo?'

He studies me, then points one long finger at my face. 'Pastry,' he says.

'You what?'

The tip of his finger wiggles. 'You got pastry on your face.'

I wipe my cheek with the back of my hand and try to smile. Normally I'd close the door, but I decide to leave it open. If Mo flies in here, I'll need witnesses and an escape route all planned. 'What can I do for you?'

'How you doing, man?' He perches himself on the edge of my desk. His foot taps the floor.

'I'm okay. Hanging in there.'

'It's tough coming out, innit? Even what – two years, wunnit?'

'Two and a half.'

'A lot changes in that time.' He takes another swig from the bottle. He has a long, trimmed fingernail on his pinkie. The bastard wants to be a coke-snorting pimp. His tongue licks away the yellow foam, then he sucks his teeth. 'I hear you're all straight an' that now.'

'Straight as I can be.'

'You working for Paulo?'

'This and that, yeah.'

''Cause I heard you was like a private eye.'

'I wouldn't go that far,' I say.

'How far would you go?'

'I've done some work like that, yeah. Word gets around, I'll do some again.'

Mo nods, but it's not an affirmative. More like the DJ in his skull just mixed in a buzzing song. 'Fuckin' hell, I wouldn't have took you for a gumshoe, eh? Things change. Been a while since I seen you. Here, what happened to your brother?'

'Declan's in Edinburgh.'

'How is he?'

'He's clean.'

'That's good. Fuckin' gear, fucks you up. Kudos to the kicker.'

'I'll tell him you said hello.'

'No need. I'll probably see him soon enough.' Mo's lips part into a yellowish grin. 'Once a Manc, always a Manc.'

A Leith lad in Manchester is a Manc now. That'll make me Liam Gallagher. I'm not about to correct him, though. My accent was beaten down by the scally tongue a long time ago. I suppose it helps me blend in.

I light a cigarette. Mo's not here for a reunion. The last

time we spoke, I called him a daft cunt and butted him sharply just above the nose. I had my reasons. I was younger, stupider and I knew I would have been too scared to do it at a later date. But the way he's sitting there, dancing along to whatever rhythm his head's picked up this time, he's not here to do me over. This is a business call and, from the looks of him, he's not happy about it.

'What's up, Mo?'

His eyes narrow for a split-second, as if he's trying to remember why he's here. Then he licks his bottom lip and says, 'Me dad wants a word.'

'Anything in particular?'

'He just wants a word. Here, don't give us that face, either. He knows you're on the level now.'

Uncle Morris wants a word. That means he'll get a word, whether you want one or not. No questions asked. You're summoned, you go. Else he'll find you.

'Where's he doing business these days?'

'Usual place, mate.'

'Okay,' I say.

Mo gets up off the desk, smiles at me as he walks out of the office. I watch him as he lopes across the club. One of the lads recognises him, looks at me. I close the door and take a seat. Feels like I've just done six rounds; my legs are shaking. I stare at the floor, light an Embassy. Breathe smoke from my nostrils, watch it billow and disappear.

So what now?

A knock at the door. Paulo comes in and looks around the office before he speaks. 'Well?'

I don't look at him. 'It was nothing.'

'You sure? Fucker looked bloody happy with himself.'

'He's Mo Tiernan. He always looks happy with himself. Pills'll do that to you.'

'You about ready?'

I shake my head. 'Can't do it today, Paulo. Got other things to do.'

'Like?'

'Business, mate.'

Paulo watches me leave; I can feel him staring.

FIVE

The Wheatsheaf is a corn-fed pub just out of town. Too close to the motorway to be anyone's local, but it gets the family day-trippers every Sunday. The kind of pub with mock antiques and a wood-chip play area for the kids. A beer garden, horse brasses and a landlord called Brian West, whose name's on the lease but that's as far as it goes. To those of us in the know, it's The Uncle's office. And if you know that, you're already ears-deep in the shit.

I pop two Nurofen and wash them down with a bottle of warm water. As I pull into the carpark, I see a fat child screaming her way down a slide shaped like an elephant. Her dad, a Pringle sweater with the look of a fortnight father about him, sups a pint of real ale and watches her out the corner of his eye. Sunday drinking. Warm and relaxed, even though the skies are streaked grey and black. Outward respectability when a storm is brewing.

The way the story goes, Morris Tiernan once had a bad debt slit from arsehole to appetite. It happened at The Wheatsheaf. In the men's toilets, right by the novelty condom machine. Someone took a sharpened screwdriver, gutted him. While the guy was bubbling his last bloody breath face down in a urinal, Morris Tiernan bought a round of drinks for a wedding party he didn't know.

And now he wants a word.

I get out of the Micra, dump my final cigarette of the

journey and crush it into the gravel until the smoke stops. Take a deep breath, check my watch. It's noon. I spent a while in my car, unable to turn the key in the ignition. My hand shook too much. Thinking that they could call me back to the 'Ways just for talking to this guy.

It's taken me all my time to get here and now I am, I'm set to turn on my heels and hit the road. Morris knows I'm straight, but he still wants a word. That doesn't make sense and my stomach knots. The guy hasn't done a legal thing in his life, so what does he want with me?

There's only one way to find out.

I walk to the pub doors, pull them open. Inside, the place is dead. As I head to the bar, the doors close behind me like a gunshot. I flinch. Brian gives me a matey smile from behind the bar. A fat, balding guy with a moon face. He's nice enough, but he's one of the defeated. He'd let the world and his dog walk all over him if it meant avoiding trouble. Which is why he's in this hole. And he won't stop digging until he's six feet under.

Brian nods to me. 'Y'alright?'

'Been better,' I say.

'Drink?'

'Nah, I'm not staying long. He here?'

'He's in the lounge. He's expecting you.'

I push open the door to the lounge. It glides across the carpet with a whisper. Morris Tiernan sits in the corner, dressed in a dark blue Adidas tracksuit. Light from the frosted window next to him catches a large scar above his left eye. He's reading *The Racing Post*, a pint of Guinness on the table next to the paper. One hand rocks a pushchair. A toddler with a face like a bag of marbles is fast asleep.

The lounge door clicks shut. Part of me thinks it just locked. The same part of me starts panicking.

Morris looks up from the paper. 'Callum.'

I smile. My cheeks hurt. 'You wanted to see me, Mr Tiernan.'

'Yeah, take a seat.'

I look around for a chair. Nothing but leather-cushioned stools, built for midgets. I pick one up, buckle a little under its weight, and drag it over to Morris' table. Then I plant myself on it as casually as I can. My knees press into my chest. I look like I'm in pain.

'Who d'you reckon in the three-thirty Chepstow?'

'I'm not much for the horses. I wouldn't know where to begin.'

He scans the paper, bright blue eyes twinkling under a heavy brow. He takes a drag off a Rothmans and rubs it out in a large ashtray. Then he raises his head, stares at me. Sizing me up. I've changed since he saw me last, and he's noting each and every difference.

'You look better,' he says. 'Strangeways ironed you out.'

'Yeah.'

'That's good. Glad it had that effect on you. Don't want to end up like your brother.'

'He's fine.'

'Is he?'

'He's clean now.'

Morris raises his eyebrows. One of them doesn't move very far thanks to the scar tissue. 'Good for him. So what you doing these days?'

'This and that. I'm still on licence.'

'That's a shitter. Your PO a prick?'

'They all are.'

'I hear you're working down Paulo Gray's club.'

'Yeah.'

'He's a good lad, Paulo. You ever see him fight?'

'Not professionally.'

'I saw him fight once down the Apollo. He had a good combination on him, but he didn't have the balls to follow through on it. He could take a knock with the best of 'em, though.'

'I heard he was a good fighter.'

'He still work out?'

'We still spar.'

'Got to keep on top of your game.' He folds the paper, drops it on the seat next to him. Then he takes a long drink from the Guinness. His Adam's apple jumps as he swallows. He replaces the pint glass on its condensation ring and regards me. 'So you're a hardboiled dick now,' he says, making it sound like a personal threat.

'Sorry?'

'You do detective work. That's what I heard.'

'Nowt as flash as that, Mr Tiernan.'

'You find runaways?'

'I have done.'

'Good. I need you to find me a runaway.'

I feel sick. 'Listen, no disrespect, Mr Tiernan —'

'People say that, Callum, then they say something really fuckin' rude.' Morris' fingers tighten around the pushchair handle. The toddler's still asleep. He looks like he'd reach into the buggy and snap the kid's neck just to prove a point. And here I am with the spit gone from my mouth, trying to think of a way to say no.

'Nah, I don't mean to be rude.' I clear my throat. 'I'm not going to be rude.' Cut myself off before I start babbling. 'All I'm saying is that I might not be the guy for the job.'

Morris lets go of the pushchair. He lights a cigarette and stares at me through the smoke, unblinking. 'You're a good lad, Callum. Don't think I forgot what you did for Mo. That was beyond the call. You're straight; I can respect that. That's why what I'm offering is on the level. I wouldn't want you to get recalled. That's a kick in the bollocks.'

I nod to myself, try to control my breathing. Jesus, why am I so scared?

Because I know what he's like. I know how dangerous he can be. It's not like Mo. Mo's just a headcase. He'd top you and then puzzle about what to do with the body. Morris is the kind of bloke who has a shallow grave already prepared. And right now, the idea of a wood-chip burial is enough to make the back of my neck sweat.

'What is it?' I ask.

'Like I said, you find me a runaway. Simple as.'

'What kind of runaway?'

Morris flicks ash from the end of the cigarette. 'He's a dealer. Used to be, anyway. He worked for me until last week. That's when he went missing. And so did a sizeable amount of my money.'

'A dealer?'

He smiles; his teeth look bleached. 'Cards. I have a vested interest in some of the clubs round here. He was a blackjack dealer.'

'How much money are we talking about?'

'Ten grand.'

I try not to look surprised. 'I thought casinos had strict security.'

'Who said anything about casinos? I said clubs.'

'Right.' So the job's not legit. I had no reason to think it would be. But it's a hell of a lot more legal than I was expecting. 'What's the dealer's name?'

'Rob Stokes.'

'Anything more formal than Rob?'

'It's short for Robbin' Bastard. Who cares? The guy took my money.'

'So this isn't a runaway. This is a thief.'

'He ran away. That makes him a runaway. The fact that he stole from me's just another reason I want him found.'

'You have any leads?'

He bristles. 'If I had leads, I'd be chasing them up myself, son. It's not my job to have leads.'

I wish I'd bought a drink now, something to calm my nerves. And I wish I'd had the guts to say no straight off the bat. 'What happens when I find him?'

'You got a mobile?'

'Yeah.'

'Then I'll give you Mo's number. You find him, you give Mo a call and he'll take care of the rest.'

SIX

'Mo! Mo money, mo *problem!*'

That were Rossie, shouting across a crowded pub at me and Baz when we came through the doors. Rossie were wearing that leather jacket he said were Ted Baker, which were fuckin' bollocks, and made him look like double the twat he already was. Honest, like, a ginger cunt like Rossie, he'd look a twat in most stuff. But this jacket were his pride and joy. It hung off him like it were three sizes too big, which it probably fuckin' were. And Rossie didn't have the kind of hardness to carry it off. He were too small to be dangerous-looking, but that's why I liked him. Cunts reckoned they could start on him until he jammed that butterfly he carried in their balls. Surprise, surprise.

The place were chocka, the lunch trade in full swing. The landlord here did a fine line in proper *Corrie* Betty hot-pots, all meat and gravy and rank veggies. I wouldn't touch 'em with yours, like. Because I knew the lad what punted the meat on to this place. And beef didn't used to fuckin' miaow, know what I mean? Rossie did his upward nod from the bar and I jerked me head in response, did a saunter through the crowd. Digged a fucker in the ribs like I wanted to. He turned with a full-on wanker face. I gave him the teeth and he backed right off. Like I reckoned, soft as shite.

'Y'alright, Mo? Baz the spaz?'

'Fuck off,' said Baz.

'Get us a Kronie,' I said.

'Kronie,' said Rossie to the barman.

'And scratchings.'

'And scratchings.'

'What's up?' said Rossie.

'Eh?' I got me Kronie and sipped it. Cleared out the shite in me mouth.

'You look like someone pissed in your porridge.'

'I'm alright,' I said.

But I weren't. That cunt Innes put us right on edge. Couldn't get to sleep last night, so I kept pilling it. Feeling bone-cracked tired now, like. And I had to go over that cunt's place and play messenger?

As the Cockneys say: 'Faaack youse.'

Got Paulo giving us the evils as soon as I got through the door. Like I were summat he just scraped off his shoe. No way does a fuckin' cock-jockey get away with that, like. But nah, not right then. I were there on business, so I had to be ice. Suffer the fucker when I wanted to break his face.

Waited on Innes and took a look round his office while I was there. Nowt, man. If the lad was a private detective, he should have a bottle in the drawer or summat, but there were nowt. There was me, I were in the need to half-inch summat, just to keep me hand in, and there were nowt. So I got fuckin' edgy. Innes had put on weight since the last time I saw him. Fat fucker. Prison's supposed to harden a lad up, innit? Strip him lean and build him out of rock. But then, what the fuck did I know, eh? I'd never seen the inside of a cell. Been too fuckin' smart.

I supped me Kronie. Cadged a snout off of Baz. He had a mate what robbed them out the Kwiksave warehouse, so he were always flush. Lit it up and, through the smoke, I saw this boat I knew.

'That Dougie Harris?' I said.

Rossie picked at his teeth, followed me stare. 'Aye,' he said.

I hadn't seen him in a coon's age. Last time were when we was kids, like. He used to hang out with us in the tram station down Piccadilly. That were when I were on the cider and the blues. Dougie were always out his fuckin' skull on pills, like. Last I heard, he were on the smack. And it looked like it an' all. He had a bowling ball for a head, nowt in the way of hair and legs that'd break in a strong wind. The kind they said had a hard paper round, know what I mean? And top that off, it looked like Dougie'd seen the wrong end of someone's fuckin' boots. Burst mouth and two shiners. He were drinking a pint like it nipped his skull.

'I'm gonna chew the fat,' I said.

'C'mon, Mo. The lad's a fuckin' ghost.'

'Get off it, Baz. He were a mate.'

'*Was*, like.'

I went over to Dougie's table and slapped him hard on the back. His eyes swivelled in their sockets. When he looked at me, the colour went from his face – from white to fuckin' see-through. 'Y'alright, Doug? Rossie, get Doug another pint.'

'Tell him to get his fuckin' own,' said Rossie.

'You what?'

'Nowt.' And Rossie went back to the bar.

'How you doing, Dougie?' I said. Baz came up and took the other seat, looked from me to Dougie, then back again. He didn't know what the fuck were going on. And neither did Doug, from the looks of him. 'You look like pan-fried shite, son.'

Doug flickered with a dirty yellow smile. 'Bad night last night.'

'Tell us about it. What you doing these days?'

Baz shook his head. I looked at him.

'Nowt much,' said Dougie. 'This and that.'

'Same here,' I said. 'This and that. More of that. You working legit?'

'Nah.'

'You working?'

'Nah.'

'You need work?'

'I'm alright, Mo,' he said.

'I'm asking 'cause I might have some work for you, you need it.'

'I'm alright.' Dougie started gulping at his pint. Tried to neck the whole fuckin' thing rather than talk to me. Now what the fuck were up with that? A lad can't have a friendly how-you-doing without some cunt getting edgy? I sipped me Kronie, slipped a hand in me pocket and watched Dougie out the corner of me eye. 'You need owt, Doug?'

He shook his head. 'Nah, I'm off it.'

'Off it? You fuckin' must be, son. Baz, you remember that time Dougie took a dump in the canal?'

'Aye.'

'By Castlefield, wunnit? You just ripped your keks down and curled one right in the canal. Man, I fuckin' ended meself.'

Rossie came over with two pints. He sat one in front of Doug. I said, 'You brew it yourself?'

'Eh?'

'Where you been?'

Rossie frowned. 'At the bar.'

'Your face looks painful,' I said to Doug. 'You want a couple pills?'

Doug glanced at his fresh pint, looked like he was gonna throw. 'Nah, Mo. I'm fine. I'm clean now.'

Clean, my arse. I didn't need to see the tracks to know he'd been trainspotting, know what I mean?

'Aye, well,' I said. 'You can have a half.' I broke a pill and slid it up close to his new pint. He drained the old Kronie and chewed his bottom lip. He shook his head.

'You don't have to pay us nowt, Dougie-son. I know you're strapped. You always was. It's a freebie.'

'I told you, Mo.' He were smiling like it were a joke.

My left eye hurt. I had all snot in me nose, so I sniffed it back and swallowed. Cleared the rest out my throat with a gulp of beer. Picked up the half-pill and held it up to Doug. Then I dropped it in his pint. Bubbles fizzed all around it, like. Dougie Harris just looked at us, big old black eyes dead to the world, not a light in 'em.

Nah, it weren't a joke.

'Tell you what, I fancy a Courvosier. You want a brandy, Baz? Rossie?'

'I could drink a brandy,' said Baz.

'You want one, Doug?'

He looked like he were about to shit his pants. I got to my feet, slapped him on the shoulder. 'Course you do,' I said. 'Who turns down a brandy?' Lit a ciggie on the way to the bar, all fuckin' swagger and shit. Doug Harris turning down a pill. Pull the other one; that one's got fuckin' bells on it. That cunt what used to knock 'em back like Smarties and now the lad had a clean-living bullshit halo over his head?

Nah, man.

Leopards. Spots.

I leaned against the bar, waiting on the brandies. Watched the back of Doug's head, looked at Baz. If anyone were gonna help the cunt out, it'd be Baz 'cause Baz were a soft cunt even though he were a big cunt. And if he helped Doug out, I'd have it out with him.

Doug were talking to Baz. I couldn't hear him. The way Baz were talking back, they both must've reckoned I were having them on. I wanted to go back over there and stove the pair of them fuckin' nobheads in.

As the brandies arrived, I saw Doug knocking back his pint. Got back to the table, and he weren't finished with it. Felt my gut knot up so I dropped a couple of full kilt moggies into Doug's brandy and necked one myself. Sat and watched until Doug swallowed the rest of his pint, one eye on the brandy in front of him. 'That's it, Dougie-son. You sup up.'

'Mo, I'm off it.'

'I know, son.'

'Nah, I mean it, Mo. Joke's a joke, innit?'

'Sup up, Dougie.'

'Mo –'

'You a simple cunt, Dougie? Fuckin' tapped or what? Sup up.'

After another couple brandies spiked with half me stash, uppers and downers, Doug were having it large in his own back yard. Rossie and Baz and me, we watched him turn all the colours of the rainbow, watched him blink slow like his brain were fizzing out hardcore. Dougie Harris had turned into a proper lightweight. He looked like one of them rats they test the vaccines on, itching like a fucker. I watched him squirm and drank some more.

'We going out tonight?' said Baz. He weren't looking at Doug. Like he couldn't stomach it.

'Aye,' I said. 'We got to go see Columbo.'

'Fuck's sake,' said Rossie. 'Columbo's a creepy cunt.'

'You ain't gonna be in there, Rossie. I need you to do us a sly one.'

'What?'

I'd been thinking about it while I watched Doug wind

down. Dad wanted Innes to do this job for him, find Stokes, I still weren't comfortable with that. Innes were a fuckin' pisshead and whether he was a proper private eye or not, he had nowt in the way of bollocks. Certainly not enough to carry out a job like this. So fuck him and fuck Dad. I needed to sort this out on me own. 'I'll tell you in the car, Johnny Nob-Rot.'

Baz spluttered on his pint, laughing. Aye, I were a funny cunt. Doug giggled like a fuckin' girl, like a *nah-ha-ha-nah*, and choked out quick.

'You heard then,' said Rossie. He had a face like a cat's arse.

'Yeah, I heard. Now sup up and let's get the fuck out of here.'

We drank 'em off as Doug leaned on the table. He were dozed right out. Before I left, I went through his wallet. The lad had a score on him so I took it.

Way I saw it; it served him right for being a cheeky cunt.

SEVEN

Half now, half when I call Mo. I haven't opened the envelope Morris gave me, but it feels heavy in my hand. He gave me the address where Stokes used to work, a tattoo parlour on Hanover Street. I didn't know people gambled there, but then that was probably the point. It's a members only club. Morris said I'll be expected. Just head to the first floor and give my name. They'll let me in, no problem.

Morris promised me that we'd be even after this. I had no choice but to believe him.

And now I'm sitting here in my local, I'm wondering. Even for what? I've never done anything to Morris, I don't owe him a bloody thing. If anything, he owes me.

Find a runaway, simple as.

It's always simple as. Do a little work for Uncle Morris. Yeah, he's a little shady, got a few fingers in a few pies, but that doesn't make him a proper criminal, does it? It's good money and you know he pays in full.

A job, simple as. Keep your mouth closed, simple as. End up doing half a five-year sentence in Strangeways so a judge can prove a point. Keep a look out over your shoulder and try not to get killed.

Simple fucking as.

I sip my pint and stare at a framed picture of Manchester in the grimy days when it had an industry that wasn't customer service. A group of blokes wearing shellsuits are at the bar, talking loud and laughing louder. I try to ignore them. Tap the envelope with the tip of my finger until it becomes too much for me and I open it up, peek inside. About five hundred in twenties. I close up the envelope. A lot of money for someone like me, too much to explain away.

I have to tell Paulo about this. That, or avoid the club altogether. I don't see that happening, though. Paulo'd get suspicious. And then what? Out on my ear.

I could tell Morris I've thought about it, but I'll have to turn down the job. Life would be easier that way.

But then, according to The Uncle, I owe him. And I'll still owe him if I turn this down. The next job he offers me might be mandatory, and it might throw me back in the 'Ways.

Fuck. I have to do this. I don't see any way around it.

This runaway dealer, he's either ballsy as fuck or just plain stupid. I'm banking on the latter. That way maybe I can clear all this up before Paulo gets wind of what I'm doing, who I'm working for. Because I know I'll be up the creek if Paulo finds out. I drain my pint and push back my chair. Tuck the envelope into my jacket pocket, reckon I might as well get to work straight away.

The sooner I'm done with this, the sooner I can get back to normal.

The pub door opens as I'm putting out my cigarette. It's Paulo. Got a face on him. He heads straight for me. Fuck.

'Cal,' he says. 'Fancy one?'

I check my watch. 'Bit early for you, isn't it?'

'You already started by the smell on you.'

He orders at the bar, two pints. He looks at his with the eyes of a guy who used to enjoy his drink too much. Paulo shouldn't be drinking, not if his doctor has anything to do with it. But having Mo at the club's put him in a drinking mood. Paulo's got a good thing going on at the club, but it's precarious. He reckons it's because he's an ex-con, and that's probably got something to do with it. No matter how open-minded people say they are, you mention either mental illness or prison and they start looking for the nearest exit.

Paulo's had both in his life. One led to the other. He used to fight. Started out amateur when he was sixteen, turned pro in his twenties, but he never rose above mediocre. The way some of the old lads tell it, Paulo had flashes of brilliance in the ring, and he could take a punch or twenty. They kept mentioning Jake La Motta with his iron jaw. The guy was a bull, built like the proverbial shithouse.

Trouble was, Paulo Gray had something in his brain that wasn't quite right. He'd zone out at times, and that left him open. He'd sit in his dressing room and stare at the wall. One night, they say, it took two guys to drag him out of there. He wasn't scared, just depressed.

After that, he couldn't get the fights. He drank. And he ended up doing a bloke in a pub in Cheetham Hill with his bare hands. Paulo says he doesn't remember it and I don't push him. He's got other stuff to worry about. Sorting out the young offenders that come through his door in droves is part of it. Taking his medication is the other part.

Normally, I'd be out of here, but he's paying.

We return to my table and it's a while before he drinks. Even then, it's a sip. He savours the taste and looks at me. 'Got a new lad started this morning,' he says. 'Reminds me of you.'

'Good-looking, is he?'

'He's fuckin' angry is what he is. Tried to pick fights outside the ring. I had to batter him, teach him some manners.'

'Spare the rod, eh?'

'You know the way I work.'

Yeah, I do. Paulo's hard but fair. Once you have him as a mate, you're sorted. Stand by you thick and thin. And Christ knows there's been a famine recently.

'What did Mo want?' he asks.

'He wanted me to see Tiernan.'

'And?'

'And I went.'

'And?'

'Fuck's sake, Paulo. He wanted a chat. Asked me to do something for him.' And my heart skips, tooth pricking. 'I told him no.'

Paulo stares at me with clear blue eyes. Doesn't blink. 'What was it?'

'Does it matter?'

'You're right. I don't want to know. And you told him no,' he says.

'Yeah.'

'Good lad.' Paulo finally lets himself blink, returns his attention to his pint. Takes a large gulp. 'I shouldn't be drinking,' he says. 'Doctor said I shouldn't. One pint is all it takes, he says.'

'You're doing alright, though.'

'Yeah, because I know when enough is enough.' Paulo looks up at me. 'Self-discipline, it's tough. But it's worth it.'

I don't say anything. I just nod like I understand. But I'm already too busy thinking about Stokes.

EIGHT

I talked to Rossie in the rear view. He were all stretched out in the back of Baz's Nova, head against the window. It fucked Baz off summat rotten, but what were he going to do 'cept whine: 'Get yer feet off me seats, dickhead.'

Rossie shuffled his hand at Baz, then made sure he wiped his trainers all over the back seat. Baz glared at him.

'You know Innes?' I said to Rossie.

'I know the name,' he said.

'You know his brother.'

'Smackhead?'

'That's the fucker.'

'He were on that job with us,' said Baz.

'I ain't seen him about,' said Rossie.

'The smackhead's up in Edinburgh. Innes says he's on the programme,' I said.

Baz laughed.

'What's so fuckin' funny?'

'A smackhead goes to Edinburgh to clean up? Fuck's sake, that's comical, man.'

'Huh.' I didn't get it. They was both Jocks, it were where they came from. Why the fuck shouldn't the smackhead go back home?

Baz pulled the car round into Columbo's street. Columbo were old-school Moss Side Massive. Didn't matter how rich he got, he'd never move out. Like me dad, except Columbo had nowt. And I didn't like going round to see the cunt, but he were cheap and he knew not to tread on the merchandise too much else I'd have his balls.

I went up to Columbo's front door and pushed the bell. It were a musical one and it went on for ages. When he came to the door, Columbo hunkered up around the peephole. Which were a waste of fuckin' time because his front door had this pane of frosted glass in it. I slapped the glass and Columbo flinched. Jumpy fuck.

He opened up. I smiled. 'Y'alright, Columbo?'

He didn't look alright. He looked like he were passing a kidney stone.

Me and Baz slumped on Columbo's shit-brown couch. It smelled like someone pissed themselves on there and no-body'd bothered to clean it up. Baz were in the middle of rolling one that'd kill the smell just as soon as he sparked it.

Rossie were outside. He were making a call for us. I had to get him to do it. Them lads, they hear it from me, they might shit it 'cause I'm such a hard cunt. That, or they feel their balls getting bigger and start giving it with the jaw that they're working for Mo Tiernan. That couldn't get out. I weren't that fuckin' stupid – this had to stay under Dad's radar. So I got Rossie to make the call and I were laughing, man.

Baz sparked and I got on that bastard like it were mother's milk. Columbo were doing nowt in the way of trade right now. Too busy giving it some gum flappage about this red-hot dog-fuck porno he borrowed off this lad he did stir with. I didn't want to hear it. We was here to score, not listen to some daft cunt getting hot under the collar 'cause he saw some skank take it up the shitter from an Alsatian. He were talking about this bird licking the dog's balls when I said, 'Here, Columbo, you selling or what?'

Columbo were a fuckin' dwarf, or as good as. Looked like

the old bloke on the telly, had a glass eye the same as him. He were the only person I knew who had a glass eye, like. And it used to fascinate us, trying to work out which one were the fake. But now I just got fucked off with him 'cause I knew it were the right eye and Columbo were a cunt about bending your ear about nowt.

I handed Baz the spliff. Columbo pushed out his bottom lip with his tongue. A second there, and I thought the fucker were calling us a spaz. All ready to spring up and cut the cunt's tongue out his head until I realised he were just getting a bit corn out his teeth. His knees cracked when he got up, went to the sideboard. Columbo said, 'How much you want?'

'Eighty notes,' I said.

'Hundred,' said Baz, coughing through the tack smoke.

'You got the extra score?' I asked him.

'Yeah.'

'A hundred, then.'

Columbo mumbled summat under his breath. I didn't catch it, said, 'You what?'

'Nowt,' he said. Columbo slid the sideboard door across, pulled out a big bag of pills and wiped his nose. Made this noise like a slow-draining sink. 'All Bruce, eh?'

'Yeah,' I said. 'Chuck in a couple tammies an' all.'

'You want some Ritalin?'

'Fuck would I do with Ritalin, Columbo?'

'Swallow it,' said Baz, so I taxed the spliff off of him.

'I ain't got ADD, fuckhead,' I said to Baz.

'Nah, Ritalin's like whizz if you ain't got ADD. Give us a couple Ritalin, Columbo.'

Columbo measured out the pills. He kept wiping his nose. Wouldn't surprise us if he'd done a few lines before we came over. And it didn't surprise me that he didn't fuckin' offer it about, either, the tight cunt. I dug the cash out me back pocket, held it out to Baz for him to slap a twenty on there, then I tossed it onto Columbo's coffee table. Columbo looked at the cash and his tongue started roaming his mouth again. He dropped the bag of pills on the table. I went for it before Baz got a chance. 'Fuck's this?'

'Hundred notes,' said Columbo.

'Fack orf, mate. Where's the rest?'

Columbo sighed. 'Mo, you do this –'

'Looking at a pound a pill, ain't we? That don't look like a hundred.'

'You do this every fuckin' time, Mo.' Columbo closed his good eye and shook his head. 'If it weren't a hundred notes' worth, you'd know it, son.'

'Fuck you think you're talking to?'

'I'm talking to Morris Tiernan's son,' he said. 'And I wouldn't fuck you over because of that.'

I gave him a glare, then smiling teeth. 'I'm just messing. You're a good lad, Columbo.'

Rossie came into the room. He were putting his mobile in his pocket.

'We sorted?' I said to him.

Rossie nodded. He were ice cold, even if he did look a twat in that jacket.

'Then we're sorted.' I got off the couch and tucked the baggie of merch in my jacket, kicked Baz's leg until he got up. Took a couple of sharp ones, the fuck was feeling The Warm too much. When we was about to go, I turned around. 'Just one more thing, Columbo.'

'Aye?' He looked sick of my shit.

'You don't fuck me over because I'm Mo Tiernan, not 'cause I'm Morris Tiernan's son. You don't fuck me over 'cause I'll fuckin' cut you up if you even think about it, you hear what I'm saying?'

Columbo just looked at me. I couldn't read him. Didn't matter as long as he got the message.

'Yeah, Mo,' he said. 'I hear what you're saying.'

'Make sure you fuckin' do,' I said.

And I took the lads and left, went back to Rossie's gaff to prepare for the night's business.

NINE

It's not easy driving in Manchester city centre. In fact, it's a pain in the arse. Minicab drivers without fear, bus drivers with more road rage than sense.

So I leave the Micra in the shadow of Victoria Station and pay for an overnighter. I shouldn't be gone that long, but I can't take the chance of the car being towed. That happens, and I might as well be in a wheelchair, the amount of work I could do. Hanover Street's not far from here and the walk'll do me good.

The wind picks up around my waist; I pull my jacket tight. Rain is in the air. And the cold is making my head throb. As I turn the corner, I see the tattoo parlour, a place called Roscoe's. A blue neon sign advertises '*peircings*'. The windows are plastered with posters, mostly bands and DJs I've never heard of. One of them has a drawing of a mean-looking Goth holding up a dripping heart. I look for the handle to the front door. It doesn't have one, so I push. A small bell rings somewhere.

An antiseptic smell in the air, the trace of lemon. The floor is covered with linoleum that makes a tacking sound as I walk across it. A couch, coffee table and dirty-looking chair dot the room. A girl sits behind a counter with more band posters stuck to it. Probably the only thing holding it together. The girl looks like she covered her face in glue and headbutted a bag of ball bearings. She's reading a well-thumbed magazine with a bored expression. When she finally looks up, I notice her eyes are purple. It's a little startling.

'Can I help you?' She shows teeth, one of them streaked with a calcium deposit. Something shines in the back of her mouth.

'My name's Callum Innes.'

She blinks. 'You expected?'

'I think so. There should have been a call.'

'Uh-huh. Well, straight up the stairs, second door on your right. You can't miss it.' The girl points to a beaded curtain to my right. I nod, rifle through my jacket for my cigarettes. When I pull the pack, she taps a sign with one purple fingernail. 'Health regulations,' she says.

'Oh, right. Sorry.'

'No biggie.'

I part the curtain, feel the strands flick against my head as I pass through. Look to my left, and there's a small room with what looks like doctor's table. In a chair next to it is a guy with a full-on Rod Steiger, stripped to the waist, a roll of fat hanging over his belt. He's leafing through a thick book of tattoo designs, more of which hang on the walls. Celtic bands, swirling multicoloured dragons, flaming Bowie knives. He looks up at me and for a moment, my arse goes into spasm. I blink and see he's wearing opaque contacts. What is it with these people and their fucking eyes?

'You my three-thirty?' he says.

'Nah,' I say. 'I'm here to do some money.'

He runs his tongue over his top teeth. 'Kay. Well, she'll have told you where to go.'

'Yeah. Up the stairs, second door on the right —'

'And straight on till morning,' he says. He smiles, but only for a second. Then he goes back to his book. Yeah, thanks, Peter.

I head up a narrow stairwell. No need for a banister, the walls are that tight on me. When the space opens up into a landing, I'm confronted by a mountain masquerading as a bouncer. He's stuffed into a tuxedo two sizes too small. His shirt cuffs ride up on his wrists, prison ink spilling out from under. I need to take a step back to look up at his face, then wish I hadn't. He's done time, this one, and it wasn't easy.

'Yeah?' he says.

'Callum Innes,' I say.

He digs into his jacket pocket, pulls out a wrinkled sheet of A4, lined. Studies it as if he needs glasses but he's too vain to get them. With a boat like that, vanity should be the last thing on his mind. I don't tell him that. I value my scrotum too much.

'You got ID?' he says.

I show him my driver's licence. He takes it, compares the picture to what's standing in front of him.

'Morris sent me,' I say.

'Big whoop. Morris sends everyone.' He hands me my licence, jerks his head. 'Go on.'

I try to give him a friendly smile, but it doesn't feel right and he doesn't offer anything in return, so I move past him into the club. A cloud of cigar smoke hits me in the eyes as soon as I step through the door. The sound of chips being click-shuffled, the muted rattle of a roulette wheel somewhere and the throbbing undercurrent of cards hitting felt. As the smoke clears, I blink through the tears and get a better look at the room. It's crowded with gamblers, most of them too dangerous to hit the legit casinos. The bad vibe of barely-concealed aggression. Low ceilings smother us from above, thick carpet threatens to do the same from the opposite direction. A small bar on my right, blackjack tables in front of me, the roulettes behind them. And right at the back, huge red curtains tied back to reveal private rooms.

I recognise a couple of scallies with temper problems drinking at the bar, but they don't recognise me, thank fuck. Tiernan's lads. The last thing I want is to get into conversation with them. I'm sick of telling people Declan's clean, sick of seeing their eyes glaze over.

Oh, right, yeah. Your brother's clean, he's off the junk. Good on him. No more gabbing to the busies for a baggie of black. No more living in his own filth. He's fine, that's a good thing.

Have a drink on me.

I head to the nearest blackjack table, find a spot and get seated. Hand over a tonne to the dealer and get twenty reds back. I sit and fiddle with the chips, try to look like a proper punter. When I see the dealer staring at me, waiting, I smile and slip a tenner onto the table. He clicks onto autopilot, starts dishing out the cards.

Five minutes later and I'm down to half my stack. The other players aren't the best conversationalists. In fact, they haven't said a thing. They came to play.

'Been a while since I been in here,' I say.

A grunt from two seats down. The dealer doesn't acknowledge me.

'Yeah, used to be a dealer here, a guy called Rob. He still about?'

'Card?' says the dealer. He stares at me intently. Something in his eyes, but I can't make out if I've hit a nerve or not. He might just hate all the punters in here. I look down at my cards. Sixteen. I take another. The dealer flips a four. I stay.

'So I don't see him about,' I say. 'What happened? He get the sack or something?'

No answer. The dealer continues as if I'm not there.

'Fine, fuckin' hell. Just trying to make a little conversation.'

The Chinese guy next to me turns his head, looks me up and down. 'No here for talking,' he says. 'You play, you no play.' He points at me with his right hand. I notice two fingers cut off at the knuckle. A tattoo on his neck, a bluebird peeking out from under the collar. He's an old-time wannabe Triad, maybe a real one. I don't want to find out which.

'Okay,' I say. 'That's fine with me.'

'Card?' says the dealer. This time, there's a twinkle in his eye. If I didn't know better, I'm sure he's laughing at me. My heart starts to beat faster.

I have seventeen in front of me. 'What do you think?' I ask him.

His lips twitch as he moves to the Chinese guy.

'Oi,' I say. 'I didn't say I was staying. Gimme a card.'

The dealer's eyes narrow for a second. Then he slaps a queen in front of me, rakes in the cards and my cash in one fluid motion. The Chinese guy is sitting there with nine, and he looks fit to cut my throat.

'What a pity. Never mind.' I get up from my seat, taking the rest of my chips with me.

Fuck the dealer. I should have known he'd keep his mouth shut. And I was hardly subtle about it, but then I'm not used to being in places like this. Word spread, obviously. Employees banding together against a common enemy. In this case, it's Morris Tiernan. And me, I stand for Morris. It's okay, though. I'll find someone with a mouth on them. I always do.

I just have to bide my time.

TEN

A couple of bottled beers later and I feel loose in my skin. I'm leaning against the bar, sipping a Becks. The scallies I know have gone, so I'm more relaxed. I'd be even more relaxed if these drinks weren't costing me so much.

The barman is a gangly lad with a perpetual stoop. Like every other employee in here, he's wearing a dress shirt and dicky bow. But the dark sweat patches under his arms and the luggage under his eyes give him away.

'You work here long?' I say.

He doesn't say anything, busies himself with the optics. I watch him. He's trying to avoid me. I slap two red chips onto the bar. 'Oi,' I say. 'I'm talking to you.'

The barman turns, clocks the chips. 'You want another drink?'

'You know a guy called Rob Stokes?'

'Nah,' he says.

I light an Embassy. 'He was a dealer here.'

The barman shakes his head.

'You don't know the dealers?'

'Nah.'

'You don't take breaks together?'

He doesn't answer. He's watching something over my shoulder. Feels like the floor just listed to one side, so I'm guessing the bruiser on the door just walked in.

'What are you, a fuckin' mute?' I say.

'Nah,' he says.

For fuck's sake. 'Fine, don't talk to me.'

I turn away from the bar, take a swig from the bottle. Sure enough, the doorman's looking at me, even though he's pretending not to. Got that shifty-eyed glance going on, as if he's not sure what he should be doing. I stare right at him. This place is tight. No wonder Morris couldn't get anything out of the staff.

'You don't have to talk to me, mate. But you will have to talk to someone sooner or later. This Rob Stokes isn't going to get away scot-free.'

I let that hang in the air. The barman's stopped moving.

'Tell you what I'm going to do. I'll leave you my number. You get over your lockjaw, you give me a bell and we'll talk about it.'

'I don't talk to the police, mate,' he says.

'I'm not the police. And I'm not your fuckin' mate.' I turn back to the bar, see he's still looking at the bouncer.

I write down my mobile number on a napkin, push it towards him. 'My name's Callum Innes. I'm a private investigator. And whatever you say to me is just that: private. You've got nothing to be afraid of.'

The barman gives me a look like who do I think I'm fooling?

He's right. It's all shite. But sometimes it works.

'Everything alright here, Kev?'

It's the bouncer. And I didn't hear him coming. He's almost right on top of me when I turn. 'Everything's fine,' I tell him. 'Me and Kev were just shooting the breeze.'

He doesn't look at me. The mountain and the barman, exchanging glances like a couple of star-crossed lovers. It's enough to make me sick. 'Here, Kev, I'll have another Becks, mate,' I say.

Kev doesn't move.

'I think you've had enough,' says the bouncer.

'You what?'

His hand opens, gestures towards the door. 'You're not welcome here. C'mon.'

'C'mon where? I've had three fuckin' beers.'

'No need to get lippy with me, son.'

'I'm not getting lippy with you. I'm stating a fact. I've had three beers. I'm a member.'

Look at the bouncer's eyes. They disappear into his skull. His piss is pure boiled about something, but his voice doesn't show it. 'I think you've had enough,' he says again, and puts one huge hand on my shoulder.

Two ways to go with this. I can kick off and get battered, or play possum. The rising heat in my face makes me want to take this empty Becks bottle to the mountain's head. His hand on my shoulder tells me to think again. He's got power in those fingers, so God knows what the whole limb's capable of.

That's what makes me bottle it. This place is far too dangerous for someone with my disposition. Fuck knows I've tried not to panic since I got out, but times like this, the fear takes over.

Keep calm, Callum.

Smile. Be nice.

I smile, but I can't be nice. 'You want to take your hand off me, pal?'

'I think it's time you left.'

'And I think you do too much fuckin' thinking.'

'I think —'

'Watch it. Your noggin might overheat. But you know what? I think you're right.'

I neck the rest of my beer and slip out from under the bouncer's grip, head to the door. Behind me, I can hear conversation, but can't make out the words.

Yeah, I think. Who was that masked man?

ELEVEN

Someone told me that the difference between a pub and a bar is that a bar has more mirrors to show you how fucked up you are.

I need a drink after my brush with the bouncer. Something to settle my heart rate. Somewhere to lie low and take stock. I'd head up to Oxford Road, bury myself in an old man pub vibe, but it's too much of a walk. So I scout around and find a place in Withy Grove that looks like Austin Powers' worst nightmare.

Beggars and choosers spring to mind.

Lines of purple and white swirl across the ceiling. I go down the stairs into a club that's already starting to fill up. Air-conditioned, dark red and pink. I feel like I've walked into a lung. A quick scan of the place then I walk over to the bar, hoping to get a drink down me before the music kicks in properly. At the moment, I can hear a low funk-jazz thing going on, the kind of music that makes me think I should be wearing a pimp suit and shoes with goldfish in the heels.

I pay for a bottle of Holsten Pils and try to look cool by leaning against the bar. From the glances I get, I'm not doing a great job. They know I'm not one of them and they're vaguely annoyed.

Yeah, these people, they're a completely different class. Seems to bother them more than it bothers me, though. I look around, not afraid to make eye contact.

A working-class hero is something to be. But then, six bullets, point blank, and not one of them hit Yoko. Think on.

The young and the restless, the upwardly mobile and sexually aware new professionals. Formal coats, suits and ties. Mobile phones that come with cameras, games and wireless broadband internet capabilities. Glasses that didn't come from Specsavers, more likely to have Red Or Dead on them.

I could have been this, I reckon. Minded my schoolwork, stayed clear of the wrong crowd. Remained in Leith, kept my head down, grown a fucking goatee and ended up doing data entry for enough money to get hammered on the weekend.

Yeah, right. Like there were data entry jobs in Leith. And I didn't have the brains to work in HMV.

I lied to myself about the chances I'd wasted. That's the way the song goes, even if the tune doesn't stick.

Rob Stokes took the chance. The only thing he lied to himself about was thinking he could get away with it. He's done a pretty good job so far, but it won't last. He got out of there, and the staff at the club won't talk. It comes back to me, that lifer look in their eyes. They don't talk about Stokes because it isn't true, *can't* be true. This phantom dealer with the balls to grab ten grand and bolt, he's a myth. Those dealers, the last thing they want to believe is that it's possible to get out of the business. And so they keep quiet and keep the cards coming.

I drain the bottle, stifle wind. Call the girl behind the bar and get her to set me up with another and, what the hell, a double Jamesons to break the gas.

A couple of blondes, one obviously more attractive than the other, are settling into a booth. Giggling, gesticulating. Career girls through and through. The attractive one has the burnt sienna skin of a sun-worshipper; her friend the Tango hue of a stand-and-tan, pale flab peeking out from under a crop top. The sad thing is, they're both out of my league.

There was a girl at school, but that was too long ago to mean anything. Some more along the line, but nothing you'd call love. Certainly nothing I'd call serious.

Sex hasn't been an issue.

They told me inside, that's all I'd want when I got out. Some lads, they became obsessed, nearly went blind with wanking. Which was a tough thing to manage, considering you didn't get a lick of privacy. But that's what they talked about, who they'd fuck their first night out. Jo Guest, Cameron Diaz, could've been Anne Widdecombe – it didn't matter who, any hole's a goal and all that. It didn't happen for me. I had other things on my mind.

Something always gets in the way.

I down the Jamesons – balls to savouring it – and finish off the burn with a swallow of beer. And Christ, I wish this place had tables. Somewhere to sit. My knees are starting to feel loose. I pull myself upright and wander about, bottle in hand.

Totally self-conscious as Bobby Womack launches into 'Across 110th Street', the volume rising, bass shaking. It's official. I'm Shaft in photo negative.

Up a flight of steps, and there's a seating area overlooking the dance floor. I take the steps two at a time, feel a creak in my knees. Halfway up, I have to take a breather. I lean against the railing and survey the dance floor.

A couple of hours, and I get my exercise going to and from the bar. My own fault – I broke the seal with that first Jamesons. When I check my watch, I have to concentrate on the numbers. Fuck. I should go home, but my legs feel like they want to stay here. Counting the drinks since this morning and it all adds up to too many.

A scally lad just walked in. He's at the bar now, counting

the change in the palm of his hand. I freeze. He sticks out like a sausage in a synagogue, and paranoia tells me it's me he's after. It doesn't make sense. But then, that's the thing about paranoia. It doesn't have to. I keep an eye on him as I climb the rest of the stairs, stick to whatever shadows I can find.

The scally turns and leans against the bar, a pint in his hand. He hasn't touched it, surveying the dance floor with all the intensity of a tail. He's long-bodied, pale in the light. And he doesn't look like he's bothered about being out of place in here. He's too busy thinking about something else. His steel face gives it away. Reading his watch would give him that same concentrated look, though.

I sit on the edge of a backless couch with a cow-print pattern as the lights in the place start to move, dappled, across the dance floor.

He looks around the place, his head bobbing as someone moves into his line of sight. He doesn't think to lift his head. He sips from his pint. I'm trapped up here.

Nah, nobody's trapping this bloke. I'm a bigger man than that.

I get up, finish my beer and put the empty bottle on the table next to me. Go straight for the stairs and down onto the dance floor, keep my head down but the scally in my peripheral vision. There's only one way to get round this, I reckon. And that's to call the bugger's bluff.

The scally rolls his shoulders back when he sees me. He's definitely a tail. I turn on my heel and make straight for the bar. His face tightens. As I reach him, he moves to one side, his trainers squeaking on the floor.

'You want a drink, mate?' I say.

'I know you?'

'I was about to ask you the same thing.'

'Dunno what you're talking about,' he says. His left eyebrow twitches; a terrible fucking liar.

'Tell Morris I'm handling it.'

'Fuck you talking about?'

I look at him, make sure I've got his full attention. 'You tell Morris I'm fine by myself. I don't need help on this.'

He shakes his head. 'Who the fuck's Morris?' His face all screwed up, not meeting my eye.

'I see you again, I'll knock you on your arse,' I say.

'Whoa, what's up with you, man? I'm just having a drink.'

'You're a fuckin' scally.'

'Who you calling a scally?'

'I don't like being tailed.'

'Tailed?' He laughs. It makes him sound like a twat.

I grab him by his tracksuit and his hand opens around his pint. The glass drops to the floor, smashes. And suddenly he's all indignant, puffed up and ready to fight. I push him hard in the chest and he slams off the bar. The scally gets his balance the same time he gets his breath and makes for me.

Someone shouts for security. But I'm already out the door.

I pull my jacket tight, shivering from the cold and maybe just a little fear, start walking back to Victoria Station. I look over my shoulder, waiting for the tail to come running after me. He doesn't. The pit of my stomach feels like it's twitching, trying to digest something that isn't there. I let loose with a loud belch, then light a cigarette to stave off the cold.

My head's whirling. Maybe I'm going nuts.

Get it together.

I find my Micra, slip behind the wheel and chew the inside of my cheek. I could go home, but I wouldn't sleep. Check my watch, and it's probably about time the dealers at Morris' club knock off. I could stop by, see if I can't have a word with that barman again, maybe chip some information out of him.

I turn the key in the ignition and Billy Bragg starts playing, a busker voice and a one-amp guitar. Twenty-one years when he wrote this song. Doesn't want to change the world. Who does? Too much work, too little respect. I'd settle for beer money and a roof over my head.

A short drive to Hanover Street, and I park behind a Ford Escort with a bad paint job. I'm guessing that the staff go in the same way as the punters, so I watch the front door, Bragg turned down.

This is how I spend most of my time these days. Sitting. Waiting. Watching. Listening to music at an inconspicuous volume and hoping to Christ I don't get spotted. When I started this job, I was prison-hard. I wasn't afraid to walk down them mean streets with a rude wit and clenched fists. I had ideas. But the streets take their toll, and I soon found out it was safer to sit in a car than be out in the open. I don't run as fast as I'd like, not as fit as I need to be. So the Micra it is.

I turn off Bragg, stick in The Smiths. I should invest in a CD player for the car. Spend some money on it. But then the kit would be worth more than the car, and I'd come out the flat one day, find a gaping hole where a Blaupunkt used to be, the rest of my motor in flames. Kids'll torch anything round our way.

So I'm sticking with tapes.

Eject Morrissey and Marr, stick in The Animals. I listen to the opening bars of 'We Gotta Get Out Of This Place' then stop it before Eric Burdon kicks in with the vocals.

Fuck's the matter with me?

You're being followed, Cal.

That's not the case, though. I know that. That bloke in the bar, he could've wandered in just like me. He could've been checking out the meagre talent on display. There are some blokes who don't realise that there are boundaries when it comes to scoring. I've seen enough pissed-up tracksuits trying it on with office totty. He might have been one of them.

It's this job. I'm not sure of anything. Doubt's a pisser.

Sitting in silence now, wishing I was home, but knowing I can't go back yet. My skin crawls with the cold. I'd turn the heater on, but it'd be like kicking this car in the bollocks. Besides, the amount of drink in me might knock me out if I get too comfortable. I crack open a window, light a cigarette and inhale.

My mouth feels dirty. I open the glove compartment; see if I can't find a mint or gum or something. A tidal wave of mix tapes spills out onto the passenger seat. Tom Waits, Joy Division, more Smiths, Warren Zevon, The Stranglers, Elvis Costello, Ian Dury and some crappy tape I got free from a magazine that promised New Wave, but gave me New Romantic. And, at the back, an opened pack of Extra. I struggle with the wrapper, take the last piece. Pop the gum in my mouth even though the coating's cracked and it tastes like an inner tube.

I start shovelling the tapes back into the glove compartment, manage to pile them all in there and close it with a dull click.

'Fuck are you doing here?'

I jump across the car. It takes me a moment to place where the voice is coming from, and when I do, all the alcohol drains from my system.

The doorman. That big bastard bouncer who chucked me out this afternoon. He's wearing a black puffer jacket. Light catches the massive sovereign rings on his fingers and a dirty twinkle in his black eyes. 'What'd I tell you?'

I try to get my cool back. 'What did you tell me? My memory's shot.'

'You're not welcome at the club.'

'I'm not at the club.'

'You're near enough. What you waiting on?'

'A bloke can't sit in his car?'

'Get out.'

'You know I'm working for Morris.'

'I don't give a shit who you're working for. Get out the car or I fuckin' drag you out.'

'Listen to me,' I say, but my voice cracks into a whine. 'Morris Tiernan hired me to find a dealer who used to work for him. His name's Rob Stokes, right? And he's fucked off with Morris' money. Now Tiernan wants –'

One hand on my mouth, the other wrapping fingers around my throat. I choke out. The bouncer removes one hand, pulls his fist back and cracks me hard with those sovereigns. I black out for a second, come back to the here and now with his fingernails digging into my neck. Blood all over my jacket and one nostril feels like it's been ripped open. I scrabble against the door, black flies instead of vision.

He gazes at me, eyes half-closed, and squeezes my throat.

I try to tell him to wait up, hold on, let me explain, but it comes out like Donald Duck with a voice box.

'Get out the car,' he says. Low, soft.

I get out the car, I'm as good as dead. I don't get out of the car, I'm as good as dead. Rock, meet hard place. My hands flap, telling him to calm down. Ease off so's I can open the door. If I get out, I might have a chance to take off running, even though my lungs feel like they're fit to burst. I know I wouldn't get far, but when the devil shits in your pillow, sometimes you've just got to pretend it's extra stuffing.

The bouncer's fingers loosen. I try to smile at him. He doesn't smile back.

I glance at the tape deck. It's still on. Which means a swift twist of the ignition, and I'm out of here. That's if I can manage it without him crushing my windpipe.

Reach across and unlock my door. The doorman removes his hand and cracks the knuckles. I rub my bruised neck, cough my voice back into action. 'I wish you'd let me explain.'

I put one hand on the door handle, click it open. My foot eases onto the accelerator.

He catches the movement. He lunges.

As I turn the key, the engine coughs. The bouncer's eyes become wide, like what the fuck do I think I'm doing? This was supposed to be a one-on-one. His top lip curls.

The engine catches as I throw open the driver door. It glances off his right knee as he makes a grab for me. One short dig in the kneecap and he twists away, his hand falling short, his face all screwed up with anger and pain.

I floor it.

Pull on the steering wheel as hard as I can, and the Micra jerks forward, pranging the car in front with a grinding shudder. I keep the pressure on until something snaps. One of the Escort's hubcaps goes spinning into the street. The Micra's engine screams at me to take it easy, but panic has taken over. I need to put as much distance between me and the bouncer as possible. I hear his hand slam the boot of the car and tense up. Keep the motor gunned, trying to do nought to sixty in first gear.

Nothing but the roar and whine of the car in my ears now. When I'm halfway up the street and the engine sounds like it's going to blow, I force myself to ease off on the accelerator. A quick look in the rear view and the bouncer's nothing but a hulking shadow. Jesus, that was close. I ease down at traffic lights, head back to Salford. Settle back into a rhythm; let my lungs catch a decent breath. My throat stings, feels like someone took a cheese grater to it. I cough up something slick that tastes of blood and spit out of the window. Check myself in the rear view mirror. I'm a fucking mess. My nose has stopped bleeding, but one nostril is torn in the middle. Those bastard rings. Big ugly bruises on my neck, and it feels like he broke the skin somewhere.

As I pull into my parking space, I light another Embassy. Something is seriously rotten in Morris' club, and I'll be fucked if I let some steroid freak stop me finding out what it is.

I get out of the Micra, inspect the damage. The left wing is scratched and battered to hell, but I suppose it adds character. I'll put it on expenses, let Morris pay for it. Maybe I'll have a word with him about his bouncer. I might even let Mo have his wicked way.

Man, my neck really hurts. And to cap it off, my tooth's started throbbing again. I get into my flat, pull the half-empty bottle of Vladivar from the freezer and take a swig. The first hit tugs on the raw nerve, the second freezes the pain. Bring it with me into the bathroom. I take drinks from it as I mop the blood from my face with a damp flannel. Dabbing, not rubbing.

Yeah, my nostril's ripped. Not a lot, but enough to give me the look of a bad boxer. I peel the back off a plaster and slip it over the tear. A couple of prods, and it looks like it might stick fast. Another drink to celebrate.

I can't do anything more tonight. Might as well try to get some sleep.

I think I deserve it.

TWELVE

'You fuckin' what?' said Rossie. His face had gone a slapped-arse red. 'You fuckin' what? You're having a fuckin' laugh aren't you, Darren?'

Baz and me looked at each other. Baz said, 'Some lads don't like to swallow. Crying shame, innit?'

'I asked you to do one thing for us, right? One fuckin' thing. And you couldn't do that, could you?'

I watched Rossie in the rear view. He had his head down. I saw a bald patch starting on the top of his head.

'Nah, don't give us that, son. And don't think you're getting a fuckin' penny, either.' Rossie beeped the lad off and sucked his teeth. 'That scally fuckin' wanker.'

'Didn't go well then,' I said.

'He fucked it up.'

'Then you ought to fuck him up, Rossie.'

'Innes spotted him.'

'Who'd you use?'

'Darren Walker.'

'Why'd you use that cunt? He couldn't find his arsehole, two hands and a map.'

'He owes us a favour,' said Rossie.

'Looks like he still owes you that fuckin' favour.'

We was in Baz's Nova, headed out for the night. Baz had turned on his *Fast and Furious* underlighter, which made the car look like shit, but Baz were proud of it. I reckoned it looked about as gay as you could get.

Normally I would've been buzzing, but that phone call Rossie just took put a proper crimp on the evening. I turned round in me seat. 'So what'd he say?'

'He says Innes saw him.'

'Where'd he go?'

'Some bar in Withy Grove.'

Baz snorted. 'Darren in Withy Grove. No wonder he got fuckin' spotted.'

'Before that,' I said.

'He was round at the club,' said Rossie. He had a sour face on him, like he didn't care for me asking all these questions. Like I gave a fuck.

'The club?' I said. 'Yeah, right. The club.' Course he would've started there, wouldn't he? Stokes worked there, it were only fuckin' right the cunt Innes would've started beaking it round there. But he would've got nowt, like. The word had already gone round that place like fuckin' wildfire. Just a rumour – Mo'll kick your fuckin' teeth in, you say owt – but a rumour well spread. Dealers, man, they fuckin' shite it at the first sniff of a pasting. And I were discreet about it. I didn't do nowt 'cept get Rossie to break a lad's wrists.

Try dealing now, cunt.

We pulled up in the NCP in town and I got out and let Rossie stretch his legs. Baz lit a ciggie. I taxed it off him after he'd had a few puffs. Baz pulled a face. 'Here y'are, nobhead.'

'I'll get you another pack laters,' I said. Took a draw, but it tasted like fuckin' socks. That were the trouble with the pills, like. They proper fucked up your tastebuds. I took another puff and chucked it at the ground. Baz pulled another face, the twisty fucker.

'What d'you want to do?' said Rossie.

''Bout what?'

'Innes.'

'Fuck him. He won't find out nowt, know what I mean? The lad might call himself a private dick, but he's a fuckin' drunk.' I tapped the side of me head. 'If he didn't whistle, he wouldn't know where to wipe his arse, the daft bastard. Fuck it. Forget it. We got other shit to be doing.'

Walked out onto Whitworth Street, got a gust of wind right in the boat. Getting cold these nights. I needed the sweat of a proper club in me armpits. We headed up towards the Village, but I weren't going to try me luck in any of them places. Aye, there were a market for the uppers and poppers in there, but fucked if I were gonna get touched up. Places was full of shirtlifters and fag hags. So nah to the pink parties and on to the student union. The students had the most money in this town. Fuckin' rich kids with Mater and Pater paying their way through Media Shite Studies. Disposable income. And they wasn't bothered about getting caught. I had that to say for fuckin' students: they didn't give two shits about the law. Most of 'em, they did one module in it, they thought they was Perry Mason.

A big bouncer with a shaved head, proper monkey goon cunt, tried feeling us up on the door. I wouldn't have minded if he were a proper bouncer, like, but you could never tell with the student nights. This big bastard had a yellow vest on and like a tight T-shirt underneath, so he could've been fruity. I bared my teeth and gave him the wild eyes. He knew us then. He knew Rossie an' all. Rossie slipped the bouncer a twenty and he let us in.

Bright lights, slick air, man. I were in me element. This were what a lad lived and breathed, like. Could kill you if you went too far down the line, but the secret for me was stamina and pills and water.

Pills for owt. Up, down, left, right, screaming singing all through the night and a couple vallies for Lorraine Kelly in the morning before the big daytime nap.

So Baz went straight for the bar with a proper thirst on and me and Rossie held back, scanned the territory. I always liked to keep Rossie with us, because he looked like a card-carrying hard fuck when he needed to. He stopped any bother before it happened. It were still early, but it seemed like they was rolling out the tunes especially for me. This one's a fuckin' thumper for the Tiernan lad, welcome to the club, and the punters'll be lining up round the fuckin' block to buy.

Oi oi, you lahky peep-holes. *N-tsh-n-tsh-n-tsh.*

Business went fast, kept the night banging underfoot. I sorted it out, got me turnover turned over sharpish, like. A half decent DJ spinning. And some blonde piece wanted a slice of Mo. I had to knock her back, like. Not that I were one not to mix business and pleasure, but she had tan lines and smelled rank.

'What's that perfume, love?' I said.

'J-Lo!' she shouted. 'Does it suit us, you think?'

'Well, you got the arse for it.'

She got all pissy at that, but what the fuck were I supposed to say? She were fat as yer mother. More in Rossie's league, know what I mean? He'd fuck mud. If mud'd have him.

'You got snow, mate?' said this fattish cunt in a black leather waistcoat. He had glasses on, thick ones. The light made his teeth look too big for his mouth.

'Nah, mate,' I said. 'Pills.'

'I don't do pills,' he said.

'You want business, you stump up. Otherwise, fuck off out of me sight, alright?'

The Waistcoat blinked like a million times. Lairy fuck, this one. Stand Up Tall, fuck arf. Rossie saw it in the cunt's eyes, even behind them glasses; Waistcoat were gearing up to go off on one. Coke flies in his head. Rossie moved towards the Waistcoat, sucked his teeth and showed the Waistcoat the butterfly in the palm of his hand. That were all it took to make the Waistcoat's bowels loose.

'Here, I didn't mean nowt,' he said.

'Fuck off,' I said.

'Get yerself a Smirnoff Ice,' said Rossie.

Baz came up behind the Waistcoat and hammered the point. Baz were a big fucker. Waistcoat turned off, went back into the crowd as Baz pushed a bottle of Becks into me hand. I necked half the beer right away. The medication I were on had dried us right out. And I were sweating like a paedo in a crèche, man. I kept some pills for meself and sold the rest on to a shorn member of the rave generation born five years after his time. I didn't even fuck about with the price. Cunt reminded me of the old school. Could he get a rewind? Certainly fuckin' could. And I rolled back the prices like fuckin' Asda.

The Becks got us a thirst, so I had to push through to the bar and got me a couple Martells. Double and trebles to clear the chalk in me throat. Baz got bleary and had to hang onto the bar, the fuckin' lightweight.

Weren't long before I started slowing right down, like. My head started getting mangled about four hours in. When I banged back the last two, washed 'em down with beer, I were ready for the floor and ready to get loved the fuck up. So I went out there, left Rossie and Baz holding their cocks while my blood were mercury on fire and the beat took the thought of Innes and Stokes and everything fuckin' else right out me head.

THIRTEEN

Normally, I'm okay when I wake up. Normally I've killed dreams with booze or a half-dozen Nytol. Normally, I get to wake up without the stifling fear that I'm back inside.

This time, it feels like the walls are coming down on me.

Eyes still closed, I can't hear anything above the sound of a jackhammer. I can't get my head straight enough to find the source, but I'm up. There's no doubt about that.

My neck clicks painfully as I reach for the alarm clock. Open my eyes and red lines blink noon at me. Pull myself out of my kip. I swallow. It hurts.

As I pad into the living room, the front door's rattling in the frame. Much more of this, and it'll come flying off its hinges. Another volley of blows make my head throb.

'Fuck's sake,' I say. 'Alright, I'm coming. Jesus . . .'

I squint through the peephole. Nothing. Black. A pause in the battery, then it sounds like someone kicking the door. Hard. I take a step back. I know that knock. Detective Sergeant Donkey Donkin of the Manchester Met. And I don't have much of a choice in the matter. I have to let him in.

Fuck.

Pull the chain off, open the door.

Donkey stands there with a sick grin on his face. His body is just like that boat of his, overstuffed. A lanky streak of piss in a uniform stands next to him, the Matchmaker to his

Creme Egg. The uniform has a sour look, probably thinks it makes him look professional, but constipation's the first thing that springs to my mind. At first glance, he's not old enough to be wearing the uniform. At second glance, he doesn't even look old enough to shave. It makes me wonder why Donkey's brought him along. If he's here to roll me, then he's best doing it without witnesses. Unless Donkey's taken up teaching his moves. Anything's possible.

'Morning, Detective.'

'It's afternoon, you lazy bastard. What's with the *Chinatown* look?'

'I cut myself shaving.'

'Don't play funny buggers, Innes. Let us in. We got something we need to talk to you about.'

'You got a warrant?' I ask.

Donkey thinks I'm serious, but only for a moment. Rage flashes across his face, but once it hits his mouth, he parts his lips in an ugly grin. 'Yeah, son. I've got a warrant. My boot up your arse. You got the kettle on?'

I don't want Detective Sergeant Donkin in here. Not that I've got anything to hide. It's just that I hate the fucker and once he gets in, he'll start playing *The Sweeney* with me. And, to be fair, he does have a touch of John Thaw about him. If John Thaw was twenty stone and smelled like a dead dog. But if I slam the door on him, he'll just kick it down.

I step back and leave the door open. It's up to him. He squeezes through, the uniform following at a safe distance. I catch the young copper glance up and down the corridor as if he's afraid of a rear attack.

'So d'you want a brew, then?' I say.

Donkey licks his thick lips and apparently finds something wedged in his teeth. 'Aye, why not? Milk and four.'

'Sweet tooth.' I walk into the kitchen, fill the kettle and

grab a couple of mugs from the draining board. 'What about your boyfriend?'

'Nah,' comes the reply. 'He's on duty.'

Click the kettle on and dump a teabag into Donkey's mug. I make sure to hawk up a fat one to keep it company. Sometimes it's the little things that brighten your day.

While the kettle boils, I lean against the doorway to the living room. Donkey's already made himself comfortable on my couch. Going for the regulation Burtons suit with the egg stain on the tie, he's also wearing one of those retro brown leather coats that stop at the arse. The sides are bunched up around his thighs. It makes him look fatter than he already is, which is some feat. His neck is thick to the collar, but when he moves, I catch a brown stain running around the inside of his shirt.

He watches me with rodent eyes.

'This business, then?' I say.

'I'm not here to admire the wallpaper.' Donkey reaches into his jacket, pulls out a tin with a Harley Davidson on the lid. Pops it open and sticks a reed-thin roll-up between his lips. 'Is that anaglypta, by the way?'

'What's this about?'

He lights the ciggie with a knock-off Zippo, takes a few puffs. The smoke smells like pipe tobacco. 'Where was you the other night?'

'The other night? You've got to be more specific than that, Detective.'

'Last night, smart arse.'

The kettle clicks off in the kitchen. 'Be right back,' I say.

I make the tea, brain ticking over. He can't have heard about my run-in with the bouncer. Doesn't make sense that the big bugger would go crying to the busies, especially considering his line of work. But stranger things have happened. Donkey's notorious for keeping his ear to the ground, mostly because he's as bent as they come. Not difficult to find out stuff happening in the underworld if you're part of it.

Make sure to give him the sugar that's congealed into a hardened lump, shot through with old coffee. He'll have to chew the last mouthful.

As I give him his mug, he says, 'You got an ashtray?'

There's one right next to him.

'Never mind,' he says, and flicks ash onto the floor. 'So where was you last night?'

I smile. 'I was out at Withy Grove.'

'Fuck me, going up in the world, eh? You'll have plenty witnesses.'

'Probably. I didn't take any names, mind. Didn't think I'd need 'em.'

'Oh, you need 'em.'

This is Donkey through and through. Thinks he's a proper hard case, reckons he should be down London and head of the Flying Squad by now. The closest he's going to get is watching Regan and Carter on Granada Plus and getting pissed up on duty. Oh yeah, and maybe the odd bit of police brutality.

He sets his mug on the table next to him, reaches into his pocket for a hip flask. He adds a nip to the brew. 'How's Declan?'

It always comes down to my brother. 'He's fine,' I say. 'He's clean.'

'Wonders never cease. Send him my best.'

'I'll do that.' Even though I won't do anything of the sort. Declan knows Donkey's been asking after him, it might be enough to throw him back to the wolves.

I take a sip of tea, look across at the uniform. He hasn't said a word so far. It bugs me. He's standing on a couple of bandy legs, his hands behind his back in a classic plod pose. Weedy bastard. If Donkey's brought him along as muscle, he needn't have bothered. This kid doesn't look like he could throw a tantrum, never mind a punch.

'You been to The Denton recently?' says Donkey.

'I was in there Bonfire Night,' I say, still staring at the uniform.

'Have any trouble?'

'You know I did. You ask me about The Denton, it's not my local, you heard someone mention my name 'cause there was bother.'

'Clever boy.'

'I'm not fuckin' daft. And what's the story with PC Haddock over there? You going to arrest me for something?'

Donkey's tone changes. He looks at the floor as if he's trying to remember the correct phrase. 'If you'd be more comfortable in custody . . .'

'You got fuck all on me, Donkey.'

He's out of the seat and at me before I know it. Hits me hard in the gut. The breath shoots out of me. I tumble to the floor, mug of tea tipped all down my front. I don't feel the burn until I try to sit up. Then it's like my chest's on fire.

'Fuckin' *wanker*.'

'You watch your mouth, Innes.' He's standing over me. Looks like he's ready to put the boot in if need be.

I pull my shirt away from the skin. Look down and my chest is lobster red.

'Call me Donkey, son, I'll kick like a fuckin' donkey.'

'That's police brutality,' I say. 'I'll have you suspended.'

'It's not police brutality, mate. You're not in custody. And you keep talking like that, you won't be until I've broke your fuckin' skull.' Donkey crouches by me. His breath smells like wet tobacco. 'You know better than to play funny buggers with me, Callum.'

He rips the plaster from my nose, takes the scab with it. I start bleeding again.

Christ.

I turn over, get to my feet. The uniform still stands there. Taking it all in like a good boy. No wonder the Met's in such a state.

'Fuck do you want, Detective?'

'Where'd you get the nose job?'

I remember the line: 'Your wife got excited. She crossed her legs a little too quick.'

Donkey sighs. 'Constable, if you'd do the honours.'

The uniform wakes up and pulls cuffs from his belt. Starts on with reading me my rights. Which he doesn't have to do, I don't think. Unless this is more serious than I thought.

'I know my rights. And one of them is that I'm allowed to get cleaned up before you two go to work on me, okay?'

I walk into the bedroom, change my shirt, grab some jeans. I catch a glimpse of myself in the mirror. Those bruises on my throat have turned nasty. My nose prickles. My tooth throbs in sympathy. I'm a wreck. Grab another plaster from the bathroom and press it onto my nostril. This is bullshit. Donkey's got nothing on me. If anything, he's heard that I'm working for Morris. He'll bring me in, sweat me down and hope that I spill whatever I'm supposed to spill. He used to do it with Declan all the time. But my brother was weaker than I am. He had a habit and a fear of dying in a dirty police cell.

I return to the living room with my arms out. The uniform obliges by cuffing me. Not too tight. Look in his eyes and there's a glint of sympathy. Yeah, mate, you probably had to endure a whole morning of the fat bastard. I hear Donkey likes Dido. And he would have insisted it was played constantly. So yeah, I pity that uniform something rotten.

'Who's grassed me up?' I say. Smiling through it all. What the hell.

'You don't get it, do you, Innes?

'I get it. You hear that I had a barney at The Denton, you come round here with Dixon of Dock Green and slap the cuffs on me, think I'll grass up anyone to stay out of jail. Bring it on, Detective. I'll be out in time for *Corrie*.'

'And I'll see you right back in the 'Ways, you little wanker.'

Something doesn't sit right. That didn't sound like an idle threat.

'Shit, that smackhead didn't die, did he?'

'Your wrestling partner? Nah. But Dennis Lang might cark it before the day's out.'

'Who's Dennis Lang?'

But I don't need Donkey to tell me; it clicks into place quick enough. The landlord at The Denton. 'That bastard?'

'That bastard. And his wife says you did it.'

Shit.

FOURTEEN

We know the steps to this dance, even when there's no music playing.

The uniform leads me outside to Donkey's Ford Granada, a car that looks like a prime candidate for a mercy killing. Someone's written UNMARKED POLICE CAR in the grime on the bonnet. It was probably Donkey. He's weird like that.

I get into the back of the Granada, the uniform sitting next to me. Donkey pulls himself behind the steering wheel and 'White Flag' starts playing. Knowing full well that anyone with a pair of ears is likely to crack with that deaf bird twittering her way through three-minute chunks of shite. Above the whine, Donkey starts to hold court on how to subdue a suspect with minimum force.

Minimum force, my arse. Donkey's a batter first, make up excuses later kind of copper. You know the type. They're the ones that end up getting the boot or hitting the top of the ladder. One of these days, DS Donkin's going to go too far. He'll beat the shit out of the wrong guy, or end up in stir himself. Then he'll be fair game to any con with a grudge.

Hope springs eternal.

We arrive at the nick and I'm bundled out of the car. Brings back sore memories of the last time I was here. Then I had puke on my shirt and shaking legs. Now I'm shaking, yeah, but it's anger.

We go into reception, Donkey too close for comfort. He

pops a Polo to hide the smell of booze on his breath. He cracks the mint between his teeth, knowing it irritates the hell out of me.

The duty sergeant looks bored and tired at the same time. One of those guys who shave their head to make up for a receding hairline. There's a scar in the right crook of his widow's peak. I stare at it.

Donkey finds a vacant interview room, hauls me towards it.

I'm innocent, but it's a small consolation. If I remember rightly, I was innocent the last time. Lot of fucking good it did me, too. Donkey's obviously done his homework, but maths was never his strong point. He's added two and two, come up with me. I have an alibi for last night, for what it's worth. I don't know if I want them to call the bar to check up on it, though. Assaulting a customer probably isn't the rosiest light that could shine on my situation.

So Dennis Lang's in critical condition. Brenda Lang thinks I did it. Why? Because we talked about it. And I said no, didn't I?

It wasn't the first time she'd talked to strangers. I got that vibe straight off the bat. She had that drunk storyteller thing going, probably spent most of her nights getting slurry and talking to anyone who'd listen. Mine can't be the first ear she's bent. So what happens? Her hubby gets done over, the police go to the wife, and who does she think of?

The person who told her no. The person who upset her.

Never talk to wannabe widows. That night is starting to have a rulebook of its own.

But Donkey doesn't have a leg to stand on. No evidence, no holding cell, at least not for long. When I finally get myself settled in an interview room that stinks of Mr Sheen and sweat, I try to relax. Donkey leans against the wall, his arse dangerously close to the panic strip. From his face, I can tell he loves every second of it. The first bona fide investigation he's had in a long time. The only reason he got this is because he knows me, reckons he's the best man for the job. The constable stands behind me, his back to the door. There in case I try to make a run for it.

The tape turns.

Donkey clears his throat. It sounds thick. 'So,' he says. 'You were in The Denton Bonfire Night.'

'That's right.'

'And you had some trouble in the toilets.'

'Correct.'

'What happened?'

'You know what happened, Detective Donkin.'

'For the benefit of the tape, Mr Innes.'

'Ah, well then. For the benefit of the tape, I was due to meet a client at The Denton.'

'A client?' There's a hint of sarcasm in Donkey's voice.

'That's right.'

'What kind of client would you meet in the gents?'

'He wanted some privacy.'

'You renting your arse these days?' He looks over at the constable and winks.

'I run a private investigation business,' I say. It sounds so weak.

Donkey grins, then: 'You licensed?'

'No.'

'Then you shouldn't be running any kind of business.'

'I didn't start like that. People ask me to look into things for them.'

Donkey pulls a roll-up out of his tin, lights it. As the flame from his Zippo catches, his lips pucker. Smoke streams into the air.

I reach for my cigarettes. Donkey shakes his head. 'Non-smoking station, Mr Innes.'

Oh, I get it.

'So you're a private detective,' he says. 'And you meet a client in the toilets.'

'Yeah.'

'You don't have an office?'

'He didn't want to come to the office.'

'Why not?'

'Because he was a smackhead,' I say. 'And he wanted to score.'

'This a sideline of yours?'

I glare at him. 'You know it's not.'

'But you agreed to meet him anyway.'

'I thought he was a real client. He didn't tell me what he wanted over the phone. Junkies don't tend to be that fuckin' open about their hopes and dreams. And when I met him, and he said what he wanted, I told him I wasn't in that business. Which I'm not.'

'And then?'

'Then I showed him the door.'

'Huh.' Donkey flicks ash onto the floor and sniffs. 'See, that's not what I heard. What I heard was that you beat the shit out of him and dumped him in the street. Quite a tumble, by all accounts.'

'He pressing charges, is he?'

'Nope. Haven't found him.'

'Then why are we talking about this?' I say, but I know exactly why we're talking about it. Donkey's trying to make me look like a scally thug. Get it all down in Dolby Digital, then black-and-white: Callum Michael Innes is a piece of work with a sideline in drug-dealing. Oh, he says he's a private dick, but the truth is he's still Morris Tiernan's errand boy. Morris says jump, Cal asks how high.

I could calm down, stop playing the hard case, but I'm so riled, it's difficult.

'I'm establishing a context,' says Donkey.

'You're wasting my time.'

'You talked to Brenda Lang that night,' he says.

'She talked to me. She was piss-drunk, came over and sat next to me, starting talking about me killing her husband for money. I told her I wasn't the bloke she was looking for.'

'You told her that.'

'After she'd finished talking. Took a while. You know how drunks like to talk, Detective.'

'And then what? You just got up and went?'

'She told me to get out.'

'And you did what she said. This drunk woman intimidated you that much.'

'Her husband was a mean-looking guy. I didn't want him throwing me out. Besides, I'd had enough of that place.'

'Again, not what I heard.'

'Then tell you what, why don't you tell the fuckin' story? Obviously you know more about it than I do and I was there. Fill me in, Detective. What did I say?'

Donkey kicks the free chair. It scrapes against the floor. 'You want to sit down, Mr Innes?'

'For the benefit of the tape, I *am* sitting down. Jesus, Donkey, what next? You going to throw that chair across the room so it sounds like I put up a fight? Get to fuck.'

His eyes flare. Donkey leans across the table, glances at his watch, and says, 'Interview suspended at three-oh-six.' He shuts off the tape. Then: 'I told you to watch your fuckin' mouth, Innes.'

'Yeah, you told me. And I heard you the first time. Now how about you do me a favour and admit you've got nothing on me?'

'You got a mouth on you, lad.'

'And you've got brass balls to try and set me up for this.'

'I'm not setting you up for anything, Innes. You're fucked enough without my help.'

'Charge me or let me go.'

'We can hold you.'

'Charge me or let me go.'

He looks at the uniform. 'Broken record.'

'You know I don't have it in me,' I say.

'I know plenty. I know your brother's a junkie grass, I know you're working for Tiernan right now, and I know you didn't get them bruises pillow-fighting. So stop the karaoke, son. Having a drink problem doesn't make you Mike fuckin' Hammer. And you might not have had it in you when you got sent away, my lad, but that's not to say you didn't learn a few tricks when you was inside, just like that phoney fuckin' Manc accent you picked up.'

Blood in my mouth. Feels like I've been punched. I fold my arms. 'Charge me. Or let me go.'

Donkey straightens up, crushes the rollie under his shoe. 'We're not going to charge you, son. Not yet. But if you think you're free as a bird, you got another thing coming. You're a scally, Innes. No brains. And you'll fuck up sooner or later, mark my words. When you do, I'll be there.'

'I'll look forward to that.'

'One word from me, and you'll be recalled,' he says.

'Christ, are you finished?'

'For now, yeah. Think on.'

FIFTEEN

I tapped the Clipper on the table and stared out the window at Piccadilly Gardens. We was in this caff what did a good fry-up, but I weren't hungry. Had a bacon barm sitting in front of us, smelled so strong it made me want to throw. So I got out my seat, pushed past Baz and went to take a shite in the bogs. Hadn't had one in three days, all backed up. When I managed it, it were a knee-trembling buckshot blast and the smell told us me guts was rotten.

Summat up in me head. Should've been cool with it, like, this whole Innes thing. But the cunt were a thorn in me side. He buzzed about. Couldn't shake him no matter how hard I tried.

Just like when he were going up in court that time.

Dad told us to leave off that time an' all, but I weren't about to let that lie. I said to Dad, I said, 'Here, c'mon, that cunt gets a deal, he'll fuckin' grass.'

Dad said, 'Leave him.'

'He'll grass us up.'

'Maybe it's what you deserve, son. Leave him.'

Leave him. Always fuckin' leave him.

Never fuckin' look after your own, eh? Keep it in the family, and now Innes were part of the fuckin' family? More trusted than me, just 'cause he kept his mouth shut. And who were that down to, eh? Who made the cunt keep it zipped?

Me.

When we did that job, me and Rossie and Baz and Innes and his smackhead brother, that were me what saved the fuckin' day. Swear to fuckin' God, that security guard, that fat piece of shite, I never hit him hard. *Tapped* him. Supposed to be a judo-chop 'cept I used me torch. You know, like you seen in the pictures. One quick hi-ya-*whap* and the fucker were out cold. And he would've been, except he twatted his head off the floor. I couldn't have seen that one coming, could I?

Dad went off it. Called us all the cunts under the sun. Like it mattered to him. I were the one up for the fuckin' charge if Innes spilled it. He were the one what got caught. Him and his smackhead junkie fuckin' brother. And I sweated big time on that one. Got so's I had to track him down and have it out with him man to man. But then he got uppity and I reckoned, what the fuck. Let him rot.

I made my point, know what I mean?

I wiped and looked in the bowl. I'd pebble-dashed the cunt, so I flushed and left it. What didn't go could fuckin' stay. Let the Paki bog cleaner deal with it.

Washed me face and looked at meself in the cracked mirror. Yeah, Innes were a problem. He'd have to be dealt with, but I didn't know how to do it. It were like the fucker had the luck of the devil. And it were like Dad liked him more than he liked me.

Well, fuck the pair of 'em.

I got out into the caff and punched Baz in the shoulder. He made out like it hurt more than it did. 'Fuck's up with you?'

'Bored, fuckin' *bored* is what's up with us, mate.'

'You wanna go down the amusements?'

'Amusements? What am I, twelve?'

'You want to call that blonde piece?' said Rossie. He had a mouthful of sausage.

'You what?'

'That blonde piece from last night. She gave us her number for you.'

'You never said that.'

'You want to?'

'Nah, she were dog rough.'

'Dog rough, but nineteen,' said Rossie. He raised his eyebrows.

Baz shook his head. He rubbed his shoulder. 'Nineteen's too old for Mo.'

Silence then. I stared at him. 'Fuck's that supposed to mean?

'You like 'em younger is all,' said Baz. He smiled.

Always smiling, that fat fuck.

'Aye, and fuck's that supposed to mean?' I had a grip on me cuppa. Some spilled onto me hand, and it was hot. I felt the burn, but it were nowt compared to what were inside. A fuckin' volcano, just waiting on that shift.

'Baz didn't mean anything by it, Mo,' said Rossie.

'Let Baz talk for his fuckin' self, Rossie. Fuck were that supposed to mean, Baz? Calling us a fuckin' paedo or summat?'

'Nah —'

'Nah, what? You call us a fuckin' paedo, I'll put your head through that fuckin' wall, how's about that?'

Baz were laughing like he always did when he weren't sure about summat, the simple fuck. Rossie put his knife and fork down. 'C'mon, Mo,' he said.

'Fat cunt's got summat to say, let's hear it,' I said.

'Hey,' said Baz. He didn't like being called fat. Which was unlucky, like, because he were the fattest cunt I knew. 'I was just messing.'

'Fuck off.' And I chucked me tea at him. Baz were fast

enough to miss the mug, but too slow not to catch the brew right in the fuckin' face. He went off it, yelled, knocked the table when he got up. I planted two fists in his chest and he slumped into his chair, nearly went over. Then I got out from the table and went outside.

I could hear Baz kicking off. Calling us out an' that. But I lit a ciggie and took a draw. Held the smoke in me lungs hard and tight.

Rossie told him to calm the fuck down, then he came outside with me. 'Fuck was all that about?'

'He wants to start summat, he better follow through,' I said. 'It's a cunt with a mouth and nowt to back him up, you know that.'

'He was just messing with you.'

'Aye, so what? You want us to take that kind of talk on the chin?'

'Fuck's the matter with you? You mashed up or what?'

'Nah, mate. I'm clean as. It's that bastard what needs sorting out. Fuck it. Go back to your boyfriend. I'm off.'

I chucked the ciggie at Rossie's feet and made for the tram. I didn't look over me shoulder or nowt.

SIXTEEN

The afternoon turns to early evening, rain to drizzle. I've been sitting in this car for two hours now with nothing to show for it apart from an empty pack of Embassy and a throaty cough.

Nothing stirring. I've toyed with the idea of calling Brenda Lang, find out what the score is, but decided against it. I don't want to get any deeper. Right now, I'm innocent of everything. If I start digging around, phoning her back, it won't look good if this ever gets to court. No contact means no evidence. I've got to watch my arse when Donkey's involved.

I get out of the car, stretch my legs. There's no use waiting for a lead to drop into my lap. Something's got to be done. I start walking towards the tattoo parlour, an idea growing in my head. If I can't talk to the dealers and that barman's nowhere to be seen, there's always another option.

The bell rings as I push open the door. As I expected, the bionic girl is still behind the counter. And she's still reading that same magazine. When she looks up, her eyes are bright blue. Her nails are the same shade. She must change colours daily.

'How you doing?' I say.

'Straight up the stairs, second door on your right,' she says. Then goes back to her magazine.

'Nah, I'm not here to punt.'

'You want a tattoo?'

'Not today, no. I wanted a quick word with you, if that's alright.'

'What about?' She looks suspicious.

'You know what goes on up there. You know the staff. You know a guy called Rob Stokes?'

'What's he look like?'

'I don't know.'

She raises her eyebrows, then scans an article on body-piercing. A photo of a guy with a face like a human gimp mask catches my eye. 'Then I don't know who you're talking about.'

'You never heard the name Rob Stokes.'

'Nah.'

'You hear anything about a guy doing a runner with casino money?'

'You think I listen to what that lot say? They're a bunch of arseholes.'

'Couldn't agree more. So you never heard the name, and you don't know anything about it.' It was worth a try.

'Am I under arrest now?' she says.

'I'm not the plod, love.'

'Then I really shouldn't be speaking to you, should I?'

'Yeah, you and everyone else,' I say.

'What do you do, then?'

'I'm a private investigator.'

She starts laughing. Too long, too hard. But I'm used to it. 'A PI? Jesus, I thought they was just in the pictures. Fuckin' hell. Where's your hat?'

'I left it in the car.'

'And you're tracking down this Rob fella.'

'That's right.'

'You're doing a shit job of it.'

'I know. And thanks for your time.' I turn to leave. Then: 'D'you know Kev?'

'The barman?'

'Yeah.'

'Yeah, I know him. Proper sleazy bastard, that one. Keeps trying to get me to go out with him.'

'Anywhere nice?'

'Place called The Basement. It's a proper dive.'

'That's his local, is it?'

'Yeah,' she says. 'They try to get him to go somewhere else, he shits it. The place is his home away from home. He told us once that he missed a night and they called his flat looking for him. Like that's something to boast about.'

I smile at her. 'What's your name?'

'Brianna,' she says. 'Why?'

'Brianna, you're a fuckin' doll.'

'And you're not my type.'

*

The Basement is a student bar, and it's as rough as the name suggests. I get past the bouncer, a skinny lad with a nice line in gold teeth, and have to duck my head as I head down the stone steps to the bar. This place looks more like a cave than a basement, all chipped walls and dim light. In one corner, a small stage with a tinsel backdrop. On it is a guy who looks about eighty. He's singing 'Golden Brown' as if it was an old-fashioned love song. Beside him, a karaoke machine blinks like it's on its last legs.

He gives me a nod as I head to the bar. I nod back, order a Coke. The place isn't busy and I could have a long wait on Kev, if he shows up at all. Get my change and a filthy look from a blonde dreadlocked barman, take my drink to a table and sit down. It's nicely shadowed here. I should be able to keep an eye on the door and not be seen.

The old guy finishes off his song with a flourish, then picks up a tumbler of whisky. He toasts us all, though most of us aren't even looking at him. Then he downs the treble. From the karaoke machine, I can hear the opening bars to 'Peaches'. The guy's a Stranglers fan, obviously. These days, somebody's got to be.

I smoke a cigarette. Kev might not turn up. That's a possibility.

Check my mobile again. Another message from Brenda Lang. I let it play and then save it.

Laters.

I sit there most of the night, sipping Coke and smoking. Students come and go. One of them, a ruddy-faced Royal wearing a rugby shirt, starts taking the piss out of the singer. I feel like smacking his head in. Yeah, the old guy's a drunk, but at least he's not obnoxious.

The crooner launches into 'Nice 'n' Sleazy'. The rest of the Royal's group sing along but fuck up the words. I get out of my seat and order a treble as a sign of solidarity. At the bar, I catch the old guy's eye and toast him. He toasts back, beaming from ear to ear. About time someone appreciated him.

The treble turns into another, this time with a pint. A few rounds later, and I'm starting to feel tired. My bones ache. But I keep drinking. It's something to do.

At two, the place starts to get busy. A group of guys wearing dicky bows make their presence known. I shake myself awake, try to focus on the bar. I should've stuck to the Coke. Curse myself for being such a fucking drunk.

I get to my feet as I see Kev at the bar. Look around for the bouncer. Nowhere in sight. I didn't expect Kev to come here with a minder, but I couldn't be sure.

I shake the deadness out of my legs and walk over to the bar, sidle up next to him. Kev doesn't notice me until I order a pint of Stella. Then I turn towards him, punch him playfully in the arm. 'You never called me.'

His face goes white.

'I'm beginning to think you don't like me much, Kev. It's almost as if you're trying to avoid me.'

He makes a move to go. I pay for my pint with one hand and grab his arm with the other. 'Where you going, mate? Me and you, we're having a chat.'

'Fuck off,' he says.

'Hey, c'mon, that's no way to behave. I'll tell you something because under that hard exterior I think you're a decent human being. I'm not fucking about here, okay? I know you know something.'

'I don't know what you're talking about.'

'I know you know something. And I will find out what you know if it takes me all fuckin' night. I'm not asking for free, either. But if you insist on playing the eel with me, Kev, I'll tell Morris Tiernan there's a barman who needs his mouth broke.'

Kev's cheek twitches. Could be a smile. Most likely, he's panicking.

'Yeah, you know *that* name, don't you?' I say. 'Now how's about I buy you a shot to go with that pint and we'll talk.'

'I don't know Rob Stokes,' he says.

'I don't care,' I say and get the barman's attention. 'But you're scared about something, and that's a fine place to start.'

SEVENTEEN

Kev sparks one of my cigarettes with a red disposable. He's already necked the shot, coughed his way through the burn. I'm patient. I just watch him get used to the situation. Part of me thought that being a good detective meant being a friendly guy; open, willing to help people. I thought that if people saw that, they'd be cool with me. Turns out, it's easier to bribe or threaten someone.

Whatever Kev needs to keep his conscience clean.

'Rob Stokes,' I say.

'Uh-huh. I told you, I don't know him.' He shrugs. The alcohol's made his posture loose. I hope it does the same to his mouth.

'Where'd he go?'

'You listening to me?'

'Just because you don't know him, doesn't mean you don't know where he went.'

'Then I don't know where he went,' he says.

'Okay.' I drink my pint and stare at him over the rim of the glass. Try to think what Donkey would do in this situation.

He'd probably break the guy's legs and piss in his mouth.

Not something I can do in a crowded bar, no matter how much it might help me. Besides, I went to the bog before I ordered my first pint. Starting to simmer down a little now in The Basement. The karaoke guy has just done his last cover for the night, stepped off the stage to a loud round of applause from the pissed-up Royals. As he comes past, I catch his eye.

'Nice work,' I say.

'Thanks, son. I try me best.'

And he goes, a smile on his face. I turn back to Kev. 'So you really don't know anything.'

'I told you.' 'Okay.' I pull out my mobile, put it on the table between us. 'I want you to call Mo.'

'Who?'

'Mo. Morris' son. I want you to pick up the phone, call him, tell him what you just told me.'

'Fuck off.'

'I'm serious, Kev. If you're telling me the truth, you've got nothing to worry about. Make yourself known. Mo will believe you, I'm sure.'

'What you playing at?'

I pick up the mobile and start punching in Mo's number. Hold it out to Kev. 'There. All you need to do is connect. Just press the wee green button and tell him what you told me.'

'I'm not gonna do that.'

'Why not?'

His voice raises an octave. 'I don't know the dealers, alright? I don't hang out with them. They're fuckin' arseholes, the lot of them.'

'Then how do you know who Rob Stokes is?'

'You mentioned him.'

'But you don't know him.' I make a show of raising a finger to my temple, proper Columbo-style. 'See, now I'm confused. You know the name, but you don't know the name. Which is it?'

'I don't know the name.'

'So you don't know he did a runner,' I say. 'You didn't hear anything like that.'

He pauses, looks at me. He's thinking. Course it's stupid to say he didn't hear anything about a dealer doing a bunk, especially when there was cash involved. Kev is slowly coming to that realisation. He works his mouth.

'Well?' I say.

'I heard someone left. They were pissing and moaning about the shifts they had to cover. And I was single-handed on the bar for a week.'

'Stokes was a dealer.'

He frowns at me. 'Yeah, and?'

'So how come you were single-handed?'

'Because Alison left too, man.'

I lean back in my chair, wait for him to follow that up. When he doesn't , I have to ask, 'Who's Alison?'

There's a moment of panic in his face. He spilled too much and he knows it. But his thirst takes hold, becomes a moment of triumph because I don't know the half of what's going on. And some blokes, no matter how scared they are, thrive on being smug. 'Tell you what,' he says. 'You get another round in and I'll tell you.'

*

Alison Tiernan.

No coincidences. Not anymore. Alison fucking Tiernan.

I keep buying the drinks, Kev keeps downing them. His mouth runs away from him, then he falls into a mumbling slur. This carries on, swings from one extreme to the other, but I end up with the whole story eventually. I have to keep asking him to repeat himself, because the rowdy Royals are singing their own songs on the other side of the bar.

Alison Tiernan, sixteen-year-old daughter of Morris Tiernan. She worked behind the bar at Morris' club. The way Kev told it, Alison was supposed to be learning the value of money, having to earn it herself. She confided in Kev. She reckoned they were the best of friends. But the barman didn't know the difference between friendship and a come-on. When she up and left, he got angry.

'I don't owe her a fuckin' thing,' he says. 'She was a fuckin' prick tease.'

'And you didn't know she was planning to leave.'

He stares at his glass, his lips puckered. 'Yeah, she talked about it. Christ, they *all* fuckin' talk about it. Not an employee in there that doesn't talk about leaving. You got to understand, we get all the shit in that place. The punters what've been thrown out of the other clubs. Punters with issues, man. Hygiene, anger management, you name it. It was no place for her. Christ's sake, she was only sixteen.'

So you know that then. It's a start. One click away from a paedo, Kev. Watch yourself.

'What about the money?' I say. I light an Embassy. His eyes flicker to the pack, so I offer him one.

'I don't normally smoke,' he says. 'I'm not a smoker.'

Social smoker, living in denial, never buys his own. This lad's not doing anything to get himself off my shit list, that's for certain. 'The money, Kev. Did she say anything about the money?'

'No.' He lights up, takes a long pull and closes his eyes. 'Gave them up five years ago, but I fuckin' miss 'em at times.'

'Where'd she go?'

He blinks through the smoke in his eyes. 'Alison? Well, I suppose she went off with Rob.' Talking to me like I'm a special needs case.

'She say where?'

'No idea. She has friends up in Newcastle. Kept mentioning them, but tell you the truth, she got a bit boring with all that. I tuned out.'

Newcastle. 'You have an address?'

'I told you, I tuned out. Why the fuck would I have an address?'

'What about Rob?'

'What about him? I told you, I didn't know him. Fuck's sake. All I know is that he fucked off with Alison, right? That's all I know. And he should be shot. She's sixteen. They could put him behind bars for a stunt like that.'

The rugby players make a loud exit, chanting that they're either going to eat pizza or Ibiza. Either way, it's good fucking riddance.

'What does he look like?' I say.

Kev looks at me, incredulous. 'You're after a bloke and you don't know what he looks like?'

'Tell me what he looks like, Kev.'

He grins, shakes his head. 'Fuckin' hell. What do I care, eh? He's tall, dark hair. Grey in it, know what I mean? Not fat, not thin.' He shrugs. 'Just looks like a bloke.'

'Oh, you're tons of help.'

Kev takes another drag. He doesn't look like he's used to smoking, got that kid playing adult thing going on. Look at me, I'm smoking. I'm a grown up. 'I didn't know they'd actually do it,' he says. 'I just thought it was talk. People are always whinging about something. And I didn't think she had the guts to do it, didn't think she'd be so bloody stupid. Listen, mate, you think what you want, but we had something going, me and her.'

I've been getting an honest-to-God Jilted John vibe from him all night. It's grown the more booze he pours down his neck. But that's the kind of drunk he is. Regretful, emotional, one step away from a Loretta Lynn song and self-pity rolling down his cheeks. He knows there was nothing between them, but the sick romantic can't give that up.

I don't give a shit as long as the information's correct.

'I knew they'd send someone, y'know,' he says. 'I knew it would happen. I even told her, said, "Look, there's not enough money in the world to make you safe".'

'Should've argued your case a bit better.'

'He's a prick, y'know. Rob. I know I said I didn't know him, but I know his fuckin' type. He'll blow the lot. He'll flush it down the bog.'

'He have a drug problem?'

Kev looks at me with a sheen on his eyes. 'He's got a losing problem. He's a punter. There's not a dealer in that place who isn't. Dealers, man. Fuckin' dealers, they reckon they've all got the inside track on the bet. Like they deal the games, they know the way they work. You watch people lose all night, and you think you're better than them?'

Not better, I think. Just different.

'You're a good lad, Kev. Don't let this place grind you down.' I get to my feet.

'What's going to happen to them?' he asks.

I rub out my cigarette. 'I don't know.'

'Then what are you doing?'

'I'm being paid to find them, Kev. After that, it's out of my hands.'

'So you're setting them up,' he says.

'I'm just hired to find them.'

'You're a fuckin' hatchet man. You're setting them up.'

'Go home. Get some sleep.'

He pulls himself out of his slump. 'You're a fuckin' *hatchet man*!' he shouts.

I walk away from the table, resist the urge to reach across and smack him hard in the nose. He repeats himself, then deflates like someone stuck a pin in him.

Hatchet man. Fuck's sake. I can't get anyone on my side.

EIGHTEEN

I were watching *Predator 2* when the doorbell went. Put me spliff in the ashtray and downed me Courvoisier and got out me beanbag, went to the door to give the cunt some grief.

Dad stabbed his Rothmans out on the doorway. 'Mo.'

'Y'alright, Dad. I were just watching a film, like.'

'Uh-huh,' he said and he went into the lounge. Danny Glover were investigating a crime scene done by the Predator. Drug dealers dead all over the shop. I didn't give a shit, like. Already seen the good bit when the Predator fucked 'em all up, Rastas getting proper splattered all over the shop and this bird with her tits hanging out giving it with the vocals. Weren't as good as the first one, mind.

Dad looked down at the telly, grabbed the remote and knocked off the volume. 'You been working, Mo?'

'This and that,' I said.

'Pills is what I heard.'

'Aye, I do some pills. Some shrooms, some resin.'

'It paying alright?' he said. 'I didn't know people were still doing pills.'

'The old school still like 'em. Sometimes I do 'em powder, like.'

'Coke?'

'Nah, the E.'

'Uh-huh.' He looked around. 'What's your mark-up?'

'On the powder?'

'On the pills.'

'Couple quid.'

Dad nodded. He looked like he were thinking about summat. 'You do the Bruce Lees, but you don't do coke.'

'Nah. Too hard to get hold of. You want some speed, I can get you some speed, Dad.'

'I'm not looking to buy, son. You be interested in the bigger deal?'

I looked at me dad. Then at the spliff and the brandy. Man, I wanted a drink and a draw right then, but it weren't right. Would've made us look like a junkie, unprofessional. 'What d'you mean?'

He were still thinking. 'I mean what I said. You interested in the bigger deal?'

'What, like smack or what?'

'Like volume, Mo.'

I didn't know what to say. So I said, 'Aye, course I would.'

Dad looked at the floor. 'Glad you said that, 'cause the way you're going, boy, you'll be lucky to keep peddling pills.'

'Eh?'

'I came over here because I wanted to offer you something. I wanted to get you involved.'

'Cheers, Dad.'

'But I get word that you don't take leave it as an answer. You stood in front of me and you promised that you'd wait on the fuckin' call from Innes; you promised that. And I said leave well enough alone, let Innes sort it out. That's what I said to you, wasn't it?' Dad lit a Rothmans. 'That's what I told you.'

'What's this got to do with −?'

'I told you to do nowt, didn't I? I said Innes was handling this.'

'Aye, and he is.'

'Then what's the score with Walker, eh?'

I shook me head. 'I don't know nowt about it, Dad.'

Me head jerked back like whiplash. Me cheek caught on fire. When I brushed the water away, I saw me dad with his hand returning to his side. 'Thought I'd raised you to be a better liar, Mo.' He walked over to me beanbag and picked up the brandy bottle. 'I told you, you took care of this, you'd fuck it up. You got Darren Walker to tail Innes, you got made.'

I gritted me teeth. Me cheek were flared, man. Fuckin' hurt like a bastard. 'Swear to God, Dad, I don't know nowt about it.'

Dad took a swig from the bottle. 'You lie to me again, son, I'll break this bottle over your skull.'

'You wanted to keep this in the family,' I said. 'You got no right to get Innes on this.'

'I had every right.'

'Alison's *my* fuckin' sister.'

'And you haven't got the nous to deal with it. You're your mother's kid, Mo. And I kept you on from the goodness of my heart. But you're old enough to get your arse kicked. So don't go pissing me off. Because I don't owe you nowt.'

'You're me *dad.*'

'I'm your dad, but I wouldn't trust you as far as I could shit you, son. You're a fuck-up. You're no good to me and you're no good to yourself. You want to get yourself a proper fuckin' job and stop playing the gangster, because you haven't got the bollocks for the real thing. You carry on playing and you're gonna get hurt. And I'm not gonna be there to kiss it better, you understand me?'

'I can handle this,' I said.

'You can handle the rough stuff if you want. You get to deal with Stokes but only when Innes finds him, alright? Don't go beaking it, Mo. You're nowt but a pair of fists and flick knife. Sooner you get that in your skull, the better.'

I didn't say nowt. I stared at him. Fuck him. I wanted to deck the fucker. Cunt. Me eyes hurt. My throat hurt. Fuck him.

'I wanted to get you involved, Mo. I really did. I thought if you could handle keeping your fuckin' nose out of this thing with Alison, you were mature enough to do some good work. But you couldn't even do that. So you're locked down, son. And if you get yourself in trouble with the law, I'll leave you to the spurs.'

'Dad –'

'You're lucky I don't call this whole thing off right now. But the deal stands because I'm a soft bastard. In the meantime, you stay well away. You get me?'

I shook me head. There were no talking to the cunt.

'I ask you a question, you answer it,' he said.

'Aye, I get you,' I said.

'Good. Make sure it sinks in this time.'

And when Dad left, he took me bottle with him. I sat on the edge of the sofa and rubbed me cheek. Fuckin' bastard, talking to me like that.

Don't touch Innes, Mo. He's far too fuckin' important to piss about with. He's fuckin' golden balls, isn't he? Moral fuckin' fibre an' all that. And a brain in his head.

He weren't the only one with a brain.

Dad didn't say nowt about Rossie and Baz. I could stay locked down, but them lads were free as fuckin' birds.

Which meant that Innes were fucked big style.

NINETEEN

Stokes is with Morris' little girl. And Alison's in Newcastle.

It explains a lot. Why Morris was so keen to use me instead of one of his scallies. He wants to keep this hushed and he knows I can keep my mouth shut. Word gets out that Tiernan's got Lolita for a daughter, well, anything could happen. It's a weakness. And Morris has got any number of enemies who'd play on that something rotten. So he's nipping the bugger in the bud before it becomes public. Keep it close, which is why I have to phone Mo when I find them. It makes sense, but something about it makes me feel sick.

So I'm going to Newcastle. I don't know anything about the place, other than it's chock full of angry Geordies and bad football. Girls with scrunchies so tight in their hair, they look permanently surprised. The same as Manchester, only colder, more hostile and all delivered in an accent that makes Glaswegian sound like Received Pronounciation. Wish you were here.

Check my mobile. More from Brenda.

'Mr Innes, it's Brenda Lang. I can understand why you don't want to talk to me, but I need to talk to you. Please call me.'

'Please, Mr Innes. I'd like you to call me at this number.'

More pleases. More Mister Innes. Then the messages become slurred.

'Call me, Callum. I need your help.'

'You promised you'd help me. You remember? You promised.'

And then finally, the heavy, throaty voice of a depressed and angry drunk: 'Fuck you.'

She's a charmer. I can see how a guy would be smitten enough to marry her.

I grab a pile of clothes that smell cleanish, chuck an extra pair of pants into my holdall. Nan always said, you got to wear clean skids in case you're ever in an accident. What she didn't mention was that it didn't matter. At the moment of impact, you shit yourself thin. But Nan's advice is hard to shift, even if she was a bampot. Clear my bathroom out and dump the essentials into the bag. I pocket some Nurofen. I get the feeling I'll need them on a regular basis. Maybe I'll see if I can get something stronger up there. Until then, I know I'll be popping these fuckers like Smarties.

I check my nose, realise it's not healed yet, and replace the plaster. Check my throat and it looks worse than it feels. Give it a few more days and I shouldn't look like I've had a fight with a hoover.

Look at my watch. It's early yet. But what the hell, I call Brenda Lang. I promised myself I wouldn't, but this is the end of the line for her. Put a full stop on the end of that sentence.

'Mrs Lang, it's Callum Innes.'

'Innes?' She sounds groggy. I must have woken her up. Sounds like she has a thumping hangover. Good. 'I've been calling you.'

'I know you have, Mrs Lang. And it's got to stop.'

'Wait, I wanted to apologise.'

'For what? Grassing me up for something I didn't do? Or leaving obscene messages on my mobile?'

'My husband's in critical condition.'

'So I hear. But if you think I'm going to head round to ICU

and hold a pillow on his face, you've got another think coming.'

She launches into a coughing fit. It sounds painful. When she's finished, she says, 'I know you didn't do it, Mr Innes.'

'That makes two of us. How's about you tell the busies that so I don't have walk around with an extra shadow, eh?'

'I *have* told them. I'm sorry. I just got scared. Is there somewhere we can meet?'

You what? 'I'm leaving town today, Mrs Lang. And we've got nowt to talk about.'

'I need to find out who did this,' she says, he voice rising into a whine.

'Then you need to trust the police.'

'If it's a question of money —'

'It's a question of being fucked over once already, Mrs Lang. Look, I'm sorry you don't have the perfect marriage, and I'm sorry that your husband got done over. But you've got to understand, you put me in a position where I can't play the PI for you. Get someone else.'

'You were the only person I talked to, you know.'

'I don't care. It was none of my business then, and it's certainly none of my business now.'

'I thought you were a professional,' she says.

'A professional what?'

And I hang up before she answers. I suck my teeth. A bad taste in my mouth. I try to swill it out with coffee, but my brew's gone cold. I spit back into the mug, go to the kitchen, drink a glass of water and stick the kettle on. As I wait for it to boil, I lean against the counter and stare at a brown stain on the lino.

That could have gone better. But fuck it; it's over with now. Hopefully. I pour the dregs from my mug into the sink and make myself another coffee. Light a cigarette as I walk back through to the living room.

Christ, what did she think I was going to do? The woman got me nicked. She think I was just going to roll over and forget it? Probably. Most people do. Brenda, Donkey, Morris fuckin' Tiernan.

But this Innes has balls.

I shouldn't be working for Morris; I know that. But it's something I have to do. I'll try to keep Paulo out of it as much as I can. Let him know that he's not involved, and this is something that I'll finish, no harm done. It won't take more than a couple of days of visiting casinos before I find Rob Stokes. The way Kev went on, the dealer has a gambling problem. And with all that cash at his disposal, the first itch he's going to get is to punt it.

It's not much of a plan, but it's something. It's a lead. And a lead's better than sitting here.

I grab cash and keys, head out of the flat. As I tuck some of Morris' money into my wallet, I notice a brown fleck on one of the notes. I pick at it with my nail and it comes away. Dirty money, blood money, it bubbles to the surface of my mind. And then I tell myself to shut up.

Yeah, keep telling yourself this is going to work out peachy, Cal.

Down the stairs, out into the carpark. My Micra looks like it's fit for the scrap yard. I only hope she can make it up to Newcastle and back. But what the hell, I'm living dangerously. The caffeine's slipped into my blood stream, got me a little hyper. As I slip behind the wheel, I slam in Hamell On Trial.

'I'm good to go, I'm good to go, y'know . . .'

*

The lads' club still has the smell of church about it, that musty odour of enforced worship hanging in the air. At first glance, you'd think Paulo was running an under-age fight club. The lads in here have scars; they fight like they mean it. All Paulo tries to do is control it, mould that rage into something that might end up in a career. That, or they tire themselves straight. Hard knocks, but it seems to work.

I walk through the middle of it, strip lighting above giving everyone jaundice, casting their eyes way back in the sockets. A couple of lads I know are in the corner, slapping gloves. As I pass, one of them turns and gives me a nod that passes for a greeting. I nod back.

Paulo's in the ring, a ginger kid's forehead against his. He's talking low and intense. Looks like they're praying together, but I know he's prepping the kid, jazzing the little fucker up. I notice that Paulo's holding up a pair of focus pads. As the kid steps back, Paulo brings up the pads and hunkers down behind them. The kid's eyebrows knot in the centre of his forehead, his eyes crinkled at the edges.

Then the kid lets fly, windmilling three wild punches into the air. His fourth connects without force. His fifth catches the edge of the pad and throws him off-balance. He stops, wheezing. As I get closer, I watch the kid wipe a mixture of tears and snot from his red cheeks. Paulo slaps him on the back, sees me, and tells the kid to get changed.

'Y'alright, Cal?' he says.

'I'm okay.'

'Just, I ain't seen you about, son. Thought you might be avoiding the place.'

'Nah, I've just been busy.'

Paulo leans against the ropes. 'You up for a spar, then?'

I check my watch. 'Nah, mate. Can't do it. I've got business.'

'Going somewhere?'

'Newcastle.'

'You'll need a warm-up, then. Them lads up there, they're not the Queensbury Rules type.'

'I don't know if I've got the time.' Check my watch again to make the point. I'd thought about telling Paulo exactly what's going on, but all that just flew right out the window. I've bottled it and, yeah, I'm a fucking coward, but what about it? I want out of here. And once this job's all over and done with, maybe I'll find the nerve to come back.

This is Paulo, this is the guy who got me out on the community visits, basically got me out of prison. And I bring the Tiernans into his club. Talk about gratitude.

'C'mon,' he says. 'We'll get you loose before you hit the road.'

As I get changed, my stomach growls. I don't feel right – this is a bad idea – but there's fuck all I can do about it. My tooth tweaks and I suck the blood from my mouth, wonder how much I can swallow before I get sick. Feels like I've already reached that stage. I look around for a gum-shield, but can't find one, so I walk out into the club hoping that Paulo's going to go easy on me.

He's already up in the ring. As I swing through the ropes, he turns and smiles at me. He's not wearing a gum-shield either. Which means he wants to talk.

As soon as he notices the bruises on my neck, Paulo says, 'What's up with that?'

'Nothing,' I say.

'Them love bites?'

'No, they're not love bites.'

He bounces on the balls of his feet, slaps his gloves together. 'Then what's up with your neck, Cal?'

'I told you.'

'What's it called? That auto-erotic stuff? You're not into that, are you? Never struck me as the kinky type.'

I throw a weak punch. 'Fuck off.'

He knocks my glove away with his right. 'I'm just asking.'

'I'm not kinky, Paulo. You know me better than that.'

'What about your nose?'

'Cut myself shaving.'

'Uh-huh.'

We circle each other. I try to concentrate on what I'm going to tell him about Morris, but he breaks it with a swing to the left. I catch the side of it with my cheek. My tooth screams. Give my head a shake and I move that little bit faster. Paulo's a big lad and he lumbers, but he can take a shitload of damage before he breaks step. Comes from taking beating on a regular basis for the last forty years, lines and scars marking his face like a roadmap of bad moves.

'Pity you weren't in yesterday,' he says. 'You had a visitor.'

'Yeah?'

'Old mate of yours.' He shakes his head, working out the kinks in his neck. 'A copper.'

He bounces to my left, and I jump too far, miss what should have been an easy blow. He punches me lightly on the shoulder. Playing with me. Testing the water.

'Donkin?' I say.

'Aye, that was his name. Fat lad, looked like he could use a spar himself. Except he had scar tissue on his knuckles.'

'What'd he want?'

'He wanted you,' says Paulo, faking a right, throwing a left. I miss it, but only just. 'And what'd you say?'

'I told him I wasn't your fuckin' secretary and he should find you his fuckin' self.'

I smile, but it gets knocked off my face with another quick left. It connects, hard. I grab a few steps and back away. Paulo meant that one.

'Why d'you think he was sniffing about?' he says.

'You know what the fuckin' busies are like, especially the likes of Donkey. Once a con, always a con. You must've had your fair share.'

'Yeah, but not without reason. What you been doing, Cal?'

'I've been busy.' Another duck, bob, smack in the head with Paulo's right. That one makes me dizzy; I have to shake it out. Takes me a second.

'Then it's to do with Morris,' he says, punctuating it with another blow to the side of my face.

I back off again. Shake my head clear. Fuck's sake.

'I'm not working for Morris.'

'What was Mo doing in here the other morning, then?'

'I didn't take that job.'

'So there was a job.'

'Yeah, but I didn't take it.' I get my vision back, hold up my gloves.

'Good lad,' says Paulo. He one-twos, batters some air. Telegraphs his right and I sneak in with mine. My glove connects with his ribs, a decent shot, but he absorbs it. 'You wouldn't bottle it and not tell me, would you?' he says.

I hunker, dodge. He doesn't even try. I feel like a ponce. 'What you getting at, mate?'

He lunges once my gloves part, lands two heavy blows in quick succession to my midriff, follows up with a corker to my mouth. The tooth goes into overdrive.

'Fuckin' *hell*,' I say, putting one glove to my cheek. 'Hang fire, Paulo.'

He doesn't. Paulo dips to my left and winds me with a deep blow to the gut. I crease, feel bile burning in my throat. Down to my knees with a thump and water in my eyes. I wheeze like a dying dog.

Can't catch my breath. I look up at him and my head's gone light. He's swirling in a mist. I blink a few times and hot water leaks down the sides of my face. My mouth hangs open. The tooth doesn't hurt so much if there's air running around it.

Paulo has stopped moving. Standing there, staring at me.

'You know what I did after I got out of the ring, Cal?' he says. 'I bounced. I worked the doors. Sometimes I worked the doors up Cheetham Hill and nearly got fuckin' shot doing it. So I tried the city, right?'

I nod, because I can't find the breath to say anything.

'I worked seven nights a week, doubles on the weekend. Got so's I couldn't look at a fuckin' beer, 'cause I knew what it did. It made lads bolshy. And I was doing the only thing I know how to do. Fight. Or break up fights by knocking heads. Most of the time it was pretty much the same thing.'

I whistle out a slow breath through my nose. Stare at the canvas. I can see drops of blood and wonder where it's coming from. Probably my nose. I'm a captive audience, just the way he wants it.

'The money was shit and the work was shittier. Then one night, Morris Tiernan comes up to me and he says do I want to work for him. Nothing harsh, like, but he needs a bloke who can handle himself. And I'm like, nah, that's alright, don't worry about it, I'm fine, right? You listening?'

My tongue goes to the tooth. It waggles in the gum. A copper taste. I pull myself to my feet and wipe a trail of bloody snot across the back of my glove. Paulo's staring at me like he's waiting on an answer, so I give him one: 'Yeah, I'm listening.'

He smacks his gloves. 'C'mon then.'

'I think I'm about done for the day, mate. My tooth's killing me.'

Paulo launches a quick left at my shoulder. I'm thrown off-balance, one foot back to steady myself.

'We're not finished yet, Cal,' he says.

'I mean it, Paulo. I've had enough.'

'Not yet,' he says. There's a weird glint in his eye. I've seen it before, normally when he's bawling out one of the kids for throwing a dirty punch or giving him shit about why they haven't attended the club. 'I'm telling a story here, Cal. And we're finished when I say we're finished.'

'Paulo, I've heard this story.'

'I know you have. But somewhere along the line you missed the point of it.'

He wants to play hard, fine. Fuck him. I sidestep as he lunges. One of his punches hits my chest. I land a strong glove on the side of his head. Paulo shakes it off. I try another. He punches my wrist.

'So I tell Morris Tiernan where to go, right?' he says. 'I tell him I'm not interested. And that should've been it, am I right?' He holds out one glove to me. I try to hit it, but he whips his hand away in time. 'You'd think he'd get the message. But no, he sends a lad round to keep asking. And this lad, he won't take no for an answer either. So he starts on with the lip, starts on with the "stupid fuckin' cunt" bit.'

I try to back up, but Paulo bears down. 'What's your point, Paulo?'

'The point, Callum, is that Morris Tiernan doesn't stop at one visit. Which means when Mo doesn't turn up here the next day and neither do you, I get to thinking. And I don't like what I come up with.'

'Paulo —'

'You took the fuckin' job,' he says. Straight out with it, deadpan.

I stand still, arms by my sides. He winds down. I can't look at him. I stare at his feet.

'Well?' he says.

'Yeah,' I say.

'Yeah, what?'

I look up at him, feeling like one of those lads of his. 'Yeah, I took the job.'

His jaw clenches, but he tries to look calm. He nods slowly, then breathes out. Says, 'That's what I thought.'

I shrug. 'I had to, mate.'

'Nah, you're alright,' he says. His eyes have glazed over. When he speaks, it's like he's reading it off a cue card: 'You think you should do this, you think you should risk another five-stretch, you go ahead and do it. You were good to keep it out of here. But you finish this off quick. This is the last time. I hear you're working full-time for the man, I'll cut you off. You play favourites and you'll find yourself out in the cold.'

'I get it.'

He looks at me, frowns. There's a brief flare, then back to glass. 'Nah, mate. I don't think you get it at all. That's the fuckin' problem.'

PART TWO

Run Boy Run

Your prison number is given to keep track of your property, files and paperwork. It remains the same even if you move to another prison. It should be written on any letters addressed to you.

I didn't get any post, didn't want any. Who was going to write to me? Declan? Nah, he was busy getting himself fucked up. Word going round was that Dec had developed a taste for downers. Besides, I told him not to visit. Told my mam the same thing. My uncle Kenny told me I'd brought shame on the family. I told him to go fuck himself.

You have a weekly allowance of £2.50, £10 or £15 based on your privilege level. Smoking is not allowed in visits areas. Exercise is thirty minutes to an hour, depending on weather and category.

Rules and regulations, the twenty-three bang-up when a knife went from the kitchen or a tool from the workshop. Locked in and pacing the cell, wanting to look like a jungle cat, but ending up like a stray dog. Afterwards, the spurs shook with aggression. Some lads didn't take to being banged up. Which was fucking unfortunate.

Some lads thrived on the aggro.

A lifer called James Figgis had taken a liking to me. The bloke was an ex-hooligan with a London Intercity firm, said he had links to the severe right-wing extremists, the real bad blood-oath bastards. He followed me about the yard, gobbing in my ear when he talked. The world, run by Jews, the New

World Order dedicated to keeping the Anglo-Saxon down, how the Pakis and wogs and chinks and the rest of those faceless, bloodless East Europeans with their hollow eyes and sticky fingers were ripping the jobs from the common white man. White was right and there weren't no black in the Union Jack.

He said he'd pegged a guy in Birmingham, a Rasta. Took a double barrel and the guy's kneecaps point blank.

'He screamed like a fuckin' coon,' he said.

That kind of attitude, it's not long before someone takes offence. The someone in question was an Asian guy Figgis took to be a terrorist. His name was Kumar, he was a Muslim, and he worked in the kitchens. One morning in the breakfast line, Figgis went to grab a bowl of Rice Krispies and Kumar threw a pan of boiling water in his face. The Asian watched me, two cons back, as Figgis dropped to the floor, screeching, steam rising off his face like piss on a cold day.

I couldn't take my eyes off Figgis. His hands up around his face, but not touching. Too afraid, his skin scalded, his eyes screwed shut and stinging red. Screaming like a bairn. Like 'a coon'.

A screw grabbed Figgis under the arms and pulled him out of the kitchen while we all looked on. Figgis' legs kicked out, his feet squeaked against the lino. Kumar returned to the back of the kitchen, but he never took his eyes off me. They had a matte finish, just completely black.

I didn't say nowt. Kept my mouth firm.

'Yeah, you better,' Kumar said to me on the spur. 'You better keep it locked, mate.'

His voice was too deep for his frame. It felt like God was speaking to me, some really nasty Old Testament cunt.

There was a bang-up after that. I would have been glad of it if Kumar hadn't spoken to me. But his voice boomed in my skull.

You will be eligible for community visits after you serve at least three-quarters of your sentence, depending on your Parole Eligibility Date (PED) and your Sentence Expiry Date (SED).

It couldn't come fast enough.

TWENTY

'You can fuck yourself,' said Baz. 'That's what you can do.'

'That's nice talk, Baz,' I said.

'You chucked a mug of fuckin' tea at us. I were just messing.'

'And so were I.'

'I know when you're messing, Mo. And you wasn't messing then.'

'Fuck off and get round here.'

'Get the bus, nobhead.'

'I told you once, Baz.'

'Get Rossie.'

'Get fucked. And get round here.'

I bleeped him off. Fuckin' Baz with a pet lip on 'cause I chucked a mug of tea at him. Fuck's sake, what were the world coming to when a mate couldn't chuck a mug at another mate without all this whiney bitch nonsense. Not like I burned him bad or owt. Fuck's sake, even if I did it'd be an improvement to that face. And the fucker had no right messing with us like that. He weren't the one worried about his fuckin' sister took up with a lad twice her age. It were embarrassing, man. *Humiliating.* What kind of family was we that'd let that happen?

So there were more to be done than pissing with Baz, know what I mean? I sat on me couch and smoked a ciggie, drank a bottle of Vittel. Did a wrap of speed to break me into the day. Me cheek were back to normal. Nothing scarred this cat.

When Baz rang the buzzer, I went downstairs, got in the passenger seat of his Nova. I laughed at Baz's face: it were bright fuckin' red and blotchy. 'Fuckin' hell, Baz,' I said. 'You want to stay out the sun, mate.'

'Where we going?' he said. He didn't look at us.

'We're going to see Innes.'

'I thought you was done with that.'

'What made you think that, Baz? I weren't finished with that.'

'But the lad –'

'The lad were a fuckin' scally. Bout time someone with some sense took this thing over.'

'Mo –'

'You gonna shut the fuck up and drive, mate? I know what I'm doing.'

Baz stuck his bottom lip out some more and started the engine. We drove and he didn't say nowt until we was near Salford. Then he said, 'You sure about this?'

'What's not to be sure about, man?'

'Your dad'll find out.'

'Me dad won't find nowt out. You think Innes is gonna go crying to him?'

'He might.'

'Nah, I'll make sure he don't. So how's about you fuckin' button it and keep your eyes on the road.'

*

I pull away from the club, and I don't feel anything. I drive in silence, head for the motorway on autopilot. Paulo's right. But it's not my decision to make.

Part of me wants to be back inside.

The lockdown was safe. I had books and a Walkman that was so battered nobody bothered to nick it. I could close my eyes in there and pretend I was somewhere else until the lights went out. It was comforting, in a way. Yeah, there was the fear of what could happen on the landings, in the yard. But if I kept my head down and my mind off it, nothing would happen. That's what I believed, anyway.

There's a hold up, traffic backed up all along the M62 outside Hull. If I'd bothered to turn the radio on, I probably would have heard about it. As it stands, I'm stuck behind Corsa with a Baby On Board sign in the back, but no sign of a kid. I stare at the woman driving. Catch her face in her rear view. She doesn't have a kid. Not unless they've found a way to stop the menopause.

Part of me wants to rear end that Corsa. My foot hovers over the accelerator until my ankle cramps.

Paulo nearly beat the shit out of me. He had no right to do that, even if he is a mate. I stood up for him enough times in the past. People giving me shit because I was working for a homosexual. Oh right, like the only way I got out of prison was because he fancied me. Get a grip. Sly innuendo and finger pointing. But the trouble with finger pointing is that someone's bound to snap it off at the knuckle.

And Christ, when did I get so angry?

The Corsa turns off at the next service area, and so do I.

The air smells like exhaust fumes. I step into a café, order a fried breakfast. When it comes, it looks like someone's thrown up on my plate and put toast by the side of it. I drink a bad cup of tea (their fault) loaded with sugar (my fault) and wish I could smoke.

My jaw aches where Paulo took a right against it. My tooth still smarts. At least the bruises on my neck feel like they're disappearing.

The knife and fork squeak against the plate like nails on a blackboard, so I don't finish my breakfast. I grab a piece of toast. Halfway through it, I realise I need a piss. When I throw the toast back, there's blood in the butter.

In the gents, I splash water on my face and try to blink back the fatigue. I'm not that far from Newcastle now, I can feel it. My stomach clenches.

Fuckin' coward.

And Tiernan knows it. That's why he's using me. And that's why Paulo let me carry on. The same reason he lets a new kid take their frustrations out on him. Sometimes you can't be told. Sometimes you have to learn it the hard way. That was never going to happen with me on my arse waiting for work.

I had work, and I blew it out. Then again, what was that work? Trawling back alleys for someone daft enough to put Dennis Lang in hospital. And whoever did that had more balls than sense.

Which rules me right out. Thanks for thinking of me though, Donkey.

I walk back out into the café, hand over cash to a woman with a face that looks like it's been put together by a four-year-old. Then I'm out in the Grim Up North. I shield my lighter with the inside of my jacket, light an Embassy. This place is Yorkshire Ripper territory. Hindley and Brady. Salesmen, truck drivers and cheapskate families barrelling up and down these motorways every day. It's depressing the fuck out of me.

I never thought I'd say this, but the sooner I'm in Newcastle, the better.

*

We pulled up and Baz were still sulking like a kid. I nabbed one of his ciggies before I got out the car and lit it with me Clipper, hand cupped round the flame. Took a couple lights, but I got the bastard smoking in a bit. Walked to the club doors, checked I had me Stanley in me trackie bottoms. Wouldn't need to use it, most likely, but a gunslinger don't leave the house without his shooting iron. Got a bad taste in me mouth and spat at the wall as I clocked a couple lads standing by the doors. They was lads I used to know from the estate. Used to be sound an' all, but gone the way of most of 'em round here. Fuckin' soft as. When the skinny one didn't move out me way, I gave him a dig. He looked like he wanted to make summat of it, so I gave him a couple seconds. 'You want summat, son?'

His shoulders dropped. 'Nah, mate.'

Mate. Fuck off. I pushed open the doors, got a whiff of the place. Christ, it stank in there. Sweat. Damp. I didn't notice it last time I was here, so they must've had a bunch of people stink the place out in the meantime. They looked like they was still working hard at it an' all. Couple kids in boxing garb in the ring, knocking the shit out of each other. Couple more on a bench. Got the *Rocky* theme in me head. Did a couple steps from me own repertoire.

And then there were Paulo Gray, come out the back office and headed straight for us. And fuckin' hell, he were ugly. I put me hand in me trackie bottoms, double-checked the Stanley. Aye, I were ready to cut this fuck up if need be.

'Help you, Mo?'

'Where's Innes?' I said.

'He's not here,' said Paulo.

'Fuck d'you mean he's not here? Fuck is he?'

'What d'you want Callum for?'

'Who gives a fuck what I want him for? Where is he?'

'You want to step in the back office, Mo?'

'Is he back there?'

'Aye, son,' said Paulo like I were a fuckin' spaz. 'He's back there. I want a word.'

I followed him. But when we went in the office, I kept the door open. Just in case he tried any of that poof shite on me. I wanted to have witnesses just in case. Paulo leaned against the desk and stared at me. 'What's going on, Mo?'

I jerked me head. 'Nowt to do with you.'

'Then why you round?'

'I were after Innes. This is his place.'

'Nah, this is my place.'

'Fuck off,' I said.

'Tell you what I think. I think you should leave and I think you should stay far far away from here.'

'Fuck do you get off talking to me like that?'

'I mean it, Mo. I'm giving you fair warning, son.'

'Fuck off. Where's Innes? You tell us where he is and I won't come round no more.'

'How about I don't tell you where he is and you don't come round no more?'

'You taking the piss, son?'

'I ain't your son, son. You keep talking to me like that, I might have to persuade you to fuck off,' he said.

'I don't swing like that.'

Paulo smiled and he got away from the desk. Then I felt the fuckin' world choke out with a bang. Next thing I knew, the door were slammed shut and he had me up against the fuckin' wall. Hand on me fuckin' neck, thumb in me Adam's apple, like. I started on at him, but I couldn't get the breath to say owt.

'If I wanted you as my fuck-puppet, Mo, you'd be toothless right now.'

I jerked at that. Nah, mate. No fuckin' way.

He held me tight and me heart started battering at me ribs.

'Don't worry yourself, Mo. You're not my type.'

I screwed me face up. Bout the only thing I could do to tell him to fuck right off. Struggled with me right hand, tried to get it into me pocket where I knew the Stanley waited.

'Cal's a good lad,' said Paulo. 'And you got the talent of everything you touch, it turns to shite. He's doing this thing right now because he thinks he has to. Don't get it into your head that he wants to do it, because I know for a fact he fuckin' doesn't.'

I shifted under his hand, felt me teeth grind together. If I could've got gob in me mouth, I would've spat at the cunt. Me fingers near the Stanley now. He caught summat in me face, though. I'd grabbed the Stanley when I heard this muffled crack and then this fuckin' agony in me hand. Paulo let us go and I dropped to the floor.

Looked up and there he were with me Stanley in his hand, staring at it like he'd found it up his arse. And he'd broke me fuckin' finger an' all, I were sure of it. I looked down and saw me first finger lean to one side. It weren't supposed to do that. Plenty of water in me eyes, but a throat that were dry as fuck.

Paulo chucked the Stanley at me. I got out the way. It clattered on the floor.

'Go on then,' he said. 'Pick it up. Billy fuckin' Big Bollocks.'

I looked at the Stanley. It shone. Looked back at Paulo. He were a big fucker for his age, like. And faster than I reckoned him.

'C'mon,' he said. 'You want to be the big man, you try coming at me.'

And if it'd been me, man, I would've told it loud and proud. But him, he were just standing there and talking dead quiet. Relaxed on the outside, but he had proper mental eyes, summat I'd never seen in him before. I cradled me hand and got up off me knees. 'You're fuckin' dead.'

'Aye, son? That right? C'mon, then.'

I shook me head. 'Nah, not now.'

'Why not now? Fuck's the matter with you? You can't take a sprained finger? Who's the fuckin' poof now?' He took a step forward; I took one towards the door.

'You're dead.'

'Keep saying it, son. One day it'll come true.'

'You're fuckin' *dead.*'

And I left the Stanley on the floor, pelted it out the club and made it back to Baz.

'What happened to you?' he said as I got in the Nova.

'Nowt,' I said. 'Just start the fuckin' car.'

*

When I hit the edge of the city, concrete blocks looming across a sickly-looking sky, I turn off The Chemical Brothers.

Down by the Quayside, I find a parking space and book myself into a Travel Inn. The place is right in the middle of development. On one side, new office buildings, all glinting glass and virgin sandstone. On the other, council flats. Somewhere it feels like a line's been drawn, and neither party is going to cross it without a damned good reason.

'Would that be a smoking room?' says the receptionist.

I take a drag on an Embassy. 'Take a wild guess, love.'

The casinos don't open for another hour so I spend my time staring at the ceiling of my room. A quick scan of the Yellow Pages, and I only find two casinos in Newcastle. The city is behind the times. Manchester's got at least six legit clubs. But I'm glad. Two casinos are easier to canvass. That's if Rob Stokes is even up here.

I open the desk drawer, find a Gideon Bible and slam it closed again. Pull myself off the bed and wander through to the bathroom. I've nothing better to do, so I have my second shower of the day. It feels like I'm being beaten up, but after a while I can feel the knots in my shoulder melt. Towel off and have to use both sachets of coffee to get a decent cup. Then I reach for my mobile and check for messages. Declan's is still on there, so I give him a ring. 'How you doing, bruv?'

'I'm good,' he says.

'Where are you?'

'I'm in the pub. I just got out of a meeting.'

Oh, that's just fantastic. A guy goes to an Outreach programme, then nips to the pub afterwards. Mind you, I can't blame him. Anything that good for you has got to give you a thirst. 'You're doing okay, then.'

'Yeah, I'm doing fine,' he says.

'How's Mam?'

'She says for you to call her.'

'I will when I can.'

'You said that last time.'

'I've got nothing to talk to her about, man.'

'Doesn't matter. She's your mam. She deserves a call every now and then. You still working for Paulo?'

'You still clean?' I say, then pause. 'Yeah, I'm still working for Paulo.'

'Can you throw a punch yet?'

'I'm trying, bruv. But I'm a lover, not a fighter.'

'Huh. When you coming up?'

'As soon as I can, mate. I'm stuck in Newcastle right now, but I'll try to get up for Christmas or New Year or something, okay?'

'What you doing in Newcastle?'

'Working,' I say. 'Look, I've got to go. Stuff to do. I'll give you a call at the end of the month, we'll sort out a session, okay?'

'Aye, alright,' he says.

'Take care.'

'You too.'

I ring off and stare at the mobile. It's hard talking to my brother. In fact, it's a fucking chore at times. My whole family's like that. We'd rather skirt around the issue than have it out head-to-head. It took me a stretch inside to face up to Dec. After all, he was my older brother. I remember him beating the crap out of me on a regular basis and even when I did floor him, he had the ability to make me feel guilty as fuck about it.

We'll see what Christmas brings. A good bevvy and maybe we'll be okay.

Right now, though, I've got more important things to do. Newcastle's casinos are open for business.

TWENTY-ONE

'I'm sorry, sir, but I can't give out that information.'

'Okay, well, I was just asking. He's a mate of mine.'

'I understand that, but I'm afraid I still can't help you.'

'That's fine,' I say. 'Two o'clock tomorrow, then?'

'We'll see you then,' says a smiley female voice. A blonde voice.

I hang up.

Gaming regulations are gaming regulations, and they mean the casino staff can't tell me if Rob or Robin or Robert Stokes is a member. They also can't let me just swing by, not until after the twenty-four hour cooling off period. Christ, it's not as if I'm trying to buy a gun. But I joined up over the phone anyway. Both places. All they ask is that I bring identification when I come in tomorrow.

Which I told them was fine. I root through my wallet for my driving licence and dump the rest of my accrued crap into the bin, slot the driving licence back into a prime place. My wallet's still plump with cash, but otherwise it looks sparse. If I was found dead, they wouldn't get much information.

Twenty-four hours. I look around the room. Bland. The travelling man's lot: dull furniture, a portable telly and a plastic kettle. Porn on pay-per-view and five channels with bad reception, sachets of coffee and tea, hot chocolate if you're lucky.

I need to get out of here. And I need a drink.

At reception, I ask a girl with braids in her hair if there's a pub nearby. She looks at me with a smile in her eyes. 'You're on the Quayside, Mr Innes. It's all pubs down here.'

Huh. Maybe Newcastle's not the shithole I was led to believe. She gives me directions and I follow them to the letter.

You can tell a lot about a place by its pubs. Judging from the stretch along the Quayside, Newcastle's desperate to please. It's just like Withy Grove, but pulled taut and facing onto a rolling brown river. Looks like I'm coming out on the tail end of the lunch hour. I pass suits and skirts; a couple of young guys in the similar colour tie-shirt combo are talking loudly about how crap their jobs are.

Tell me about it, fellas. At least I don't have to dress up.

The first place I come to, The Pitcher & Piano, looks too expensive. I give it a glance, but when I realise the piano isn't real and the clientele look like twats, I move on. That's the trouble with this place. The bars are like those that have cropped up in Manchester. Ball-less, soul-less, all glass coffee tables, animal print sofas and bottled beers. Jukeboxes playing Joss Stone and cocktails with 'ironic' names. Wine bars for the noughties.

Fifteen minutes of walking, and I finally find a pub. Inside, the place is decorated with black-and-white pictures of famous Geordies. I only recognise some of them, and that's mostly because they look like stills from *Get Carter* and *The Likely Lads*. At the bar, they've got a few lagers on tap, which is a good start. I order a Stella and it comes without fuss. The price isn't too bad, either. I settle at a table and watch the pub. A guy in a suit is eating a burger and managing to get most of it on his tie. When he catches me staring, I turn away and light up. There's nothing like flicking ash into a pristine ashtray.

My stomach growls, but I'm not about to chance pub grub. I don't think I've got the constitution for it.

But I'm calmer now. This place isn't exactly heaven, but it's better than Manchester. For the moment, at least.

'Anyone sitting here?'

I look up. She's a brunette, looks a little rough around the edges. Like that drunk bird from *Will and Grace*. And from the way she's handling the chair, it looks like she's already had a few today. She's smiling and that's about all I can see. That, and a stunner with a good few years on me.

Course, it could be the drink talking.

'Nah, y'alright,' I say. Thinking she'll just pull the chair away somewhere else.

She sits down and places her drink on the table. 'You okay?'

'Yeah, fine,' I say. 'Couldn't be better.'

'Funny that.'

'Yeah?'

'Because you look like someone pissed on your chips.'

A mouth on this one. I smile, say, 'I don't have any chips to ruin.'

'Aw,' she says. 'Tell you what, I'll buy you a drink.'

'Why?'

'You don't look like the kind of guy who'd ask that.'

Known me five seconds and she's already got me pegged.

'I'm getting drunk,' she announces after she comes back with the drinks, a couple of chasers lined up.

'Looks like you already are.'

'Are what?'

'Drunk.'

'Are you?'

'Not me. You.'

'You got drunk fast,' she says.

'I'm not. Why're you getting drunk?'

'Because I hate my job.' She crosses her legs and pulls her skirt over her knees.

'Everyone hates their job. That's why it's called a job.'

'Oh, you're funny,' she says, deadpan. She drinks, then: 'I've decided. I'm going to take a half-day.'

'It's already three.'

'A quarter-day. Whatever. I didn't go back after lunch. You up for getting sloshed?'

'You don't know me,' I say. 'I could be anyone.'

'Yeah, you could be a murderer. What's your sign?'

'Leo.'

She breaks into a beaming smile, shows fantastic teeth. 'You actually know your sign. Jesus, I was joking. What's your name?'

'Cal.'

'Like the Helen Mirren movie.'

'Can't say I saw it.'

'You didn't miss much. Love story set in Ireland. She's the widow of a murdered Proddy copper, he's skirting about with the IRA. I'm Donna.'

'Pleased to meet you. So what's so bad about your job?'

She sighs dramatically. 'I'm a PA for a director of a PR company. It's all initials to make a job sound more important. What do you do?'

'I'm a PI.'

Donna laughs. 'So we're in the same boat. What does PI stand for, anyway?'

'Private investigator.'

'*That* kind of PI? Fuckin' hell, I thought you meant personal injury. I was about to say, you don't look like a lawyer, like. Wow.' She seems genuinely impressed. But then, she's slurring. 'So you're like a two-fisted kinda guy, right?

You do the cheating spouses, fraud claims? You solve the murders?'

'The first two sometimes. The police solve murders.'

'Sometimes. I heard there was this gadgie, they slit his throat and dumped him on the beach at Tynemouth. They never solved that one. But a PI, wow. How'd you get into that racket? That's the right lingo, isn't it? Racket?'

'I sort of fell into it. Did favours for a few people, they paid me for it. I discovered I had a knack for it. Not something I can explain. And yeah, your lingo's spot on.'

'Cool. You don't look like a private dick.'

'What am I supposed to look like?'

She thinks, then opens her hands and says, 'Mickey Spillane.'

'You know what Mickey Spillane looks like?'

'Alright, Humphrey Bogart.'

'Well, I'm sorry to disappoint you.'

'I didn't say I was disappointed. So what you working on, Shamus?'

I shake my head. Too much for polite conversation, no matter how much the drink seems to be flowing. 'Nothing,' I say.

'Unemployed, eh? Looks like I'll be getting the drinks in, then.'

'You don't have to do that,' I say.

'I'm a modern woman, Cal. I can do whatever the fuck I want.'

And as we tan those chasers, I don't doubt it.

TWENTY-TWO

Came out Accident & Emergency with a splint on me finger.
Doctor said it weren't broke, like, but what did that cunt
know? It felt broke. And I were boiling over with things I'd do
to Paulo given half the chance. The look on me face were
enough to get the doctor rushing me through. And the
bastard didn't prescribe any painkillers, either. Fucker.

Baz were outside in his Nova. He didn't want to come in;
the lad had issues with hospitals. Said his mam died in one.
When I got in the car, he said, 'Y'alright?'

I held up me splint. 'Do I look alright?'

Baz nodded to himself, started the engine. 'Where you
want to go?'

'Pub,' I said. 'We got business to discuss.'

'What business?' said Baz.

'Alison.'

Baz sighed. 'Why you always got to go on about that, man?
Christ, look at you: your finger's broke.'

'It's sprained.'

'You got X-rays. It's broke.'

'It's *sprained*. And I'm gonna fuckin' kill that Paulo.'

'Leave it, Mo. He's not worth it.'

'What do you know who's worth it? I'll do the cunt.'

I knew I were a daft bastard for going round the club, but
what else could I do? Summat had to be done. Summat had to
be said. I had to tell me dad that I weren't fuckin' happy with

this situation, not one fuckin' bit. And going round the club were the best way of doing it. You tell us not to interfere, Dad, here's what I think of that. Fuck yourself.

Course, the whizz helped matters, gave us that extra touch of rock'n'roll. Trouble was it got snapped out of us when Paulo did his fuckin' finger trick.

I stared out the window. Fuck it. Reached in me trackie bottoms and pulled out me mobile. Realised I couldn't dial worth shit so I chucked it at Baz. He nearly lost control of the car.

'What's this?' he said.

'Call Rossie. We got to get a plan B.'

'You call him.'

I held up me finger. 'You been in a fuckin' coma, Baz? How'm I supposed to press buttons with this?'

'Aye, alright,' he said. 'Jesus.' He searched for Rossie's number on me mobile, one eye on the road.

And I started working on that Plan B.

TWENTY-THREE

At seven, Donna gets the bright idea to call a cab and pick up a bottle on the way back to her place. I try to put up a gentlemanly fight, but the booze has taken hold. She wants company, and if I get to thinking about it, so do I. So we keep each other upright and take the taxi. It's already dark by the time we get through the front door. The place smells like lavender. I feel my eyelids getting heavy.

I trip over a cat in her living room, end up on the couch. I think it's a cat, anyway. Could be a child or a midget. Whatever it is, it barrels out into the hall with a screech. Donna starts laughing. It's a great sound, and infectious. 'Stella doesn't like you,' she says.

'Stella?'

'The cat.'

So it was a cat. 'Why'd you call your cat Stella?'

She comes into the living room, screws up her face and puts on a bloke's voice. 'Stelllllllllla . . . Hey, Stelllllllllllaaaaaa . . .'

'*Rocky*?'

'*Streetcar Named Desire*, you prole,' she says and returns to the kitchen. 'Or *Seinfeld*, whatever you prefer.'

'I think I'm pissed,' I say.

There's a clatter from the kitchen. 'Yeah, well, Mr Innes. I believe I'm in a similar state.' The sound of ice in glasses, and she emerges with a bottle of Glenfiddich and two tumblers.

She sets one of them on the coffee table in front of me and sways as she makes her way over to a chair. I gaze at the glass, watching her splash the single malt.

'The good stuff,' I say.

'I save the crap for special occasions.'

'You know how to make a guy feel wanted.'

'Chin chin,' she says, and sips from her glass.

'Cheers.'

We drink in silence. I look around her flat. Lots of books. Lots of CDs. Church candles skewered in wrought iron candlesticks. The place looks like an Ikea showroom. When I look at her, I notice she's staring at me. 'What?' I say.

'You look lonely,' she says.

'I always look lonely,' I say. 'The wind changed.'

'And you stayed like that.'

'Exactly.'

'I think I jacked in my job today,' she says.

'Really?'

'I should have gone back to work after lunch. If I'd had any sense, I would have gone back to work.'

'Tell them you were sick.'

'I've been sick a lot recently.' She picks out an ice cube and sucks on it, then drops it back in her glass. 'I hate my job.'

'Get another one.'

'I might have to. You need a secretary?'

'I can't pay you.'

'Cheap bastard.' She smiles. She has really great teeth. American teeth. She stretches in the chair and then shifts position, throwing her legs up over the arm and tugs at the hem of her skirt. I try not to look. 'I don't think I could be a secretary, anyway,' she says. 'Too close to being a PA. Besides, my shorthand stinks.'

'So what do you want to do with your life?' I say.

'I don't know. I suppose I could be a lady of leisure.'

'That's not a career.'

'It's a *vocation*.' She knocks back the rest of her Glenfiddich and pours another. 'See?'

'Yeah, I see. Very leisurely.'

Donna pulls herself up in the chair, narrows her eyes at me. 'You don't like me, do you?'

'Don't know what you mean.'

'I mean, you haven't tried anything.'

'You what?'

She gets up with some effort, walks over to me and sits on the couch. 'I mean, you haven't tried chatting me up.'

'You want me to chat you up?'

'Ach, you're right. We're probably past that stage now.'

'I think you're probably right,' I say, shifting in my seat. 'I should go back to my hotel, really.'

'Hotel? You're staying in a hotel?'

'Yeah.'

'You're not from Newcastle. I knew that, but I thought you lived up here. Why're you staying in a hotel?'

'I'm up here on business,' I say.

'So you are working. You owe me drinks, pal.'

'Kind of. It's too complicated to explain.'

'I've got all night.'

We sit in silence. She pours me another drink. It glugs into the glass, a heavy measure. Too heavy for me, but I give it my best shot. After a few drinks, I'm sitting back in the couch and we're both listening to John Lee Hooker.

My eyes start closing. Then I say, 'I can't stay, y'know. Things to do tomorrow.'

'You don't have to,' she says. She's leaning against me, has her hand on the inside of my thigh. It hasn't moved for three songs and I haven't had the heart to remove it. In a way, it's comforting. In another, it ties my stomach into a half-hitch.

'I should call a cab,' I say as the song finishes.

'Be my guest,' she says.

*

Donna follows me downstairs when the taxi arrives. I turn to talk to her, and she snakes her arms around my waist. The alcohol on her breath makes me lazy.

'You've got my number,' she says. 'You call me, okay?'

'I'll call you.'

'Course you will. You love me.'

I blink. If there's a reply to that statement that doesn't make me look like a soppy get or a complete shithead, I don't know what it is. So I keep my mouth shut. She reaches up, plants a smacker on my cheek, another on my bottom lip. 'Don't think so much, Cal.'

She has the clearest blue eyes I've ever seen. Maybe it's the booze, but I'm transfixed. She shakes me gently. 'Taxi's waiting. And from the look of him, he's already flipped the meter.'

'Course. Sorry. Look, I will call you, okay?'

'I know. And look, I'm glad you're a gentleman. I think I have a yeast infection.'

Who says romance is dead?

I get in the cab and she watches from her door as the car pulls away. Then the whole weight of the night's drinking comes crashing down on me. I give my head a shake and wipe my nose.

How's that, Cal?

Things could have been different back there. She wanted me to stay the night, and not in a slumber party sense. It wasn't as if I'm not attracted to her.

No, that's not it. I was being a gentleman. Let's face it, she was drunk. I'm drunk. And brewer's droop is a real mood-killer.

And telling her I was a PI, for fuck's sake, what brought that on? Who the hell was I trying to impress? Private investigators have steel in their pocket and iron in their spit. Me, I've got shit in my pants and blood in my mouth. Maybe if I'd met her a couple of months down the line, when I was more settled. It could have worked then.

'*Don't think so much, Cal.*'

When I get back to the hotel, I head straight for my room. As straight as I can, anyway – my legs are intent on following separate paths. I lock the door behind me, turn on the television. The volume makes my head hurt, so I tap the remote until all I hear is a murmur. Then I grab my mobile out of my inside pocket and sling my jacket onto the bed.

I need to harden up.

'Who's this?' says Mo.

'It's Cal,' I say.

'Cal?' He's shouting into the phone. From the noise in the background, I'd swear he was in a pub.

'Callum Innes, Mo. You know me.'

'Right. Where are you?'

'Newcastle.'

'Fuck you doing in Newcastle?'

'Stokes is here.'

'Fuckin' hell, you *are* a detective, ain't you? Wait, I'll get summat to write this down.'

'I don't have an address yet.'

'Then why you calling me?'

'I need to negotiate a fee.'

Mo laughs, a high-pitched cackle. 'You're taking the piss, mate. You already negotiated your fee with me dad.'

'The case has changed.'

'The *case*? Fuck are you on, Innes? The *case* isn't a fuckin' case. You're up there to find the cunt. There's no fuckin' *mystery* to it. You're not out to nail Colonel Mustard because he topped some daft bastard in the conservatory with the fuckin' candlestick. You're up there to *scout*, you're up there to find a fuckin' thief, so don't go getting ideas above your station, mate.'

Okay, so this was a bad idea, but I plough on. 'You seem to forget, Mo. I'm straight. And when I find this guy, give you the address, you'll come up here and fuck him over. That makes me an accessory. He'll be able to identify me. And while you might be able to get out of a fuckin' sentence because some weak cunt keeps his mouth shut, I don't have that much sway, do I?'

'What d'you want me to tell you? You knew what this were about.'

'I want more money.'

There's a pause at the other end. 'You're drunk.'

'Expenses, Mo.'

'You're fuckin' drunk. I knew it. I told Dad, don't hire a pisshead. Christ.'

'I give it up here, Mo.'

'Don't think you're threatening us, Innes. Get bolshy with me and I'll nail you to the fuckin' floor. Tell you what, I'll be the gentleman and think you're just pissed out of your tiny little mind. I'll put it down to the booze and I won't bear a grudge. Now get back under your rock and don't call us until you got an address.'

Click, and he's gone.

I sit on the edge of the bed. Look across at the telly. It's Bogart and Lorre in fuzzy black-and-white.

Bogie says, 'When you're slapped, you'll take it and like it.'

Never a truer word, but it doesn't stop that slap from hurting.

TWENTY-FOUR

I grabbed Rossie round the back of his baldy ginger head and shouted in his ear: 'We's in business, muckaaaa.'

Rossie struggled, said, 'Fuck off.'

I slapped his bald spot. 'Language, Timothy. Get us a brandy, muh man. I'm celebrating.'

Rossie went off to the bar and I slumped into me seat, grinned at Baz. He were rolling a fat stick. Had to hand it to him, he were a fuckin' craftsman when it came to rolling. He smoothed the edges and lit it with his Clipper. The big lad puffed hard, the smell of singed eyebrows and fine Northern Lights high in the air. When Rossie came back from the bar, he looked at Baz like the big lad had just farted loud and smelly.

I downed me brandy and banged me glass on the table. 'I call this meeting to order. Who's up for a fuckin' trip?'

'Nah, me head's halfway to the shed already, Mo.'

'Innes. He's gone to Newcastle.'

'*Ya gan doon toon,*' said Baz. Then he laughed. He sounded like a proper cunt when he laughed; looked like one too.

'You want to go to Newcastle,' said Rossie. He were squinting at us.

'I can't go anywhere. Me dad's got us locked down. And I can't trust Darren fuckin' Walker, can I? Nah, youse two are going to Newcastle. You're gonna keep an eye on the cunt.'

'I don't wanna gan tee Nyow-cassil,' said Baz.

'You got the accent down, Baz,' I said.

'Aye, but –'

'You're going to Newcastle.' I didn't want to hear a fuckin' argument.

'How comes your dad's got you locked down, Mo?' said Rossie. 'You're a grown bloke. You can do owt you want.'

'Aye, but not about this. I need to keep the old man sweet as, else he'll put the kibosh on it.'

'Fuck off the kibosh,' said Baz. His eyes had gone webbed and dark. Fucker was mashed already. 'You want to go to Newcastle, you go your fuckin' self, know what I mean?'

Rossie looked down at the table. Looked right through it.

I stared at Baz until he stopped drawing on the stick. The fucker knew he was in the shite, like. I were going to say summat, but this bloke in a Pringle jumper came over before I got the chance. 'Sorry, lads. Can't do that in here.'

I turned the stare on the Pringle. He had a gold chain around his neck. Hair poked through the links.

'You what?' I said.

'Your mate there. I can't have him smoking that in here.'

I frowned. 'You tooting rocks in there, Baz?'

'Nah, man. Just resin.'

'It's just fuckin' resin,' I said to the Pringle. He weren't happy about this. He were red in the throat, like he'd got burnt.

'It's still illegal,' he said. And if he were sure of anything, it were that little fuckin' nugget of information.

'Give it time.'

'It's illegal now,' he said.

Baz looked at his spliff like he were shocked to learn that. I had to keep me blood cold to stop from smiling. So I pretended like I were thinking it over, what the Pringle had said. But what I were really thinking about were that five seconds ago I were ready to put me boot in Baz's ringpiece, and now this twat in the sweater were giving us reason to leather the fuck out of him. Choices, fuckin' choices. And just like a pair of cunts to spoil what were turning into a good night. When I'd made up me mind, I said to the Pringle: 'Where's your respect, man?'

'You what?' he said.

'I said, where's your respect? You come over here, I'm in the middle of a conversation with a couple mates of mine, you don't give a fuck, where's your fuckin' respect?'

The Pringle got balls then. I saw him glance at me finger. Reckoned I weren't much of a threat, obviously. 'He puts that out, or I put you out.'

'Ah, you're threatening now,' I said. 'You're fuckin' threatening us.' I kicked me chair back and it crashed to the floor. I were on me feet, in the cunt's face. 'What's your fuckin' problem, you have to come round here starting shit?'

'Put it out,' the Pringle said to Baz. But his voice were wavering.

'You put us out, nobhead,' I said.

'You want to get nicked?'

'You want to get fuckin' cut?'

I reached for me Stanley, then remembered where I'd left it. Felt me heart skip. But it didn't show in me face. Rossie were getting up slow and quiet.

'Maureen, call the police.'

Baz grinned through the sweet smoke, set his spliff down in the ashtray. He reached into his jacket like he were reaching for his wallet, ticked out the blade of his Stanley and slapped the knife hard on the table. 'Fuck off out of it,' he said.

'Maureen –'

Rossie took his pint and broke it over the Pringle's head before he could shout double-knit. The Pringle swayed, but I went at the cunt's gut before he got his feet. And there weren't a bastard in the place ready to jump for his love. The Pringle hit the floor, brought the table down with him. Rossie lashed at him with his butterfly. The blade cut slight, but the Pringle rolled like he'd been shot. Baz sucked his gut and made it round in time for the Pringle to sway up to his knees. When the Pringle opened his eyes, he had to blink from the light bouncing off Baz's Stanley blade.

I dusted meself down, wiped me nose. 'Cut his fuckin' eyeballs open.'

'Wait a sec,' said the Pringle. And his bladder emptied out onto the carpet. I loved that smell of piss in the air. Smelled like . . . victory.

'You know me,' I said. 'You know me now.'

Blood ran down the Pringle's face. Glass in his head shone like stars.

'Aye you know me, son.' I pointed at him with me finger-splint. 'I'm Mo Tiernan. And I'll have you buried in less time it takes to have a dump.'

It were fuckin' good to be me sometimes.

TWENTY-FIVE

There's nothing as bright and painful as the morning after sunlight.

The walk to Central Station, and the casino near it, is a long one. My legs aren't happy about it, and neither's my stomach. But I pop into a café on the way, sit down with a cup of coffee and a bacon buttie. Smoke a few cigarettes. The owner, a camp guy with a Greek accent, welcomes me with a smile, but as soon as he smells the drink on me, he buttons up.

I don't want small talk. Just food.

The bacon is almost burnt, but I like it that way. The coffee is black and sugared. I drink it slowly and rub my eyes. I shouldn't drink so much. Or I should stay away from the spirits.

The drink-shakes private dick, a walking, talking cliché. I should be shot for crimes against reality. But instead I'm stuck looking for a dealer who may be somewhere in this city. Or I may be chasing up a lead from a Jilted John who'd tell me anything to stop Morris Tiernan coming after him.

I dump my Embassy, push away from the table. Stop your whining and get to work, Cal.

The place on St James Boulevard is new by the looks of it, purpose-built. It looks like a tombstone in a sea of concrete. I arrive at reception, all plate glass and plastic ferns. If they're going for the classy look, they've failed. Mostly because the girl behind the counter has yellow teeth and dead eyes. She smiles at me with her mouth only and it's an ugly sight.

'My name's Callum Innes. I called yesterday.'

She asks for ID and I hand it over. After a quick scan, she gets me to fill out a membership form. I lie about everything apart from my name. She gives me a card which I tuck in my back pocket, and I catch the smile slip from her face as she reaches under the desk. Probably caught the whiff of drink on my breath. Or vomit. Maybe just the stench of failure. You would have thought she'd be used to it by now. Besides, it's better than whatever Avon shite she bathed in this morning. A low buzz as the double doors unlock, and I push through into the casino.

The place is a space-age warehouse. Tables stretch back as far as I can see, most of them unmanned. The room is airy to the point of goose pimples. Looks like only three tables are open: one roulette, one blackjack, one poker. At the card tables, the blackjack dealer stares off into space, the poker dealer has something in his nose. An inspector stands between them.

If Rob Stokes comes in here, it's not during the day.

I head to the bar, order a pint and take a seat on a stool that threatens to examine my prostate. Looking over at the roulette table, I can make out an elderly couple playing the outside bets. Red or black, even money, but it means the dealer has to spin up for the sake of a fiver. He clears it; they'll get it back on the next spin. It's dull to watch. I can't imagine how dull it must be to play.

Sip my pint, light a cigarette. The hangover's gone into a slight remission; the beer takes effect but the Embassy turns my stomach if I inhale too deeply. The guy behind the bar wears a blue shirt with forced pleats down the front and a cock-eyed name badge that reads 'George'.

'How you doing, George?'

He bristles at his name. One of the many people who hate the informality of the service industry. 'Fine,' he says.

'How long you been working here?'

'A while. Couple of years.'

'Huh. You know many of the punters?'

George's left eye closes halfway. He's either trying to work me out, or it's a nervous thing. 'Some of them,' he says.

'How well?'

'We're not allowed to fraternise.'

'I know the dealers aren't.'

'Nobody is. It's a security risk.'

'Right.' I drink from my pint. 'No, I get it. You have friends who aren't in the business, you're a criminal, am I right?'

'Something like that.'

'Yeah, I know all about that,' I say. Shake my head and watch the old couple at the roulette table. 'Listen, you know your punters by name?'

'Some of them.'

'Rob Stokes ring a bell?'

'What's he look like?'

'A bloke. Salt and pepper hair. Tall. Bad attitude. A chip-chaser.'

'Mate, you just described ninety percent of the blokes we get in here.'

I finish my pint, order another. 'Take one for yourself.'

'So how much does this Stokes guy owe you?' says George.

'Owe me? Nowt. He's a mate. I heard he came in here. Why?'

'You're not police,' he says.

'Nah, I'm not police –'

'And you're not a mate of his. Otherwise you wouldn't be asking questions.'

'Maybe I just lost his number. You have it?'

'I don't know who you're talking about,' he says. Smiling like he's really enjoying this. And he knows the guy, I can feel it. I dig out a business card – one of those I got done at my local Shell – and bang my mobile number on the back with a wee bookie pen.

'Tell you what,' I say. 'If anything springs to mind, or your memory comes back, you give me a ring, okay?'

He looks at the card and the smile turns upside down. 'You're a private detective.'

'Investigator,' I say.

'What's the difference?'

'A private detective solves the case. A private investigator just looks into it. I'm not the type to gather suspects in the drawing room. I'm the poor bastard who follows cheating husbands, wives, runaways. I'm the one sitting in the car with fuck all else to do. And I'm the one who'll slip you a wad if you can point the finger, George.'

He blinks. 'You practise that speech in the mirror?'

'Twice a day. But the deal stands.' I down half the pint and leave the glass on the bar. 'You see him, let me know. I'll make it worth your while.'

'I'm not daft, Mr Innes.'

'Good lad,' I say. 'Make sure you stay that way.'

And I leave. Glad I got something out of him, even though I'm not sure what it is. A feeling, but sometimes that's all it takes. Most of all, though, I'm glad I could leave that pint unfinished. No self-respecting alkie would let that happen.

Which makes me one step on the road to normal.

TWENTY-SIX

So I had to go with them. No skin off my cock. They wouldn't go up without us, the born fuckin' leader that I were. So I said alright, what the fuck. I could keep Dad off me back for as long as it took. And I knew I wouldn't be able to keep meself from going mental if I'd stayed down here.

Call me a control freak.

Standing outside this garage in Moss Side, and Baz were with us. Rossie were inside talking to this lad with a swallow tattoo on his neck. He looked like a proper hard cunt, like. I wished I had him with us instead of Baz, who were griping again.

'Why we got to be here, man? What's the matter with my car?'

'Your car's a fuckin' shitheap, Baz. Couldn't make it to Chester in your car. Besides, it's too suspicious. It looks like a gangster's vehicle.'

Baz looked a bit happier at that. Like he were the real deal. Like fuck he were.

Rossie came out the garage. 'Jimmy says he's got a Bedford we can use.'

'How much?' I said.

'Nowt. Just a favour for a mate.'

'You're kidding.'

'Nah, I help him out sometimes.'

We went through into the garage. Jimmy were waiting for us, didn't look like he wanted owt to do with us. Clocked me once and reckoned me a soft cunt. I wanted to prove him different. As we went to the back of the place, I heard all these dogs barking somewhere. 'Fuck's that?' I said.

'Them's Jimmy's dogs,' said Rossie.

'Animal lover.'

'Nah,' said Jimmy. He had a growl of a voice, sounded like them dogs. You know what they say about pets and their owners, like. He had a rollie in the corner of his mouth that didn't smoke, but it moved when he talked. 'Them's me fighting dogs. I fight 'em.'

'Fuckin' hell, Jimmy. That's not much of a match, is it?'

'They fight each other, Mo,' said Rossie.

'Your mate simple?'

'I ain't simple, Jimmy-son. Where's this fuckin' wreck you want us to drive?'

'I don't know if I like his tone,' Jimmy said to Rossie.

Rossie looked at us to shut up. At the back of the garage, there were this dirty-looking heap. Jimmy kicked one of the tyres. 'This is it. How long you need it?'

'Couple days,' said Rossie.

I kept me mouth shut. Didn't like the way Rossie were handling all this, like. I were the one in charge. I looked at Baz, but he were already looking around for a way out, the bottling bastard. Went up to the Bedford and pulled open the back door. In the back of the van, there were a mattress that stank of dog and a cage between that and the cab.

'I keep me bitches in there,' said Jimmy.

'Good,' I said. 'Cause that's what we're gonna be using it for an' all.'

'I want it back in good nick.'

We all looked at him then. Like we could trash this fuckin' heap any more than it already was. Rossie said, 'Yeah, no problem, Jimmy.'

And as we was driving away, the engine coughing, I said to Rossie, 'And the cunt called *me* simple.'

TWENTY-SEVEN

The receptionist at the Grey Street casino has black make-up clogged in the corner of her eye. She looks at me with resigned recognition and it's strangely comforting. A uniform that's been washed too much, a spare tyre around her waist and the gnarly hands of the serial drinker.

If I was a gambler, I'd be in here all the time. It's all faded glamour. Like the receptionist, the furnishings used to be lush, but now they're a little threadbare. A group of Chinese guys are crowded round a blackjack table. Every so often one of them yells. Then there's laughter, the kind that follows excitement. All over a steady rhythm of Mah Jong tiles being shuffled by some Chinese ladies in the far corner. It's difficult to see through the cigarette smoke. I add to it with another Embassy. My lungs are starting to scratch, but the nicotine helps keep that down.

I can hear 'Spanish Eyes' being sung by a guy with a whisky-soaked voice.

The bar's at the back of the room, so I start walking. With the music, I feel like I should be carrying a six-shooter. I hope nobody notices that I'm walking to a rhythm.

There's a girl behind the bar, cleaning something out of sight. She doesn't look up as I come over. I lean against the bar and try to look nonchalant. She carries on cleaning. I don't see her face, just the expanse of her arse and a visible panty line. But I try not to stare too hard at that. When she straightens up, she starts. Colour rises in her puppy-fat cheeks. I can't place her age. She could be anywhere from sixteen to thirty. According to her name tag, she's called Pauline.

'Y'alright?' I say.

'Aye,' she says. 'Sorry, you gave me a fright.'

I smile my charming smile. It doesn't sit right, obviously, because she looks a little intimidated. I tone it down. 'Sorry. You open?'

'What you after?'

'Bottle of Becks.'

She smiles. There's no need for it, and her smile is like a bonny baby in a morgue. It makes me wonder why she works here. She fetches my beer and sets it on the bar. I pay, take a long swallow. 'It's dead in here,' I say.

'Always is this time of day.'

Another yell from the Chinese guys. Yeah, it's dead. Nice one, Innes.

'I just joined. Thought it might be a laugh.'

'Don't get too attached to the place,' she says.

'They knocking it down or something?'

'Nah. Just don't get too attached to the place.'

'Right. I get you.' I take a swig. 'You just work in the afternoons?'

She blushes again. Probably thinks I'm flirting. And maybe I am. The beer's got me lazy.

'Why d'you ask?'

'I'm looking for a guy. I heard he might come in here.'

'What's his name?'

'You know names?'

'I know some names.'

'Rob Stokes. He'll be a new punter. Probably started coming in a week or so ago. Manc accent.'

Pauline pours herself a Coke from the draught. Sips it, thinking. Then: 'What's he look like?'

I give her the description I was given. 'Apparently, he's got a temper on him.'

'They've all got tempers on them if they lose.'

'Fair enough.'

'What'd he do?' she says.

'He owes a friend of mine money.'

Her eyes sparkle. 'You're going to break his legs, is that it?'

I smile. 'Nothing like that. Do I look like a legbreaker?'

'You don't look like much of anything,' she says.

'Cheers.'

'I didn't mean it like that. I just meant you don't look like a legbreaker. I should think before I say stuff.' She drinks her Coke and leans against the bar. 'My boyfriend says that.'

'Your boyfriend sounds like a wanker,' I say.

'He is.' She looks out at the pit and yawns. 'He's a lazy bastard, right enough. Supposed to be at home right now looking after the bairn, right? Bet you he's out drinking.'

'You want to call him?'

'And get disappointed? Nah. I'll wait till I get home.'

'He doesn't work?'

'Does he fuck. He's on disability. Reckons he's depressed.'

'Aren't we all?'

'Aye. That's why he's down the pub or smoking tack in the house. Depression. Fuck's sake, he wants to get himself a job.' Her voice hardens, and for a moment, she looks a lot older. 'What do you do, though? He's a free babysitter.'

'A babysitter who smokes tack in the house.'

'Better than nothing. Christ, look at me. You want another drink?'

I drain the bottle. 'Why not, eh?'

She cracks the top off another bottle, says, 'So you just joined. What d'you think of the place?'

'I think it's a shithole.'

'Aye, that's about right. So why are you really looking for this guy?'

I smile. 'He dropped his wallet. I have to give it back to him.'

'Uh-huh. And another.'

'He's my estranged brother. I just want to make up with him for Mam's sake.'

She laughs. 'That's sweet.'

'That's the kind of guy I am.'

'You're fuckin' nuts,' she says.

'Are they showing?'

'Give me your number, then.'

'Your bloke might have something to say about that.'

'For when this Rob gadgie comes in,' she says.

I hand her a card. She cocks an eyebrow. 'You're a PI?'

'That's right, sweetheart,' I say in my best Bogart. I do a full-on Mike Yarwood bad impersonation, the quivering top lip, the whole bit.

'You alright?' she says.

I stop the lip thing. 'Yeah.'

'I thought you were having a turn.'

'Look, you see anything, hear anything, you drop a dime, okay?'

Maybe it's just the beer buzz, but I feel pretty good about myself, despite the fact the Bogie didn't go down well. She laughs again. It sounds too natural for a place like this. I leave the bar, cross the casino. On the way out, the receptionist heaves her way through a nasty coughing fit.

Now I just have to wait.

TWENTY-EIGHT

Three hours in a van with Rossie and Baz, man. Not my idea of a sharp time. I banged back a couple moggies on the way up 'cause Baz stuck in this tape of shite tunes and I wanted to sleep through it. So I went to kip in the middle, heard Rossie and Baz bitch at each other about the tape. Then Rossie got all pissy and chucked the tape out the window onto the road and Baz started bleating.

'Oi, Fatboy Fat, fuck up, will you?'

When we got to Newcastle, there weren't no vacancies. I said, 'What the fuck's this, like?'

'Westlife are playing at the Arena,' said the bloke on reception. He smiled and it were like his baby teeth never fell out.

'Westlife, fuckin' Westlife.'

'Fuckin' shithole this is, like,' said Rossie. 'Who's playing next week? Fuckin' Girls Aloud?'

'I like that Geordie one,' said Baz. 'She looks well fuckin' dirty.'

'I think there are some rooms at the airport,' said the bloke. Helpful cunt, this one.

'The airport? How far away's the airport?' I said.

'About forty-five minutes.'

Rossie kicked the reception desk. The bloke jumped.

'Aye, fine,' I said. 'We'll go up the airport.'

'You're kidding,' said Baz.

I punched him in the arm. 'C'mon.'

We went out the hotel and I clocked a bunch of girls with backpacks. Looked like proper tourists. 'Alright, girls?' said Rossie.

They didn't say nowt, just walked past.

'Fuckin' lezzes.'

'So what now?' said Baz. 'I ain't sleeping in the back of the van, I tell you that right now.'

'We go up the airport,' I said. 'Before that, I want a pint.'

Left the van in an NCP and wandered about in the town. Fat fuckin' Geordies everywhere I looked, man. Some proper ugly in this town. Saw this place called Dobsons and we went inside 'cause it had cheap pints an' that. Got settled at a table by the window and I rubbed some whizz on me gums 'cause the moggies were still in me system, slowing us right down. I supped me pint and wiped me mouth. Looked around at me posse, but they was looking down, bags under the eyes.

'Cheer up,' I said. 'Might never happen.'

Rossie said, 'What we doing up here, Mo?'

'I told you.'

'I thought your dad had you locked down.'

'And I thought you said I were a grown fuckin' man.'

'I said that?'

'Aye, Rossie. You said that. No more fuckin' doves for you, man. Your short-term's fucked. Summat you got to learn, mate. I *am* a grown fuckin' man. I do what I want to do because I can. I don't give a shit what me dad says because you know what? He's not gonna be around forever. One day some cunt's gonna bury a hatchet in his fuckin' head and they're gonna need someone to help 'em do it.'

Baz stared at us. 'You'd do your dad?'

'If I got the right offer.'

'That's fucked up.'

'You'd do Morris Tiernan,' said Rossie. His mouth were twitching into a grin.

'What's Morris Tiernan, man? It's a name. It's a bloke with a rep. But a rep only goes so far, know what I mean?'

'*You're* fucked up,' said Rossie. He shook his head and took a sup.

'You don't think I'd do it?'

'I think you better stop with the pills, Mo. You sound mashed.'

'You don't think I'd do it.'

'Nah, mate. I don't think you'd do your own dad. Don't make sense.'

I gulped me pint, wiped me mouth. Me throat were still all dry. 'Don't make sense. Lot of things don't make sense. You don't know what he's like. And I'm not saying any day soon, but you mark mine, Rossie, one day I'll get an offer and I'm saying that when that day comes, I might just fuckin' take it with a smile on me face.'

'You're full of shit,' said Rossie.

The speed kicked in with a twitch and I wanted to go drink-chucking again, but I kept it down. I wouldn't have got a decent throw in, not with me finger in a splint. Proper fucked me up that one.

Go round Paulo's in the middle of the night with a couple cans of petrol, torch that fuckin' place to the ground, watch it burn from across the street with five doses in me blood. Paulo lived there, even better. I wondered what a fuckin' cock-jockey smelled like when he burned. Probably fuckin' lilacs or some shite.

Or give the outside of the club a new coat of paint. Me and Baz, we went to Homebase and I picked up an armful of spray cans. I had it all planned out in me mind. PAEDO PAULO, sprayed ten feet fuckin' tall in red paint. AIDS SCUM right next to it. I had visions of mobs with flaming torches 'cause of that one. They'd come storming down on his club like it was Frankenstein's castle, smoke the fuckin' monster out into the street and crucify him. Just the thought of that made me balls jump.

But I kept it buzzing under the skin. That were for later. I couldn't be a fuckin' kid about it. A lad what gets knocked and knocks straight back, he's a fuckin' chump, know what I mean? It takes time for payback. Time makes it sit better. Until I could pay Paulo back for me fuckin' finger I had Innes on me mind.

And I weren't the only one. I beamed back to the pub, saw Rossie staring out the window. 'What?'

'Is that Innes?' he said.

I got out me seat, knocked me pint over. Lucky it only had a couple thumbs of beer in it. Nudged Rossie out the way and looked out at the street.

Well, fuck me. 'Rossie, get out there and follow the cunt.'

'You what?'

I gave him bug eyes. 'Get. Out. There.'

TWENTY-NINE

More time to kill, and the beer is wearing off. I think about another drink, maybe something stronger, but I don't want to chance it after last night. It's a short step from that first shot to becoming a bloodstain on a bed sheet.

Instead, I wander into town, looking for something free to pass the time. Pass a pub that looks too dingy for me and check my watch. Just after four. I find myself outside a gallery, then inside. Not my usual cup of tea, but it'll while away a couple of hours. A sign says I have to turn my mobile off. I ignore it.

An exhibition of portraits, or so the posters say. I follow the signs, stop in front of a huge painting. Proper Old Testament stuff, it looks like. When I read the plaque, it tells me it's the destruction of Sodom. From the looks of it, a Catholic put that bastard on canvas, probably Scottish. Fear and sadism. I remember it from my childhood. Sometimes I thought about telling my dad I was gay, just to see him hit the roof. But cowardice kept the thought at bay.

I move away from the painting, scan a couple of country-side landscapes that don't do anything for me. Usual sheep and lakes. An England that never existed except in the imaginations of those rich enough to buy this shite.

A guy in a black leather jacket shows the same distaste. I don't blame him. Then I head upstairs for the portraits.

The door to the exhibition has a blackout curtain over the

glass panes. Looks like it's closed, but I try the handle anyway. When I step inside, it's dark apart from a circle of upturned televisions in the centre of the floor. And this white noise of voices, sounds like screaming, and they're all out of sync. Movement catches my eye, and there's a young guy bent almost double, walking around the circle.

For some reason, I can't breathe.

I stare at the young guy, wary of him. It sounds like a killing floor in here and the way he moves – slow, deliberate steps backwards, thrown into relief by the flickering tellies – he looks like something out of *Twin Peaks*. Jerky, but purposeful. I can't quite make out his face, not sure if he has one.

He looks straight at me and I nearly shit myself.

Not as much as he does, though. He twitches with fright, then straightens up, makes for the door.

Christ. The guy was just like me. And we scared the hell out of each other. I stay in the room for a while longer, crane to see what's showing on the televisions. A choir, different shots, looks like old footage from the Proms.

No wonder he got a fright. This is some creepy stuff.

The door squeals open again, and the guy in the black leather jacket steps into the room. He doesn't flinch, doesn't look at the televisions.

He just watches me.

I watch him right back.

I stay where I am. Don't want to confront the bloke. In the light, he looks bigger than he should be, flickering large like a nightmare. Besides, I've got a bad track record when it comes to dealing with people who might be following me. But he doesn't look like a scally. This bloke looks like a professional.

We stand there. The voices mesh into one strangled shriek. He doesn't even glance at the televisions.

Something catches the light in his right hand. Then it flips out of sight.

I make my way towards the door, my ears ringing. This got bad really fast. And I know for a fact that this guy is a tail. Who he's working for, what he wants, I'm not about to stick around to find out. I push open the door and the hinges screech. A plaque on the wall tells me that those tellies were Mark Wallinger's idea of hell.

Close, but no cigar, Mark.

I head for the stairs as the door squeaks open again. Taking them two at a time, I'm down in the gift shop before I get a chance to catch my breath. I pretend to look through some postcards, but keep an eye on the staircase. If the guy's following me, he'll be down in a minute or two.

He appears just as I head into the landscape section again. I keep my head down, but I can hear his footsteps against the floor. He's wearing boots.

I return to the gift shop, and he comes with me. He looks like he might be a copper. If that's the case, then Donkey's determined to bring me in. And if Donkey's determined to bring me in, then things in Manchester have taken a turn for the worse.

A crowd has developed outside a club down the street. I head straight for it. The reek of bad aftershave and flowery perfume battles with the smell of beer and bad Italian meals for air space. I keep my head down, light a cigarette. A Bruce Banner lookalike bears down on me, crisp Fred Perry shirt on his back. I swerve out of the way before I accidentally get a Regal in the eye.

I take a quick look over my shoulder, and the black leather jacket is nowhere to be seen. I take a moment to breathe.

Friday nights, the same everywhere. Hordes of chequered shirts and women with love handles and bad halter tops. I can hear the chorus of a group of Welsh lads pissed off their faces. The women are all white, shivering legs and high-pitched curses. I can't make out what they're saying, but it's probably bad.

This is hell, Wallinger. Look around you.

Up the spiral steps, across the bridges that criss-cross the motorway, cars roaring by on the edge of the city. It's a clear night. I stop by the barrier and watch the traffic for a moment. After a while, the headlights stream into long red lines. I find enough phlegm to gob a fat one onto the motorway from the bridge. It doesn't have the same sense of satisfaction it did when I was ten. I try it again, but it's a poor effort. I have to wipe the spittle from my chin.

Me and Declan used to do it when we were kids. Spent hours gobbing at cars, people, whatever passed under our bridge. It didn't make much difference. Now the kids lob concrete blocks from these places, kill guys my age. Times change.

I lean against the barrier and ditch my cigarette. I should get back to the hotel, but I don't want to. The heaviness in my legs might spread to the rest of me. And I need to stay awake, just in case. Knowing my luck, I'd stretch out for a second and wake up nine hours later with nothing to show for it.

My mobile rings. I answer it.

'Mr Innes, it's George.'

'George,' I say.

'I work at the casino. You gave me your card. I think Rob Stokes is here.'

'You're sure,' I say. But I know he's sure. He knows who Rob Stokes is. I knew that when I talked to him.

'As sure as I can be. He matches your description.'

'Uh-huh. He just walk in?'

'He's been in a while. I had to wait until I got my break.'

'Right, I'll be there in a bit. Try to keep an eye on him for me. Let me know if he leaves, okay?'

I disconnect, start back towards town. My legs ache and my bad tooth starts to throb. So Rob Stokes is at the casino, that's great. But something doesn't add up. Things are happening too quickly for me to get my head round them. I've been in town two days and found the bugger, so why couldn't Morris?

Because he never got this far. Gave up at the first hurdle, maybe.

I shouldn't think about it. Just go with the flow, see where the current takes me. If George says Stokes is there, he's probably there. If it's a mistake, then we're back to square one.

I check my wallet. If it's the right guy, I should pay George. Yeah, I've got enough. A couple of hundred should do it. And then all I need to do is keep an eye on Stokes and follow him home.

Then I call Mo and I'm out of here.

And then what happens to Stokes? I can't afford to care. At least if I'm out of Newcastle, I won't have to hear about it. Not unless Mo feels like bragging. But then, I'll be off the hook with Tiernan. There'll be no reason to see any of that lot again.

Keep telling yourself that, Cal.

I take the long way round, skirt the drunks and avoid eye contact. Outside a fun pub two lads in Hilfiger shirts shower each other with spit when they talk. One of them wears more jewellery than my mam. It throws light off his arms when he flaps his hands.

I press on. Hit Central Station, and the line for black cabs is already growing. People have started to walk up to the casino now, either beered-up and looking to blow the rest of their money, or out to impress whoever they have on their arm. I fall back from the herd, take my time. There's no need to rush. From what I know about Rob Stokes, he'll be there all night. It's not like he doesn't have enough money to lose.

'So I says to him, get the fuck out my way, like. Then I stots him right in the fuckin' face . . .'

This from a couple of bruisers in suits walking behind me.

'And he's like all bleeding an' that, fuckin' bubbling like a bairn. So I gives him a kick in the knackers for good measure.'

'Might as well put the cunt to the floor, like.'

I don't turn around. They speak like a certain copper I know, but they've got the greasy sadism of a couple of bouncers. If I didn't get the point before, it's soon hammered home.

'I told him, I said to him, nae fuckin' students.'

'Cunts think they're special.'

'Not too special to avoid a slap.'

We get to the casino, and I hang back as the bouncers head straight for the guys on the door. It's all backslaps and missing-tooth grins. I slip past, unnoticed. Into the reception and I get caught up in a gang of young guys and girls who think this place is a proper hoot. One guy with spiky hair and oily skin is trying to sign them all in. Another guy sorts out the memberships while the girls giggle to themselves. The musk of aftershave is overpowering; before I know it, my eyes are watering.

I hand over my membership card. The receptionist gives it a quick once-over and buzzes me in. When I step into the casino, it's like the place has been transformed. Blue-and-white lights fill the place. The Friday night crowd are out in force. The hum of conversation, the clatter of balls hitting roulette wheels, excitement in the air. The brand new, hip and happening gambling experience. It's a far cry from

Tiernan's club, but then that's probably the point. This is the new school.

George is still behind the bar. I catch his eye and walk over. He nods towards a guy, tall and reedy, playing roulette. I can only see him from the back, but his hair is speckled grey.

I stop, find a seat at the edge of the pit. A valet crosses in front of me, asks if I want a drink. I order a coffee. When it comes back, it tastes like someone shat in it. And judging from the look I get when I don't tip the valet, they probably wished they had.

The guy at the roulette table, he's hunched over the layout, his hands a blur. He has a dealer's reflexes, and a punter's mixture of bad luck and worse temper. When the dealer calls out a number, he falls back from the table like someone punched him in the face. When he's watching for the spin to stop, he plays with his chips, clipping them over each other. It's a nervous action, and one that gives him away as an ex-croup.

He turns his head and I get a look at his face. Too many wrinkles, a sign of stressful living. I'm starting to see the same lines on my face these days.

I finish the coffee and make my way up to the bar. George needs to be paid. And I need a good place to watch Rob Stokes in action.

THIRTY

'You got a room?' I said to the receptionist at the Premier Inn. I tried to be nice and cool about it, but me heart were skipping all over the shop. Tracked the fucker down. Once Rossie managed to work out that he had to stay out of sight, he got the whole tailing thing sorted. Saw Innes come back across the bridge. And we had a wander about. And there were Innes' Micra in the Premier Inn carpark.

'Sorry, sir. We're full.'

She were lying. And that weren't nice. But then I looked at Baz and took her side. Baz were standing by the door looking like he were after summat to nick.

'Westlife,' I said.

'Sorry?'

'Westlife're playing, am I right?'

'At the Arena, yeah,' she said.

'You like Westlife?'

She smiled. 'Not really.'

'Nah, you're too old for them.'

She just kept smiling.

'And she's too old for you,' said Baz.

'Leave it,' I said. Then, to the receptionist: 'Ta for your time, love.'

Breath of fresh air outside. I nudged Baz for a ciggie and he handed one over. I lit it and stood looking at the hotel.

'I told you, Mo,' said Baz. 'I ain't sleeping in the back of that van. It stinks.'

'You fuckin' stink,' I said. 'And nah, we ain't kipping down in the back of the van. We ain't kipping down anywhere. We're going to wait until Innes shows his face and then we're going to scare the fucker off.'

'What's the point in that?' said Rossie.

'It'll make me feel better,' I said. 'What the fuck d'you think the point is? We scare him off, we can go looking for Stokes ourselves.'

'You think we can scare him off?' said Baz.

'If there's one thing I know about Innes it's that he's a fuckin' bottler. And he don't want to be doing this anyway. So all we're gonna do is give him an excuse to get the fuck out of Dodge, know what I mean?'

I grabbed the pair of them and pushed 'em back towards the van.

THIRTY-ONE

I stay away from the hard stuff, maintain a buzz with the watered-down Kronenburg the place has on tap. George busies himself with other punters. A guy at the end of the bar has his flies open, but nobody seems to have told him. He watches a plasma screen above the bar. Sky Sports is on, a wealth of stats and breaking news sailing across the bottom of the screen. He's transfixed, until something breaks the mood and he scribbles on a napkin.

At about nine, the music kicks up in volume. What was Dionne Warwick and Kenny Rogers slips into The Who and David Bowie. Right now, Bowie's singing 'Heroes'. It's an odd choice, considering the clientele. They're young and stupid enough to think the song's from a mobile phone advert.

Stokes is at the same table as before, but the dealer's changed twice since I came in. I've watched him rake in a couple of decent wins, but it means nothing in the long run. Any winnings go right back onto the layout. He's tapping his knuckles against the edge of table. The woman next to him resembles a tanned skeleton. She looks down at the sound, her face creasing up like a cat's arse. Then she realises she has to get some chips down before the balls stops and panics, shoves a couple of reds onto a column.

The dealer rakes them in. She looks fit to spit.

I order another pint, a Coke to go with it, just to keep me alert. 'How long are your shifts, George?'

'What d'you mean?'

'It just struck me, you were in this afternoon. How many hours do you work?'

'I'm on a double,' he says. 'I'm stuck here till the bar closes.'

'When's that?'

'Two.'

'Right. That's harsh.'

'Tell me about it. It's the only way to make decent money, though.'

'How long does Stokes usually stay?'

'Until he's pissed away his cash, Mr Innes.'

It doesn't look like I'll have too long to wait. A quick glance at the roulette table, and I can see Stokes is short-stacked already. His back is all knotted up, giving him a stoop and a concentrated look. One more spin, and that look becomes desperate. He sticks the last of his stack on an outside bet.

True to form, it doesn't come in.

'Fuckin' *bastard*,' he says. Loud enough for everyone to hear. I take a drink from my pint. He'll be popular with the dealers in here, no doubt about it. That kind of showboating marks him out, especially on a night where most of the punters aren't taking the games too seriously. And for a guy on the run with someone else's money, he's suspiciously high profile.

But then, he's a gambler. And from what I know about Stokes already, he's stupid and arrogant enough to think he's invincible. Suddenly the idea of letting Mo off his leash doesn't sound too bad at all.

I stifle a belch as Stokes pulls himself away from the table, and storms out of the pit.

Straight for me.

I turn away, try to be cool about it. He looks too wound-up to pay me any attention, but I pretend to fade into the cigarette smoke anyway. He pulls out his wallet and I get a glimpse of enough cash to make my tongue feel thick in my mouth. I take a sip of my pint and watch the plasma screen.

Stokes sucks his teeth and slaps a fiver on the bar. 'Georgie, I'm having a shitty night.'

'Sorry to hear that, Mr Stokes.'

I catch a twitch in George's face, see him glance at me.

'I'll have the usual,' says Stokes.

George shifts his weight from one foot to the other as he's pouring a John Smith's for Stokes. Sets the pint down and cranks a double Johnny Walker from an optic. He takes the fiver and dumps silver on the bar. Stokes takes a long pull on the bitter. 'You lot in here, you might as well fuckin' mug me. It'd be faster.'

'But less fun,' says George. He has a fake smile plastered on his face, like someone put vinegar on the roof of his mouth. This is banter to go with the drinks. About as friendly as he wants to get with me watching.

'You're right,' says Stokes. 'You're always right, man. The house has the advantage. I should know fuckin' better. It's not like you don't tell me that.'

George doesn't hear him. Or if he does, he doesn't show it. He moves to the other end of the bar. Out of the way. And I know why.

I don't know who you're talking about, mate.

Georgie doesn't know Rob Stokes. The lying bastard. The question now is how well does he know him. I make a mental note not to pay the barman. Fuck him. And his glance at me when Stokes arrived at the bar bothers me. I didn't get a look at Stokes' face, but I'm sure it was for his benefit. Like, here's the guy who's looking for you, Rob. Gets me thinking that George set the pair of us up.

Stokes drinks his bitter, then knocks back the whisky. He turns to me, says, 'I know you?'

I'm shaken out of it. 'Don't think so, mate.'

'You're a Manc,' he says.

'Salford.'

'Fuckin' hell, small world. I used to live down Manchester.'

'Whereabouts?' I ask.

He takes a moment. 'All over.'

If there's any fear in Stokes, he's not giving it up. As far as he's concerned, I'm just another transplanted Manc. How he knows that from my accent, I don't know. The more I drink, the more I sound like a Leith lad. Which means he's probably been briefed.

'Why're you up here?' I say.

His eyes flash, then he drinks. 'Girlfriend wanted to move up here. I fancied a change of scenery.'

'And what do you think of the place?'

'Newcastle? It's a shit pit.' Stokes leans against the bar, regards me with red-rimmed eyes. 'But it's better for me right now.'

'Why's that?'

'Just because.' He finishes his pint, sucks his teeth again. 'What's with the Coke?'

'Stops me getting drunk.'

'Expensive, though.'

'It does the job.'

'Why you scared of getting drunk?' he says.

Because I'll end up twatting people like you, I think. 'I just hate hangovers.'

'Uh,' he says. He opens his wallet again, sorts out his cash. He removes a wad and nods to me. 'Nice talking to you.'

'And you,' I say.

I finish my pint as he strides back down to the pit and heads for a blackjack table. I order another drink, sip at my Coke while I wait for George to get his arse in gear.

When he finally hands over the pint, I look at him. He's gone white.

'You feeling alright, George?' I say.

'I'm okay.'

'Good.' I reach into my pocket. 'You want me to pay you now?'

He shakes his head. 'No good here. There's cameras all over the place. Just meet me outside after work.'

'Right,' I say. 'Wouldn't want you to get into trouble.'

'Thanks. Is it the right guy?'

'I think you know fine well it's the right guy, Georgie.'

He looks at the floor. I notice his hairline is receding. Older than I thought. Not that it matters much. He has to serve another customer, so I let him go.

I call for a cab when it looks like Stokes is hitting rock bottom. It's outside waiting for me at ten-thirty when he calls it a night. As I get in, a Ford Escort's headlights go up full blaze and Stokes tears out of the carpark.

'That's my mate there. I got to follow him home,' I say to the driver.

The cab driver looks at me in the rear view.

'I mean it.'

'Uh-huh,' he says and breaks into a smug grin, pulls the cab out of the carpark and makes sure he keeps two cars behind all the way.

As Stokes turns off towards Benton, I check the clock on the cab dashboard. It's getting towards eleven. I can picture George hanging around outside the casino after his shift ends at two. Waiting for me to turn up and hand over the cash. He can go fuck himself.

I wonder how long he'll wait there before he realises he's been stood up.

And I can't help smiling to myself.

THIRTY-TWO

Stokes turns off Benton Road before he hits the Metro station into a residential area. Mostly bungalows and semi-detached. Nice gardens, well-kept. Obviously owned, no council.

But as soon as I see the block of flats, I know that's where he lives. This is definitely rented accommodation, but the council tax is probably a bigger expense. He turns left into the block carpark.

'Right here's fine, mate,' I say to the driver.

The cabbie lets me out. I tip him well and make a note of the firm's number. I'm going to need a ride back. As he pulls away from the kerb, I sink into the shadows on a patch of wasteground, squint through the gloom.

Stokes appears, goes into the door nearest the end of the building.

So he lives in one of six flats. It's a start. When I'm sure he's inside, I cross the grass towards the block of flats. I check the windows for any sign of life. The one at the far end has the door to the balcony open and a flickering blue light behind curtains, probably a television. The one below has a lit window, too. I scan the rest of the flats for any signs of someone coming home.

Nothing.

I keep watching.

I wait. Watch. Listen. The television keeps blaring out. Sounds like the theme tune to *Sex and the City*.

Georgie, I'm having a shitty night.

That bothers me. Something I've missed. Yeah, I know George knows Stokes. That's a given. But does it go any further than that? Something's niggling at me, something about the way George's face tightened when Stokes came over. Something about the way he kept his distance when Stokes was at the bar, like he didn't want to be associated with him.

They'd know each other. Obviously. If Stokes is a regular, and a regular loser at that, of course he'd know George. And the barman's a shift junkie, so he'd be in most nights. But something about that glance, that twitch of the face. It wasn't just the knowledge that I'd caught him out.

It was like he was scared of Stokes.

Fuck it, forget it. It's nothing. The barrage of an approaching hangover, the twinge in my tooth, the idea I'm doing something wrong, that's what it is. It adds up to paranoia. Nobody's setting me up.

A shadow crosses in front of the curtains, thrown into strobed distortion. From the flat I can hear voices, but I can't make out what they're saying. I try to get closer. The grass squelches underfoot and I hope to hell I didn't step in dog shit.

The voices aren't American. Male and female. When the male voice starts shouting, I know it's Stokes. The female voice hits the same volume, but I still can't make out what's being said. The television almost drowns them out.

Almost. When he hits her, the smack is enough to make the breath catch in my throat.

It goes silent apart from the girls in New York.

A low male voice, saying something that tries to be soothing.

The soft sound of someone crying. Probably Alison.

A temper like his, I shouldn't have thought he'd save it for the tables. Nah, he's a guy who likes to bring it home with him. And Alison's on the other end of it. Money's a bitch for bringing the worst out of people, especially when they've got an addiction to feed.

I should call Mo right now, tell him to get his arse in gear and up to Newcastle. I've got an idea where Stokes lives. I can wait for Mo to arrive, then point him in the right direction.

Something stops me, though. I don't know if it's fear, duty or the idea that, fuck it, I might have the wrong place. I should double-check that before I even think about calling Mo. Then when I'm sure that this is the place, I'll give him the address and go home. If I'm not sure, I'll have to hang around. And if Mo finds out what Stokes has been doing to his little sister, he'll make it messier than usual.

And as much as Stokes is doing nothing to get off my shitlist, I don't want to be responsible for that. It's not in my job description.

Yeah right, Cal. That *is* your job description.

I walk away from the flat, pull my jacket tight, head out to the sounds of a main road just up the way. I think I've got enough information. Anything more than that, Mo can sort it out.

But the white knight in me won't give it up. I've got to do something to help Alison. I should sort this out so nobody else gets hurt.

Hurt any more than necessary, that is.

There's a moral decision to make here, and I'm not sure I'm the right man to make it. Too many things don't add up the way I need them to. The more I think about it, the more I think George knows Stokes of old. I mean, Christ, the guy's only been in town a week or so. And a man like him doesn't strike me as the type to make friends easily, no matter how loose that friendship is.

No, George has got to be one of those friends that Kev mentioned to me. One of Alison's mates. And the only reason he would have for grassing Stokes to me is that he knows what's going on in that flat. Maybe he's playing the white knight himself. Or maybe he's just like Kev, besotted with Alison Tiernan and hoping I'll get Stokes out of the way. Grab himself a handful of the Tiernan family and end up being next on Mo's list.

Jesus, I really hope that's not the case.

I pull out my mobile and ring for a cab. Light an Embassy and take a long drag on it.

No, I won't be calling Mo just yet. I have too many questions.

And Alison Tiernan's the only person who can answer them.

THIRTY-THREE

Rossie were sparked out in the middle seat of the van, Baz all cloudy-eyed at the wheel. I'd just done another wrap and it kept me night vision proper enabled. Glared at Innes' Micra like it were sitting there teasing us. We knew Innes weren't there. We knew he were out and about, but he'd have to come back for his car. I checked me mobile to see if there were any messages, but a big fat zero blinked at us.

He knew the deal. He found Stokes, he had to call us. I felt like calling me dad and telling him what the fuck were transpiring. But then what did I know? Nowt. Far as I knew, Innes were holed up in a pub somewhere fucked out his brains.

But nah, he came to Newcastle for a reason.

I seen the cab coming down the hill and I fuckin' knew. 'That's him,' I said. 'He's got summat.'

Baz snorted. Fucker were half-asleep. I gave him a nudge. 'Baz. Wake up, man.'

He opened his mouth, then turned away. Bastard.

The cab pulled in the carpark and I got close to the window, squinted right up so's I could see what were happening. I watched Innes fuck about in the car, then he got out and started walking to the hotel. Felt like tearing across the street and leathering the cunt in the back of the head, but I stayed put. Mature, that were me. Fuckin' mature. Mature enough to handle ten times this job.

'There y'are, you cunt,' I said. I watched for a new light in one of the windows, but nowt came. Muttered to meself and gave up after a couple minutes. Fuck it. We didn't need to go in his room and work him over. I nicked one of Baz's Regals and got out the van, lit up and watched the hotel through the smoke.

I could've burned the whole place down. I wanted to. Summat in us wanted to see the sky lit up like that, knowing that Innes was in the middle of it all. Proper hellfire damnation. Try that on for size, you Catholic fuck.

But nah, that were the kind of thing the old Mo would do. He'd go in there like guns blazing, kick arse all over the shop and leave no man standing. But this now, this were the New Mo. This were Mature Mo. I went in there and burned, there'd be consequences, and I heard me dad in the back of me head telling us that he weren't gonna stand by us no more. He'd leave us to the spurs.

I stayed out the 'Ways this long. I didn't fancy a trip now.

I opened up the van door and gave Baz a knuckle knock on his head.

'Ow, ya bastard. Fuck was that for?'

'I thought you was asleep.'

'I *was* asleep.'

'And now you're awake.'

Baz yawned, then his face went all fat and rumpled again. 'What'd you wake us up for, Mo?'

'You still got them spray cans?'

'What fuckin' spray cans?' said Baz.

'The ones we was going to do Paulo's place with.'

'Yeah.'

'C'mon then.'

'They're in the back of me car,' said Baz.

'You're fuckin' kidding.'

'I didn't know we was supposed to bring 'em with us.'

I kicked the side of the van. The bang echoed in the street.

'Here, Mo, if you'd let us bring me car, we'd be sound right now.'

'Oh, you just figured that out, did you? I knew I kept you round for a reason. Get the engine going. We're gonna buy some spray paint.'

'Where the fuck are we gonna get spray paint this time of night?'

'I don't give a shit. We keep driving until we find a fuckin' garage, alright?' I got in the van. Rossie made a noise like he were waking up. 'Now let's get going, Baz.'

Baz shook his head, tried to get awake as he twisted the ignition. When the engine caught, Rossie woke right up. 'What's going on?'

'We're going to a garage,' said Baz.

'Sweet. I'll have a pasty if they got 'em.'

This were what I had to fuckin' deal with. No wonder I were so pissed off.

THIRTY-FOUR

I don't get much sleep. It's too warm, the air too heavy. I open the windows in my hotel room and slump back onto the bed. Stare at the ceiling. Lights pass across it as cars go by outside. I reach for my mobile and sit with Donna's number in my hand. I don't know if I should call her. She might not remember me. She might put me down as a bad mistake. And it's late.

Press in her number, but I don't follow through.

Come on, Cal. Grow some fucking balls.

Then I connect.

It rings. And then rings some more. My throat goes dry. I take a drink from the glass of water next to me, but it doesn't seem to make it better. When she picks up, my mouth is full, and I realise I don't know what I'm supposed to say. I swallow.

'It's Callum.' Which is better than nothing, I suppose.

'Callum?' she says.

'Yeah, Callum. Cal. Sorry, it's *Cal*. Like the Helen Mirren movie. We met the other night, remember?'

'Course I remember. You were supposed to call me. Did you forget, or is it a bloke thing?'

'I . . . Well, I thought I *was* calling you.'

'I expected a next-day service,' says Donna.

'Sorry. I've been busy.'

'Stop apologising. I'm joking.' She laughs. It should hurt, that sound. 'So what are you doing tonight?'

I check my watch. It's a scratch past midnight. 'What, you mean now?'

'No, I mean tonight.'

'I don't know. I have to work.'

'And then?'

'Then I'm going back to Manchester.'

'Right.'

'But we can meet up before I go,' I say.

She doesn't say anything.

'You still there?'

'Yeah,' she says. 'Well. You have my number. Call me if you want. I'll understand if you don't.'

'I'll give you a ring.'

'Okay.' She doesn't believe me. Before I get a chance to say anything else, she rings off and I'm left holding a dead line.

Forget it.

I do. For the moment, anyway. And the rest of the night falls into blackness.

*

I wake up at noon, pull myself from the bed and stumble into the bathroom. Brush my teeth. The brush catches my bad tooth and I grunt, chuck the toothbrush into the sink as blood mingles with minty freshness. Look up at myself in the mirror and realise that a good night's sleep has still left me looking like death.

I grab my mobile and call Paulo. Something about that tail yesterday put me on edge. When he picks up, I ask him if Donkey's been round the club.

'Yeah, he's been round, Cal. Every fuckin' morning he's been round. The bloke's got a doctorate in mithering.'

'What'd you tell him?'

'What d'you think I told him? I told him you were out of town.'

'How'd he take it?'

'He told me to let him know the second I got off the phone to you. Said you were in deep shit. What'd you do?'

'Hey, what makes you think I did something?'

'Because you're asking more questions than you're answering. What'd you do?'

'I didn't do anything. Donkey's got a fuckin' stiffy for me because I'm an ex-con. I told you about that.'

'He's leaning on me, Cal.'

'So lean back. You're a big boy.'

There's a silence on the other end. Then Paulo clears his throat. 'Who the fuck do you think you're talking to?'

'I'm sorry, mate. I just . . . I've got enough on my plate at the moment. I need your help on this, Paulo. Just fob him off or something, okay? I'll be back in a couple of days.'

'I got my club to think about. I'm not doing you any more fuckin' favours, Cal. Mo's one thing, but the police? That's a whole other story.'

'He thinks I did over this bloke, alright? He hasn't got a stitch of evidence, but he's after my blood.'

'You leaving town's not helped matters.'

'I know that. Look, tell you what. He left you a number, right? Give me the number and I'll call him myself.'

As Paulo grumbles to himself, it sounds like he's shifting furniture. I need to talk to Donkey, just to get the bastard off my back. I've got a throbbing pain in the back of my neck.

The guy in the black leather jacket, he must have been a copper. Donkey's watching me, just like he said he would. And this is the worst possible time for it. But me losing him in the crowd has tweaked Donkey where it hurts, so he's making things tough for Paulo. Typical Donkey.

'Got it,' says Paulo. And he gives me the number.

'Cheers, mate. I'm sorry. I'll sort this out.'

'Be sure you do.'

I hang up. As I'm pressing in Donkey's number, there's a light knock at my door. My arse clenches. He couldn't have found me already. Part of me wants to bolt for the window, but that's a stupid move. I'm not dressed enough for a getaway, and if it's the police, I wouldn't get far after hitting the concrete. They'd be on me like flies on shit and I'd be in even more trouble than I already am. So I cancel the call, stuff my mobile into my jacket and open the door.

The braided blonde from reception stares at me. She looks like she just swallowed a pint glass of brine. I look up the corridor to make sure she's alone.

'Mr Innes?' she says.

'Yeah.'

'Do you own a white Micra?'

Takes me a moment to get my head straight. 'Uh, yeah, I do.'

'I'm really sorry,' she says. 'I mean, *we're* really sorry.'

'Fuck. Give me a second to get dressed.'

And before I leave the room, I make sure I dry-swallow a couple of Nurofen to kill the toothache. Grabbing my jacket, I notice that the bin's empty. It could be house-keeping, but something tells me they're not the ones who have taken out the rubbish.

I can't think about it now. The receptionist has bad news for me.

THIRTY-FIVE

They're sorry. That about sums it up. Out here in the carpark, it's starting to rain. I feel the weight of the car keys in the palm of my hand, stare at my car. The metal part of the key is cold against my skin.

'We're all really sorry,' says the receptionist. She's been saying that on and off for the past ten minutes. I'm getting a little sick of being apologised to.

'Not a problem,' I say.

My warhorse Micra. The windscreen's still in one piece, as are the wing mirrors. The bodywork is fine apart from that prang.

But someone's taken a spray to the paintwork and a blade to the front two tyres. Across the side of the car in stark red letters it reads: 'RIP'.

'I think it might be a tag,' says the receptionist. 'Some of the kids round here have them.'

'I think it's Rest In Peace, but thanks anyway.'

'I didn't want to say that,' she says. 'It doesn't bear thinking about.'

'Easy for you to say. It's not your car.'

'I'm sorry?'

'Yeah, I know.' I crouch down by the side of the car. The front two tyres, they're shredded. Someone took their time over this.

'I mean, we have CCTV,' she says. 'We'll be forwarding the tapes to the police.'

'Don't bother,' I say. 'It's not worth it. Only a couple of tyres.'

Put the rubber together, you'd have a Westwood dress. Carved up.

'I hope this won't reflect badly on us.'

'It doesn't reflect badly on you, love. It reflects badly on this shithole area.'

Back in reception, I leaf through the Yellow Pages, find a garage in Benton and give them a ring. It'll cost me, they say. If I want them today, that is. And am I sure I want them to pick the car up from the middle of town? That'll cost too. I mean, they really want to be sure. The mechanic's voice has a twist of amusement about it, like he can't believe the kind of fish he's got on the line.

I'm sure. But there's one thing: I want a lift to Benton.

'Oh aye, that's not a problem, mate.'

'It better not be, the amount you'll skin me out of.'

Just because the Micra's out of action, doesn't make me a cripple. I still have work to do, still have questions that need to be answered. And I don't have much time.

Somehow that pissed-off dealer found out where I was staying, found out which car was mine and decided to take a knife to the wheels. If he'd left well enough alone, I wouldn't have been that arsed to wrap this up. But you mess with a man's motor, you get his attention. From what I've seen of Newcastle, it's populated with the same kind of narrow-minded scallies we have in Manchester. But at least when it rains back home, it really rains.

I turn to the receptionist. 'I'll be checking out today.'

She nods to herself. It's like she snapped out of sympathy, become this sterile jobsworth. I don't care, though. If they know where I'm staying, then it's just a matter of time before they get in my room, if they haven't already. And I don't want to be at the mercy of anyone.

It was the wind, Cal. Don't think so much.

I open my wallet, take out Donna's number, think about a pint. It's still too early, and I've got too much to do. Christ, I wish I'd met her somewhere else down the line. Somewhere I wasn't acting like a complete prat, playing detective. I crumple up her number, stick it in my back pocket and make a mental note not to take it out the next time I wash these jeans.

In my room, I pack the holdall and make sure I've got everything I came in with. Back out on reception the braided blonde hands me the bill and I pay it, no questions asked. Then I'm out on the street, waiting on the tow truck. I light up and think I couldn't be fucking this up more.

I'm not a private investigator. That's a fact. I'm a guy who tells people he's a PI, and that's as far as it goes. The job's not something I ever really wanted to do, but I admit that urban white-knight shit appealed after a while. I started off running errands for Paulo. Not much, really. If a kid didn't turn up to the club, he'd send me out after him, bring him back in. Sometimes they'd kick up a fuss, but most of the time they didn't reckon on Paulo sending someone after them. Those kids, they were used to pansy social workers, men and women getting paid too little to care too much. As long as they weren't robbing cars or shoplifting, the social couldn't care less. And why should they? Those poor bastards had enough on their books. What the kids didn't realise, though, was that the club was a labour of love for Paulo. He lost one kid, he lost a bit of himself.

And the job progressed from there. I got good at tracking down ex-offenders, maybe because I was one. This guy, Don Plummer, he was a local landlord. Had some houses in Hulme and Moss Side, a couple more in Longsight. And sometimes, he had problem tenants. I did him a legit favour every now and then by handing over eviction notices. Paulo didn't mind. It was legal, and it kept me working.

These things snowball. Next thing I know, I'm calling myself a PI and getting all kinds of shit for it. Donkey on my back for one.

I look up the street, see my lift coming over the hill. I nod to the driver as the truck pulls into the carpark. A skinny guy with a belly that looks like he's smuggling a bowling ball under his shirt gets out and looks at my car with practised disgust.

'Now that's a shame,' he says. 'That's a real shame.'

'Yeah, it's all I can do to keep the tears in,' I say.

He looks at me. When he realises I'm not serious, he sets about hooking the Micra to the truck. I get in and it's a short drive to Benton. Once we're at the garage, the skinny guy joins his colleagues and they take turns in surveying the damage. A chorus of tuts and sighs, the usual mechanic beatbox karaoke.

'I know it's bad,' I say. 'But you've got a day to replace the tyres. How's about that?'

'What about the paintwork?' says the skinny guy.

'I couldn't give a fuck. You just sort me out with some tyres.' I give him my mobile number and tell him to give me a call when the car's ready to go.

'We got other jobs on, mate. We can't just drop everything.'

'I'll make it worth your while,' I say as I walk out the door.

I light another Embassy as I head down the main road, away from the Metro station. Once I've got the cigarette on the go, I fish around for my mobile and call Donkey. Best to get this out of the way. It's the last thing I want to do, but I might as well do something for Paulo.

'Detective Sergeant Ian Donkin,' he says. His phone voice is official. For a moment I think I'm talking to a real copper instead of a fuck-up with a badge.

'It's Cal Innes,' I say.

'Innes, where the fuck are you, son?'

'You know where I am, Detective.'

'Nah, I mean it. Where the fuck are you? You any idea what kind of trouble you're in?'

'I thought you were keeping an eye on me.'

'Don't play funny buggers, Innes. I find you, you're in custody. And your poof mate won't be able to suck your way out of it, either.'

Poof mate. I'm sure Paulo'd get a kick out of that. And he'd aim it for Donkey's teeth, most likely. 'What's the deal with the tail, Donkey?'

'What tail?'

'The lad in the black leather jacket. The lad that smelled like the inside of a black maria.'

'Where are you?'

'You listening to me?'

'Where are you? I'll get someone to come and pick you up.'

'Jesus, Donkey, you *know* where I am.'

'If I knew, I wouldn't be asking.'

Okay, now I need to think about this. 'You know I'm in Newcastle, Detective. You sent a lad up here to follow me around.'

'You think I have them kind of resources, Innes?'

I can't say anything. If it's not Donkey following me around, then it's someone else and I don't want to think that through. 'Listen, I want you to stop going round the club.'

'You don't make the rules, Innes.'

'This shit between you and me, it's got nowt to do with Paulo.'

'Now that's sweet, but I don't care. You get your arse back to Manchester and turn yourself in, and maybe we'll talk about it. Until that time, I'll go wherever the fuck I want and cause trouble for whoever the fuck I want.'

'You're not bothering to investigate this, are you?'

Donkey coughs into the phone. 'I'm investigating. Trouble is, my prime suspect did a fuckin' bunk. Now what does that say to you about their innocence, eh?'

'I didn't do a thing to Dennis Lang. If you'd bothered to ask questions –'

'Don't tell me how to do my job, Innes. I don't come to your work and slap Mo's cock out of your mouth, do I?'

'Fuck's that supposed to mean?'

'It means, you don't get back to Manchester quick-smart, I'll have a word with the police up in Newcastle and tell them what you're up to. And in the meantime, I'll make sure I do everything in my power to have your mate's club shut down.'

'You don't know a fuckin' thing.'

'Never stopped me before,' he says.

Don't I know it. 'I'll be back when I'm back, Detective.'

'I'll look forward to it.'

'In the meantime, you might want to get off your arse and ask some questions at The Denton. In fact, you might want to start off with Mrs Lang.'

Donkey starts to say something, but I cut him off. I realise I've been gritting my teeth.

As I turn the corner, the reason for me coming to Benton comes into view.

Alison Tiernan lives in that block. Enough running around. It's time I found out what the fuck's going on.

THIRTY-SIX

I look around for Stokes' Escort, but it's nowhere in sight. Which means I'm okay for the time being. I don't know how long that's going to be the case, though.

I walk round to the front of the building just as a fat guy wearing an anorak comes out of the block. I make a show of looking for my keys, and give him a smile when he holds the door open for me. He doesn't return it.

When I get into the hallway, my mobile starts ringing. It's George and he sounds like someone slapped him.

'Where the fuck were you?' he says.

'Sorry?'

'Last night, you were supposed to meet me. You owe me money, Mr Innes.'

'I owe you fuck all, pal. In fact, you owe me for a couple of tyres.'

'What?'

I click him off. The mobile starts ringing again almost immediately.

'Listen, George, I don't owe you a fuckin' thing. Sue me.'

'Mr Innes?' It's not George. A female voice.

'Who is this?'

'Um, it's Pauline. Remember?'

Shit. 'Yeah, Pauline. Sorry about that. What can I do for you?'

'That bloke you were after, he's in the casino right now.'

'You sure?'

'He just threw a strop with one of the dealers, grey in his hair. Yeah, he's the guy. You want to come over and take a look?'

'I can't right now, Pauline. Listen to me, try to keep him there if you can. Tell him he can have free drinks or something and I'll pay you later, okay?'

'I can't do that, Mr Innes.'

'Well, just try to stall him.'

'How?'

'You're a bright girl. You'll think of something.'

'Don't patronise me. You sound like —'

'Bye, Pauline.'

I hang up on her. If she's got any sense, she'll leave Stokes alone. But I'm counting on her not knowing what kind of arsehole the guy is and playing it my way. It might buy me a little more time with Alison.

I take the concrete steps two at a time, and I realise that this block has a ground-floor flat and a first-floor maisonette. I walk towards the end of the landing, look out over the balcony and check out the carpark. Then round again to face the door.

This has to be it. It's the only one that could correspond to the window I was watching last night. I take a deep breath, adjust my jacket and knock on the door.

At first, I'm not sure if there's anyone in. I knock again, harder this time. I hear a voice from somewhere behind the door. For a brief second, I think it's Stokes and my gut tightens.

It can't be. He's at the casino.

The sound of a chain being put on the door. I brace myself just in case Pauline got it wrong. Thinking, well, if it's Stokes, I'll peg it and call Mo. That'll be the end of it, questions or no questions. I am the self-preservation society.

The door opens a crack. I can see one side of a girl's face. 'Alison Tiernan?' I say.

She starts to say something, then makes to close the door. I jam my foot in the gap. She slams the door on it and pain shoots up my shin. I curl my fingers round the door and pull it as far as I can off my foot. 'Listen to me, Alison. My name is Callum Innes –'

'I don't know you. Get your foot out my door.'

'Your dad sent me.'

'Fuck off.'

'You've got to let me in, Alison. I'm not going to hurt you, alright?'

'I'll call the police.'

'We both know you won't.'

'I'm not letting you in.'

I keep my foot where it is, but I let go of the door. 'Fine. Then I do this from out here. I know what Rob's been doing. And I know you two took some cash that didn't belong to you. But I'm here to help. If I wasn't, then I wouldn't have bothered knocking, would I?'

She stops trying to slam the door. Her lips purse and she looks at me through the crack. Figuring me out, wondering if I pose a threat.

'I mean it, Alison. If I didn't need to sort some stuff out, I wouldn't be here, believe me. I would've called Mo by now.'

We stand there in silence for a few seconds. Then she says, 'Get your foot out of the door.'

'Are you going to let me in?'

'Just get your foot out of the door.'

'I'm not moving until I get a chance to talk about this properly.'

Her face suddenly twitches into animation. 'Fine, okay?

Yes, fine, I'll let you in. Now get your fuckin' foot out of my fuckin' door, alright?'

I remove my foot, try to ignore the pain. She closes the door, slides the chain off and opens it up again.

'Come on,' she says. 'But if you're after a cuppa, you can fuck right off.'

I follow Alison down a dim hallway into a living room that looks like it's been decorated by a bunch of drunken students. The curtains are held up with drawing pins. Unframed posters dot the walls, a thin layer of dust on them. Alison heads straight for a ratty-looking easy chair with a throw rug on it, and sits on the arm. A small lamp provides the only light in the room, even though I catch a whiff of a scented candle.

'I've still got some things I need to ask you,' I say, taking a seat on the couch. I can't make her out. Sitting there on the arm of the chair, an oversized Elvis T-shirt stretched over her knees, she looks her age. I think. I can hear her biting her nails, but the light in this place makes her look like one of those anonymous witnesses, her features hidden in a half-shadow.

After a long silence, punctuated with her gnawing, she finally sniffs. 'Why didn't you call Mo?'

'I told you. I've got questions for you.'

'Fuck do you care?'

'I don't know. Got some stuff to get straight, that's all.'

'So you're still going to call him?'

'You don't want me to? Way I see it, I'd have thought you'd be eager to leave.'

There's a sound that could pass for a laugh, but I'm not sure. 'You don't know the first fuckin' thing, do you?'

'That's why I'm here, Alison.'

She leans over to grab a cigarette from a gold Bensons pack

and the light from the lamp catches her face. A flash of recognition, but I can't place who. It's not Mo. Her face is round, her body type a far cry from Mo's streak of piss physique. And she doesn't have Morris Tiernan's hard features. In fact, it's difficult to believe she's related to either man. Her face is softer, like a child. Mousy hair, mousy eyes. She must get her looks from her mother.

That is, what little looks she has left. A big ugly bruise covers her right cheek. It looks fresh and painful.

'Rob do that to you?'

She glances at me, then lights the Benson. 'What do you think?' She blows smoke at me. 'Who did your nose?'

'A bouncer at that club you used to work at.'

She smiles with the healthy side of her face. 'Good.'

'What was the fight about?' I say.

'What fight?'

'The fight that landed you with that. The barney you had last night.'

'I didn't fight last night.'

'I was outside, Alison.'

She takes a long drag on her cigarette, stares at me as she exhales through her teeth. 'Then why didn't you come up? You might've been able to help me out a bit.'

'I thought about it.'

'Thanks for that. A lot of fuckin' good thoughts do me.'

'What are you going to do?'

'About what?'

'About Rob.'

'What can I do? It depends on you, dunnit? I don't have much of a say in the matter, do I? I'm fucked. So's Rob. But I'm not going without a fight.'

'Don't push it, Alison.'

She leans across the light again, sits back with an ashtray

shaped like a seashell and flicks ash. 'What'd you say your name was?'

'Callum Innes.'

She purses her lips, looks like a kid about to have a tantrum. 'Well, Mr Innes, I'm not going back to Manchester. You don't know the half of what's going on here.'

'Then how about you wipe that fuckin' pout off your face and tell me?'

Alison shakes her head. The pout's gone, but she's fallen silent.

'Nah, look. When I walk out of here, I'm calling Mo. That's a given, right? And I'm going to be watching this place to make sure you two don't do a flit and make me look bad because Christ knows it's been a hard slog getting to this point and I'll be fucked if I let some brat tell me how to do my job. Now all I can do right now is listen to your side of things. You want to keep your mouth shut, I can understand that. I'll just walk out of here and call your brother.'

'We shouldn't have done it,' she says.

'I know.'

'I can't go back.'

'You're going to have to.'

'Mo's a fuckin' bampot. I can't go back to him.'

'And Rob's any better?'

'You don't know Mo, Mr Innes.' She flicks more ash and sets the cigarette in one of the shell's grooves. 'You don't know what he's like.'

'I know exactly what he's like. He's a psycho. And I'm not saying going back to Manchester's going to be easy, Alison, but it's got to be better than staying here, isn't it? How much of the cash has Rob done so far?'

'It's not that.' A sigh breaks out of her. 'Rob's got his problems, yeah, but we're working on them. And you know what Mo's gonna do to him when he gets up here. He's a jealous fucker.'

'What's he got to be jealous about?' I say as I light up.

Alison blinks. 'What's he got to be jealous about? How about – I dunno – the mother of his kid rips off his dad and buggers off to Newcastle with some bloke she's been fucking?'

'What kid?'

But I know the answer. That's where I've seen her before, that's where that spark of recognition came from. The toddler with Uncle Morris. The sleeping kid in the pushchair.

The kid looked just like his mother.

'Mo's your brother,' I say.

'He's my half-brother. My mam wasn't his mam.' She starts picking at something on her top lip. 'Dad doesn't know about it. Thought I got myself knocked up by some lad on the estate. But he went mental about it. And as much as I wanted to tell him the truth – y'know, see Mo get the same treatment – I couldn't do it. I kept my mouth shut.'

'Why?'

'I'm not a grass. And, fuck's sake, why would I tell him? It's not like it was rape.'

'You're sixteen,' I say.

'Seventeen next month,' she says. 'And Christ, it wasn't as if Mo was the first.'

Find me a runaway . . .

I exhale smoke, shift in my seat. Something rages under my skin and I can't get a grip on it, one of those internal itches. 'So, what? You run out on the kid and –'

'Make a new life up here.' Alison looks at me. Her right eye is half-closed. 'I'm not proud, Mr Innes. But you're right. I'm sixteen and I'm fucked if I go back to Manchester. You've got to understand, it was a mistake, me and Mo. It shouldn't have happened, but I'm a big girl now.'

'Yeah, a big girl getting the shit knocked out of her in a Newcastle council flat. That's a big step up, Alison.'

'You judging me?'

I shake my head. She has fire in that one good eye.

'Who the fuck are you, eh? Hold on, let me guess, you're an ex-con with a favour to pay back, am I right? That, or you're one of Dad's hatchet men, a fuckin' monkey with itchy fists.'

'That's not true.'

She grinds out her cigarette. 'Whatever you are, you've got a nerve playing the good guy.'

'You're going back, Alison. There's nothing I can do.'

'And what about Rob?'

'What about him?'

'What'll they do to him?'

'Use your imagination.'

Alison looks away, stares at a faded stain on the curtain. She bites her bottom lip. 'I don't want to go back.'

'Like you said, it's not up to you. That's a nasty bruise, but next time it could be a lot nastier.'

'That's not the point.'

'It's exactly the point. Look, you want to be an adult, you start acting like one. And I know it's none of my business, but doing a runner isn't the adult thing to do. It's being a fuckin' coward, and I know enough about that. You want to be a big girl, you stand up and face your responsibilities. Morris isn't going to do anything to you. He's your dad, for fuck's sake. He just wants you back safe.'

'You know that, huh?'

'Yeah, I know that.'

'What about Mo?'

'I can pick you up and take you back myself. I can call Mo from the road. That way you don't have to be around when he arrives, and you'll be settled in Manchester before he gets back.'

She looks like she's thinking about it. 'What if Rob doesn't stay put?'

'If he does another bunk, I'll find him. I'm not the brightest spark, but I got this far, didn't I?'

'Why would you take me back?'

'Because I don't want to be around when Mo arrives. I don't know what he's going to do, and I don't want to know. And what's Rob going to think? That you grassed him up.'

Alison starts biting her fingernails again. 'He'd be right an' all.'

'Not your fault. But I don't think he'll see it that way.'

She takes a deep breath, lets it out as if it's her last. When she reaches for another cigarette, I notice her eyes are red. She sniffs and wipes at her cheek as she lights up.

'Well?'

'Okay,' she says.

'Okay?'

'Call it eight tonight. Ring the buzzer for thirty-five. I'll be ready.'

THIRTY-SEVEN

Couldn't be doing with this anymore, man.

Yeah, doing his car over gave us summat to chew on. Fuckin' loved that, like. Rossie made with the tyres and me and Baz did the paint job. That were fun. Got a buzz out of that, but it didn't sit still long enough. Grabbed at it, and the fuckin' fun went poof, out the window. I couldn't hang onto owt these days. Because none of it were bringing us closer to Alison. Felt like I were being fucked around is what it felt like.

Summat had to be done and done right. We was watching Innes ponce about, but it were like watching a film on Channel Five – I kept missing stuff 'cause I couldn't hear or I couldn't see. And when the fuck came out the flats, he had this look on his boat like he'd sorted summat out.

'Take it easy,' said Rossie.

'How the fuck can I take it easy? You think he's in there?'

'If he was in there, Innes would've called you.'

'I dunno, Rossie. I don't fuckin' know. I don't trust that cunt.'

'Hang tight, Mo.'

'Fuck off.' I tapped the seat. Wrap of billy long gone and me nerves were fuckin' shot. 'We got to do summat. I can't be fuckin' waiting around forever. Christ, as bad as him, innit?'

'What d'you want to do?' said Baz.

'I want a word with him. Give us your butterfly, Rossie.'

'Nah.'

I looked at him. 'Give us your fuckin' butterfly, ginger nuts.'

'You talk with your mouth, not my blade. Use your own.'

'He don't have it,' said Baz.

'What happened?'

'Give us your fuckin' butterfly,' I said.

'He's gone,' said Baz.

'You what?' I looked out the window. 'Fuck did he go?'

'Dunno.'

'You're lying.'

'I'm telling you, Mo, I didn't see.'

'You're a fuckin' *liar*,' I said. And the speed were scratching us up inside. 'Fuck's the matter with you lads, anyway? You bottling this?'

Rossie yawned. 'We're not bottling owt, Mo. You need to chill.'

'Fuck off. You're bottling it, the pair of ya. Fuckin' bottling cunts. Simple as, know what I mean? You supposed to come up here with me and we scope the fucker out and find out where Stokes is and we get my fuckin' sister back and that's the end of the story, right?'

'So why d'you want Innes?' said Baz. He had his mouth hanging open.

'Why do I want Innes?' My eyes fuckin' hurt, like they'd dried out. And I wanted a weapon, anything, wanted to slam the pair of cunts in the nose with it, whatever it was. A double whap and have 'em screaming blood all over. Why did I want Innes? 'Cause he's a cunt, like the pair of youse. He thinks he can take care of this, he's out of his fuckin' league. He don't know the first fuckin' thing what's going on here. And I want him out the picture, you hear me? I want him in the fuckin' hospital and away from us. He cocks it up and we're sorted.'

Rossie shook his head.

'Nah, you don't get it. Dad's got shit *planned* for us. *Planned.* Big stuff, know what I mean? We'll be working for the man. We'll be fuckin' untouchable.'

'Mo, you was ready to kill him before.'

I leaned in close to Rossie and said, 'Whatever it fuckin' takes, Rossie. Whatever it fuckin' takes. You lads, you can go through life just getting fucked up and nobody gives a shit, am I right? Me, I got plans, I got ambitions. And they don't need to be fuckin' scuppered by some jailbird. You know why Dad got him in on this? He did it to piss me off. Because he don't think that a bunch of scallies like us can carry summat like this off. And we can. As long as you bastards don't bottle it the first chance you get. Which is what you're doing right now.'

'What d'you want us to do, Mo?' said Baz. He looked tired.

'I want more than just fucking up his car. I want *him* fucked up. I want a message sent out to him. You don't step on Mo Tiernan's toes.'

'Then what you got planned?'

I clicked me teeth together, looked for some gum. 'I'll tell you what I got planned. And you bottle this, I'll cut you both up.'

THIRTY-EIGHT

I walk away from Alison's flat on aching legs. Feels like I've accomplished something and when I get to the garage, it looks like I'm not the only one. I fork out for the new tyres, turn down the offer of new paint, and call Donna.

I ask her if she wants to meet up before I head back to Manchester. She agrees because, according to her, there's something we have to talk about. She tells me to meet her in the Egypt Cottage. Not her flat, and I get the feeling I'm about to be brushed off. It was bound to happen. A woman gets drunk, invites a bloke back to her place and she maybe thinks she said something she didn't mean, and sometimes it's easier to cut these things short before they get a chance to take root. The quiet fear of the blackout drunk.

Just another loose end to tie up.

Donna's already there by the time I step through the door. She's got a gin on the go and a cigarette in her mouth. When she sees me, she attempts a smile, but it doesn't register in her eyes. Yeah, this is going to be a bad one.

I grab a pint, sit next to her. She shifts position.

'I thought you'd be back in Manchester by now,' she says. 'That's what you said, right?'

Straight in with it. 'I'm not going back until tonight.'

'So it's all finished, then.'

'A couple of wee things to tie up. But, yeah, I'm pretty much done here.'

'Huh.'

We drink. I stare at the pictures on the wall. When I glance back at her, she looks like she's about to say something. Staring into her gin like the answer's at the bottom of her glass. Her mouth is open. Then she says, 'I was drunk the other night, okay?'

'Okay.' Setting myself up now, preparing for the kick into touch.

'I don't normally do that. I don't normally bring people back to my flat, y'know? It's not what I do. But I'd had a really bad morning, and sometimes you just want a drink. Sometimes that's the only thing on your mind and fuck responsibility. I was in one of those moods.'

'That's okay,' I say. 'I think I know where this is going.'

When she looks at me, her eyes are glassy. Gin'll do that to the best. It's industrial-strength mascara-thinner. 'Let me finish, Cal. This isn't easy.'

'Okay.'

'So when you don't call me the next day, and all I've got is like a few snapshots of the night, I get to wondering, like, how far did I go? And I remember you leaving, but I don't remember why you left. And I don't want you to think I'm some sort of slag, y'know?'

'I know.'

'Because I'm not, Cal. I'm really fucking not.'

'I never thought you were.'

'So . . . did we?'

'No, we didn't. I had to leave.'

Donna laughs to herself, but she catches the sound in the back of her throat. She dabs at one eye, smudging her make-up. 'I do have some pride left, you know.'

'It's me, Donna. Don't worry about it.'

'So what do you want to do?' she says.

I drink my pint, swallow and sit back in my seat. 'What do you want to do?'

'I like you, Cal. I just think we got off on the wrong foot. Bad first impressions and that.'

'Maybe.'

'I don't know how it can work.'

'You don't know how what can work?'

'Us,' she says.

'You want to chalk it up.'

'Pretty much.'

*

You can prepare yourself all you want, be as hard as you want. But at the end of the day, rejection is still a kick in the neck.

This is absolutely fine, I tell myself. This is just spot on. Tickety-fuckin'-boo. I don't hang around much after that first pint, make my excuses and leave, because I can't rationalise being dumped before a relationship begins.

Behind the wheel of the Micra, I stick in a tape and let it play out. I want to scream 'bitch', I want to call her and yell spiteful things down the phone, but that won't make much of a difference.

Chalk it up.

And if I'd slept with her? Maybe that would have been different. Or maybe she would have felt worse and not answered the phone. Depending on what she remembered. Christ, she gets drunk and I pay the price because I'm too much of a gentleman.

Like anything could have come from it. The age difference, the distance between Manchester and Newcastle, a million different reasons why it wouldn't work. Like the sex issue.

Fuck's sake, it always comes down to that. The sex is the thing, another *Marie Claire* myth. It doesn't matter that the guys who handed a scalding to James Figgis thought they'd teach me a lesson too. It doesn't matter that they bitched me. That kind of truth isn't first-date material, but then neither's sex. At least it wasn't when I was growing up. I feel like I've been out of the game so long, they changed the rules on me.

I stop by a chippy and sit with my dinner wrapped in newspaper. I stop by an off-licence, grab a half-bottle of cheap vodka and stick it in the glove compartment. It's a tic, an unconscious action. Something I do when I don't know what to do. The world just pissed on you? Buy booze. A nice little defence mechanism. I can't touch it, though. Not when I'm supposed to be driving Alison back to Manchester tonight. Give it three and a bit hours on the motorway, though, and I'll be gagging for a decent drink.

And a hot shower, my own bed. Some decent music on the CD player. Then back to my old life, for what it's worth.

I eat most of the chips; sling the rest out of the window. By the time I reach Alison's flat again, it's quarter to eight and I'm early enough to sit for a while and stare through the windscreen. Trying to be calm. Knowing that it's just a matter of time before I'm back home and all of this is memory.

Johnny Cash sings 'Solitary Man' as rain spots the glass. I click him off. I don't need to be reminded.

And I can't wait any longer. I get out of the Micra, hunch my shoulders to the rain, and trot across the road towards the block of flats. The place is dead, the way it should be. When I get to the front door, I press the buzzer for thirty-five.

I wait.

Nothing.

I buzz again, lean hard this time in case something's not connected. Then wait. And again, nothing. Check my watch and it's eight on the dot now. I take a step back and look up at her window. It's dark. Which means something's fucked here. Rob found out and beat her to death. Or she changed her mind. I check my mobile for messages. Nothing.

She's in the shower, she's asleep, she's knocked to the floor, gagged and bound and screaming for help in a dark flat.

Shut up, man.

So I buzz again, because it might just be that she can't hear it. And because it's something else to do. I'm out of ideas. Why wouldn't she be there? Unless someone got to her.

The guy in the black leather jacket, maybe. He's not a copper. He could be working for Morris, but then why would Morris check up on me?

I walk round to the carpark. Stokes' Escort isn't there. No lights in any of the windows, so either Stokes has found out and done something stupid, or he's managed to persuade her to do another bunk.

If that's the case, then I'm back to the drawing board. Even worse, they're going to be looking out for me, and they know what I look like, the pair of them. Christ, Alison, why'd you have to go and piss me around? I mean, she knows what's at stake here and it's certainly not a chunk of stolen money.

I should have kept my mouth shut. I shouldn't have gone up there; I shouldn't have talked to her. She's still a bloody kid, and she's not about to trust one of Morris' goons over her own boyfriend, even if he is a prize prick. If I was any kind of detective, I'd have known that. But I had to play Sir Galahad.

Bollocks to the job. I've had enough. Let Mo handle it from here on out. I'll get the scally on the phone, let him know the situation. As far as I'm concerned, I'm finished with it. I'm gone. Their fucked-up little family, their problem.

I start to cross the grass, hit pavement. I'll ring Mo from the car, then drive home. There's nothing more I can do here. And if he wants to get hard with me, I'll remind him that I have dirt to dish. Let's see how Morris reacts when he finds out his son's been keeping it in the family.

Somewhere, there's the sound of an engine. I don't hear it properly until I'm in the middle of the road. Then this horrible grating sound rises above the rain and I have to cock my head to figure out where it's coming from. It gets louder, closer. I narrow my eyes, peer up the road.

Definite movement.

And then two headlights blaze up like a couple of fiery white eyes. Roaring, the engine gunned for all it's worth.

I'm stuck. Caught and frozen in the glare, thinking daft thoughts like wasn't this the beginning of *Randall & Hopkirk (Deceased)*? And, fuck me, but tyres do squeal. I thought it was just the movies.

Too scared to move, too scared to stay put.

A small car with a grinding engine. Bearing down on me. Fucking *aiming* for me.

The whole world shudders to a halt.

It's a full car. I can make out passengers, silhouetted.

I should jump. I should get out of the way.

And I try, just as a sudden wind whips around my legs. It feels like someone kicked me in the ribs. Twist up onto the bonnet. Clatter over the roof, and I'm thinking, hey, I'm going to be fine. It hurts like a bastard, but the impact didn't kill me, so I'm fine. I'm going to be –

I tumble off the roof of the car, slam off the boot and hit the tarmac with the top of my head.

The world goes grey for a second, but I'm brought back by the pain. I let out the breath I've been holding with a whine. Open my eyes to see nothing but the black of the road. Blink as much as I can, but I can't shake the blur.

I let myself go limp on the road. A fuzzy mental check and I don't think anything's broken, just battered. My head's bleeding, though. Something warm and sticky is gumming up my eyes.

My tooth throbs.

That little fucker just can't give it up for a second.

THIRTY-NINE

I don't think about where I am. I don't think about what just happened. All I think about is whether I need to change my boxers. When I move my leg, the skin stings with urine.

So yeah, I do. So much for Nan's advice.

I want to sleep, but I know I can't. More advice from Nan, that one. You go to sleep after a knock to the head, you'll end up in a coma. And I've got to stay alive. I concentrate on my breathing, try to keep it from slowing. My head spins. I've got blood on my tongue and the smell of my own piss makes me want to heave.

'I think I got him.' A whining voice. I know it from somewhere. I keep my eyes half-closed, playing possum. Like there's anything else I can do.

'Good.' Man, I know that voice too, but my brain's so fogged up I can't make any connections. 'Get him in the back of the car.'

'Fuck that. I'm not sitting next to him.'

'Stick him in the fuckin' boot, man.'

A pair of market trainers come into view. Pumas with a mucky red stripe. Old jeans swim into focus, the kind that look pre-distressed. Whoever knocked me over is a ponce. Hands grab me under the arms, pull me up with my feet dragging in front of me. My head lolls forward. One of my leg buckles and I hope it isn't broken. My back screams and I want to scream with it.

'C'mon, man, hold him straight. Don't dance with the fucker.'

A breeze dries the blood on my face. I can feel it start to crust up. It itches.

'I'm not dancing with the fucker, but if you'd take some of the fuckin' weight . . .'

I hear the boot being opened, feel myself turned. I keep my eyes closed now, but I can see light through my eyelids. They dump me head first into the boot. I crumple, double up and someone pushes my foot so it's twisted against my leg. Then the boot lid comes down with a thump.

No use in kicking up a fuss, not yet. Give myself a chance to heal first, get my head straight. Difficult to do when it feels like I've been pushed arseways through a woodchipper. I can hear muffled sounds outside the car. They're talking, arguing.

I recognised those voices, but I still can't place them.

Fuck. *Think*, Cal.

Can't. Too tired.

Then I pass out.

*

Coach class.

I open my eyes to darkness, feel a jolt and think I've gone blind. Then I remember where I am. The boot vibrates under me, jiggling me about. So we're moving, which means they meant to hit me, as if I didn't know that already.

When I try to move, I can't. Pressed up by the back seats, there's a weight holding me to the floor of the boot. Someone's sitting in the back seat, and he's a heavy bugger. That makes three in the car, at least. From the flash in the dark, I thought I could make out more, but it could have been the shock and the light.

I run my tongue over my throbbing tooth. It throbs harder, but it keeps me awake.

So that's three. At least. Maybe a couple more. Which means I'm fucked.

My knees knock together, my gut pitches, my spine feels out of whack. The boot has filled up with the smell of me and it's almost unbearable, the stench of urine and fear high in my nostrils.

God, I've got to try and think straight here. Okay, at the most, there's five guys in this car, not counting me. That's five guys who pose a threat. More than likely, there's three. Unless the driver didn't get out after they ran me down.

Fuck. Concentrate.

That weak voice, he's my first point of call if this gets nasty. *When* this gets nasty. I'll be able to connect that voice to a build, no bother. And if I know him, and I recognise the voice, it'll give me the extra fire I need to kick the cunt in the jewels. Because I'm not about to wade into big bloke and hope the rest of them go running scared. I do that, the big bloke'll just stomp on my neck while the rest of them wade in.

So nah, go for the weakling, aim a swing at that big fucking mouth.

Feels like my gums are on fire. Want to go back to sleep. Want to pass out.

I poke the tooth.

Keep thinking, Cal. This is important. Keep awake, son.

Okay, so Stokes finds out about my visit to Alison. He gets scared and stupid, reckons the best thing to do would be to take me out of the equation. Fair enough, but how did he find out about me?

He smelled a rat at the casino. Placed me by the Manc accent I never knew I had. Another time I should have kept my mouth shut. But then he talked to me first. What was I supposed to do? Another punter could have told him. The guy with his flies open. Or Pauline could have spilled something to keep him at the other casino. But I know who it was. It's as clear as crystal who grassed me.

Georgie.

He tipped off Stokes. Just like he tipped me off, playing both sides to see who'd pay him more. Or maybe he did it because I stood him up.

And that weak voice, that's George. A high-pitched version of him, anyway. A George scared out of his mind. And it would make sense that he was driving too.

'I think I got him.'

That's about right. This car's too small for Stokes' Escort. If it had been Stokes behind the wheel, I get the feeling I wouldn't be breathing now.

It was George.

He sets me up, tells Stokes. Stokes goes home, talks to Alison. And guess who just paid her a visit? But then, why would she mention that? I'm missing something.

So here I am, rattling about like the last Pringle in the tube, coming up with theories left, right and centre. But then, when you're trapped in the boot of a car that knocked the shit out of you, you tend to take stock. Alison, George, Stokes, Mo, Morris, even Donna. The whole lot of them, whirling around my head and it's difficult to stop them colliding with insane conclusions. I've been stitched up, I'm in pain. I can't think straight and all I want to do is go to sleep. Because I know the worst is just around the corner. I know as soon as this car stops, I'm going to be dragged out of this car and get a kicking I won't be able to crawl away from.

I can take a beating with the best of them. I've proved that since I started pretending to be a PI. But I like to have a good reason to get knocked about. I do something drunk and stupid, that's fine. I pick a fight with the wrong lad, that's also fine. That's a lesson learned and chalk it up to bad decision-making on my part.

But this? A car ploughs into me and I get bundled off somewhere remote, cloak-and-dagger style, it doesn't fit with me. It's too serious, too fucking life-threatening. It's not something I've experienced, and the thought of it becoming a reality makes my bowels loose.

I'll be buggered if I shit myself too. I clench.

The engine growls, the rumble under me slowing to a dull vibration. I can hear the click of the indicator light.

We're pulling in somewhere.

This is it. I tell myself to buckle up.

FORTY

The first punch lands heavy against my cheek, the second fires up a ball of pain where I think my nose used to be.

I hit the road in a heap, hands in my armpits, legs curled under me, dead to the world.

It's cold out here, the middle of nowhere. Some motor-way, surrounded by black trees and all the life sucked out of the scene by the cars that whoosh by. It's hardly private, but who's going to stop when they're going sixty. And it affords these guys a convenient hard-shoulder burial if they need it.

My right eye is closing up. Through the slit, I can make out three of them. One of them is Stokes. I recognised his voice as soon as I could fit it to a figure. One of the others is George, I know it. The third is a mystery to me, but he's doing most of the grunt work and he's got power in his fists.

I try to sit up. Another blow to the head makes me reconsider. And fuck, I can't see again. It hurts, but doesn't add too much. If this big guy knew how to beat the shit out of someone, to keep the pain going, he'd be dangerous. As it stands, he's just here to batter me into submission, which shouldn't take too long.

I cough up blood and spit. Christ, I'd kill for a cigarette. A passing car throws a light over George. He's skinnier than I remember. I smile at him as best I can, say, 'You're fuckin' dead, mate.' But it comes out like *gawfaggagekmay* . . .

He gets the point. His face creases up and he pushes the big guy out of the way, launches a weak right at my head. It connects with my scalp, but it hurts him more than it hurts me. He takes a step back, a pained expression on his face. He blows on his knuckles, eyes sparking at me from the shadows.

'Salford, eh?' says Stokes.

I turn my head to the sound of his voice, but I can't look up. I concentrate on the sparkling tarmac. A light rain is falling. It's the only thing keeping me conscious.

'What d'you wanna do with him?' A Geordie voice. Must be the big guy. Sounds like a big guy, but not the voice of a muscleman. More like he's having trouble breathing. If I can keep him battering me, maybe he'll have a heart attack or something.

Jesus, get your head together.

'Fuckin' Salford,' says Stokes. 'Not what I expected, like. Has to be said. I expected Mo.'

I jerk my head up and grin at him. I can taste blood in my mouth and my lips are wet. I must be a right looker.

'You like that?'

I keep grinning.

'You think that's funny?'

I push bloody spittle through my teeth and shake my head slowly. Fuck am I doing? Slap-happy, punch-drunk, that one-way ticket to Palookaville checked and stamped. Whatever it is, it's messed up my coordination.

Stokes steps forward and crouches down in front of me. Streaming headlights carve clarity in his face. I can make out a deep scratch on his cheek, a bruise swelling his bottom lip. He reaches into his jacket and I automatically flinch.

He smiles. Getting off at playing the hard man.

When his hand emerges from his jacket pocket, it's holding my mobile.

Ah, for fuck's sake . . .

'You know Mo's number off by heart, do you, Innes?'

My head falls forward.

'Lad like you,' he says, 'a fuck-up scally like you, I don't think you've written it down, have you? Nah, what you did was just stick it on your mobile and leave it at that.'

I shake my head, bring up some blood-laced lung butter and let it fly full in his face. He recoils, stands and kicks me in the throat. I drop back, end up sprawled on the tarmac, staring through a haemorrhage at a moonless sky. Choking. I can't breathe. Trying to cough, but my vision starts closing in.

I roll onto my side. Stokes plants another size eleven in my gut. I spew onto the road, tears searing the cuts around my eyes. I try to blink, but it hurts too much. Coughing, spluttering air out of my lungs, bile burning the back of my throat.

Stokes drops my mobile in front of my face, makes sure I'm paying attention. Then he brings his foot down on it. I flinch hard, my body jerking. Once cracks the fascia, twice kills the display. The third smashes the mobile to pieces. He grinds his heel on the plastic then leans over. I feel the wet slap of gob hit my cheek.

'*Tou*-fuckin'-*ché*,' he says.

I want to weep. He's right. I just saved Mo's number onto the mobile and left it. There are other ways of getting it again, but that would be admitting failure. And Stokes must know I didn't call Mo yet. Which means something that I didn't want to admit to myself.

Alison's the one that fucked me over.

Another volley of kicks, and I'm on my back. I keep wanting to draw my knees up over my stomach, but I don't have the strength.

'What d'you wanna do with him?' The big guy. Yeah, answer him, tell him. Let's get this over and done with.

'We kill him, he'll be out of the picture,' says George.

Thanks, mate. You'll get yours.

'We kill him, we'll have to deal with his body.'

'Howeh, Rob, he's fucked up. Might as well follow through. What's to deal with? We dump him in a fuckin' ditch and call it a night.'

'It's too risky. People know he's up here,' says Stokes.

'Aye, but we'll be gone.'

'*I'll* be gone, George.'

'He's grassed you right up,' says George.

'Nah,' says Stokes. 'He hasn't told Mo where I am. Least that's what Alison says.'

'Who gives a fuck? Better safe than sorry.'

'Take it down a notch, Georgie. You're beginning to sound like a proper psycho. Far as I'm concerned, this isn't worth the bother.'

'And I'm saying better safe than – '

'How about you shut up, George? You're not the bloke Morris wants. You're a fuckin' tourist, so hang onto yourself.'

My lips start flapping. In my mind I'm calling George all the bastards under the sun, but it comes out as a gurgling wheeze. George doesn't like it. He kicks me hard. I roll over onto my other side, curl up into a ball. Shut the world out, try to keep breathing.

Best to keep my mouth shut. Let them sort this out.

Stokes says, 'We'll dump him in a ditch. By the time he makes it back to Newcastle, we'll be long gone.' He leans close to me. 'You hear that, Innes? Long fucking gone. You messed up, son. You dropped the ball.'

I can't see him anymore.

'Pick him up,' says Stokes.

'Fuck that, I'm not touching him.'

'George, don't make me tell you twice, mate.'

I feel hands under me again, feel the sky get that little bit closer before my head falls to my chest. The world starts spinning and I have to blink to keep myself from throwing up again. I'm upright, looking down now. I notice my shoelaces are untied. Wondering how the fuck that happened. My ankle turns, a stabbing pain at the top of my foot. Then I drop face forward into a ditch by the side of the road. The mud is cool against my face. If I close my eyes, I can pretend it's my bed.

Footsteps disappearing, the sound of the engine.

They're not going to kill me, but they've left me for dead. Small mercies.

I wait for the engine sound to fade away. All that's left are the sounds of passing cars and my own whistling breath. It's cold out here, getting colder all the time. I should make a move, but I don't want to. Not yet. Enjoy the rest.

My head starts feeling heavy, then the fear of coma spikes me with adrenaline. I put my hands out into the mud, sinking them deep. I try to push myself to my knees. It takes a couple of attempts, and when I get there, my head's thumping. Keep my eyes narrowed, because the world's going to get bright soon, I know it. It might be dark here, but the headlights of oncoming cars feel like they're burning my eyes right out of their sockets.

I concentrate on the road, lit up, raindrops like stars. They burst as my focus shifts.

And something catches my eye. It shines white against the tarmac. I pull myself closer on my hands and knees.

A tooth.

That tooth.

I finally got the bastard out.

And it hurts to laugh, but I do it anyway.

PART THREE

Blue Skies for Everyone

Parole is granted on the basis of reports by prison and probation staff, on the nature of your offences, your home circumstances, your plans for release and your behaviour in prison.

An Irish guy with a soft voice gave me a book about the American penal system.

'Read this,' he said. 'But I want it back. It's part of my library.'

I read it in a day.

Six months before the Parole Eligibility Dates and thereafter annually you will be asked whether you wish to apply for parole.

This book was about the Depression in America, made up of all these first-hand accounts of convicts over there. And they were fucked from the start. See, these guys had no education, they were mostly black, and had fuck all in the way of civil rights. No money in your pocket, you're sent down for vagrancy. You stay too long in one place, you're loitering.

Four months before your PED you will have the opportunity to see the reports and to make written representations stating why you believe you should get parole and what you will do on release.

God help you if you wanted a little action. The girls might have been pros, but they were being employed by the law to snare these guys. You got drunk, thought that girl with the come-to-bed eyes actually wanted a slice of you, the next thing you knew you were behind bars.

Three months before PED you will be seen by a member of the Parole Board who will write a report for the Board. You can see and comment on the report. He will be a kindly-looking guy in a beige shirt, white collar. He won't ask you if you feel like you've been rehabilitated, because that's a bullshit question.

In '30s America, convicts were leased out as slave labour to wealthy landowners. When their sentences were up, they were pressured into signing contracts they couldn't read. Then they were slaves for another ten years. Couldn't leave, either. Not unless they wanted armed guards with hounds on their tail.

Two months before PED – a panel of Board members will consider your case. You will not attend. They will focus primarily on the risk to public of a further offence being committed were you released, although they will consider the benefits of early release under supervision.

A Glaswegian called Harry Beggs collared me when the news filtered along the spur. He threw an arm around my shoulder and said quietly, 'Don't think about it, son. You think about it, you'll go nuts instead of flying, ken? Dinnae let them clip yer wings before you get a chance tae use 'em.'

I didn't, which is why I read so much in those final months. But it weighed on me. When I heard I'd been approved on condition that I report to Paulo's club, it felt like my stomach was lined with lead. This was what freedom was about, moving from one cage to another. When I gave the Irish guy his book back, he said, 'The Irish are the niggers of Europe.'

'What about the Scots?'

'The Scots are the Irish who could swim.'

Bloke had an answer for everything.

When Paulo came by before that final hearing, I was in no state for his usual bullshit. We argued hard. Part of me wanted to tell him to go fuck himself, that I'd wait until the last moment of my sentence before I agreed to work for him.

We fell into silence. I focused on the tattoo on Paulo's arm. A blue heart with three names: Mam, Dad and Keith.

It was fear that kept me inside, but a greater fear that made me back down and agree to his terms.

Back then, I was my own worst enemy.

Nothing's changed.

FORTY-ONE

It's a long night and a longer limp back to civilisation. Or Sunderland, which is the next best thing. Road signs point the way north, and the freezing wind lets me know I'm getting there. As much as I want to slump into a ditch by the side of the road and sleep for forty hours, I know I can't. Things to be done, loose ends flapping in the breeze.

So I follow the signs along the side of the road, a constant whoosh of cars flying by. I watch the night crack into morning, grey skies above. Dishrag clouds. More rain. I let a downpour wash away the self-pity, replaced it with anger once I started walking, and now all I have are images of Stokes, George and Alison. The rage keeps me limping, even though every bone in my body wants to rest. Muttering to myself, it's no wonder people don't give me a ride. Well, shit on 'em. If they don't fancy giving a lift to a stranger covered in blood and mud and piss, then that's their loss. I could have paid them well, made their day with a stack of cash, but no. The great British public, otherwise known as It's None Of My Fucking Business.

Another thing to keep me going: the promise of a service station. The signs have been pointing to one for the past six miles, and I'm desperate enough to believe in them. Anything to get out of the cold for a while, get myself cleaned up and rested before I work out my next move.

When I finally get to the service station, it's in the arse end of nowhere and somewhere in my battered head I wonder if it's the same one I passed when I drove up here. I hobble into the carpark, lean against the side of an articulated lorry and catch my breath. I've resisted smoking until now, but after the walk, I think I've deserved it. I light up an Embassy and break into a nasty, painful cough.

I ditch the cigarette. I haven't healed enough to enjoy it, but it kills me to see it wasted, so I move on.

Into the rest area, past the blaring arcade machines and into the Granary Restaurant. The woman behind the counter looks like she just caught a nostril full of something rancid. It's probably me. I make the mistake of talking to her, and her top lip pushes further into her nose.

'I'm sorry, sir. But the toilets are for customers only.'

'I just want to clean myself up, love.'

'And I'm sorry, but the facilities are for customers.'

'I'm a customer.' I look around, grab a muffin wrapped in plastic and slam it onto the counter. 'There you go.'

She looks down at the muffin. When I follow her gaze, I notice the muffin's all mashed up. And when I look up again, she's staring at me like I'm a psycho.

'How much?' I say.

'Three pounds.'

'For a fuckin' muffin?'

Her face crinkles. One step from calling the police or hammering a panic strip. I root around in my jacket, pull out my wallet. Stokes and his mates are a bunch of amateurs: from the looks of the wad in my wallet, they didn't even have the sense to rob me. I hand the woman a tenner. When she takes it, there's dirt on the note.

'Have you anything smaller?' she says.

'Is testing my fuckin' patience part of your job description?'

'I just asked –'

'Keep the change. Call it a tip. Customer service like yours, you deserve one.'

She points to a sign for the toilets and I drag myself across the restaurant. I manage to stun a couple of kids in the process. They were happy enough throwing their breakfast around, but one sniff of me seems to have killed their appetites stone dead. As I push open the door to the toilets, I hear the mother say, 'Don't stare.'

Listen to your mother, kids.

It's too bright in the gents. I think about knocking one of the lights out with my shoe, but I'm too knackered to do it. I move to the basin, feel a wave of nausea rise and crash in my gut. Run the cold water and splash some on my face. I watch the dried blood streak and feel my cheeks go numb. It looks like my face is melting. My fingers brush stubble as I wipe the excess water away and the bruise on my jaw aches.

What a fucking state.

I grab a fistful of paper towels, run the hot water and start dabbing at the cuts around my eye. It's no good, though. I can't focus properly.

Count them off: a battered nose, swollen; major damage to the cheek and my right eye; the left eye swelling in sympathy; a nasty purple bruise where I got kicked in the throat.

Oh, there's plenty to pay back here. And I haven't even checked below the collar.

Back in the restaurant, I don't get as many stares. I grab my muffin from the counter, give a cracked smile to the woman and make my way out to the phones. I have a plan. But it requires equipment, and it requires that I get some rest first. But I can't phone Mo without his number. And there's nobody else I can trust up here.

Well, there's one.

I feed a handful of change into the payphone and listen to it ring.

'Donna, it's me.'

'Cal. How are you? How's Manchester?'

'I'm not in Manchester.'

'What's up with your voice? Sounds like you had the shit kicked out of you.'

'That'll be because I had the shit kicked out of me.'

'Are you okay?'

'I'll live. I think. Look, Donna, I really need some help. Can you come and pick me up?'

'Where are you?'

'I'm at the services south of Sunderland, I think. I'm near Sunderland. I saw a sign for Darlington, too. I don't know. I'm near somewhere, but I can't see it.'

'Calm down.'

'I'm calm. It's been a rough night, that's all.' I close my eyes for a second and feel my legs start to buckle. Snap awake. 'Please, Donna. I swear. This'll be the last time.'

'Give me an hour,' she says.

I wander out into the lobby of the station and watch the carpark. Another hour and I'll be out of here. And then what?

Knocking me down and beating the shit out of me stank of desperation, like Stokes didn't know what to do with me. He's just another scared amateur trying to make things better but fucking them up worse.

Rob Stokes, playing the hard arse, the proper gangster. What he's seen in hip-hop videos and Al Pacino movies. All posture with none of the balls to back him up. I'm working for the real thing here, and whatever movie Stokes has been watching, it just bubbles and flares on the screen. He's not living in the real world.

Uncle Morris Tiernan has been linked to the deaths of over

thirty-seven men in his career. Some of them used to be mates. And Tiernan hasn't done a day behind bars for any of them.

Rob Stokes has no idea who he's fucking with.

He's about to find out, though.

I bite into the toffee muffin and feel like throwing up. Drop the muffin onto the ground, put my head between my legs and spend all my time trying not to pass out. The sound of an engine makes me look up. Donna gets out of her car and looks at me with a mixture of disgust and pity on her face. When I get into her Fiesta, she tells me to open the window.

'You're minging,' she says.

'I know,' I say. 'And thanks for this.'

'No problem,' she says.

And for a moment, I actually believe her.

FORTY-TWO

I couldn't fuckin' stomach talking to them cunts. I sat in the corner of Dobsons by meself, had a large double brandy. Them bastards was useless, fuckin' useless. Bottlers.

I said we did summat to Innes, they looked at us like I was going mental.

'Enough with the speed, Mo,' said Rossie.

'Aye, c'mon, Mo. You're off your tits,' said Baz. 'We did his car. That could be enough, right?'

'His car? His fuckin' car? What's the matter with youse cunts? Where's your balls?' And I were raging in that van, felt like knocking both their skulls off the bonnet until they went limp. And maybe it were the speed what made us itchy, but it weren't just that, couldn't have been. I looked in their faces and I knew that them bastards weren't up for the real deal. Aye, it were alright if you needed someone cut or knocked about, but you talked about killing a fucker, then they shit it. Didn't mind blood on their hands, unless it were the last drop spilled. Leave that to some other poor bastard like me.

I weren't given up. Nah, I just had to factor in their cowardice. Just like everything, man. You want summat done, you got to do it yourself.

Always been the same. Back when we was kids, I were always the one with the ideas. Rossie and Baz, they was followers. Fuckin' sheep. But now I were drinking, slowing, I realised summat: they wasn't sheep no more, they was pawns.

They did like I said, else they'd end up the same way as Stokes were gonna be. I had me plans already drawn up for that cunt. And Innes. And Alison.

Alison most of all. Who the fuck did she think she were, eh? Little bitch, little fuckin' slag bitch, all playing the grown-up one minute and spreading for any fuck and then sucking on a wowwy-pop the next. I didn't mind when she up and said she wanted nowt to do with us. Nah, I didn't mind. Bitch were fuckin' pregnant, anyways. So I just gave her a fuckin' kick in the gut and left it at that.

Homemade abortion, right?

Nah. Didn't kick the bitch hard enough.

And I kept me mouth shut and so did Alison, 'cause if Dad found out it were me what stuck it to her, we'd both be out. Alison's mam was a whore, and her little girl were just the same, but she were still a little girl and Dad always liked her more than he liked me. I must've reminded him of the fuckin' shack-job what spawned us or summat 'cause when I were a kid I used to look at meself in the mirror and I never looked a bit like me dad.

I drunk the brandy right down, like a warm hand on me gut. I'd bought a pack of Rothmans at the Paki shop and I lit one now, got out me seat and went to the bar. Got a pint of Guinness and brought it back to me table. You smoke like The Man, you drink like The Man, you *become* The Man. Rossie tried to say summat to us, but I ignored him.

Slipped behind me table and took a sip of the black stuff.

This were it. Like I'd ripped me dad's heart out and ate it, wore his skin like a fuckin' suit.

All I'd wanted to do were take the fucker out. That were all. Simple operation. Nobody would've missed Innes. Way I heard it, he had family in Jocksville, but he never talked to them no more.

Maybe Paulo would've said summat.

Fuck, I didn't know no more. It might've been a risk worth taking, like. But then maybe it were the billy and the fuckin' pills mangling me head and not letting us think right. And I had to think right.

But what the fuck, eh? Top and bottom were that because them bottling cunts didn't let us do what I wanted, we lost the bastard. We'd swung by the hotel, I went inside, asked, 'Did Mr Innes check out yet?'

The receptionist said that she couldn't give out that information.

'Nah,' I said. 'I'm a mate of his. We was out last night on the piss and we lost him somewhere in town. I just wanted to make sure he got in alright, know what I mean? I'm his best man. He's getting married. I'm his best man.'

Fuckin' speed.

But she didn't give up nowt.

So we was stuck here. All I could do was wait. Hoped the fucker hadn't spotted us and hoped to fuck he gave us the call when he were supposed to.

FORTY-THREE

The bath water is a notch too hot for comfort, but it feels like it's easing some of the tension away. I'm laying back, my head on a blue flannel, staring at the shower that overhangs the bath. It smells good in here, despite my presence. Donna's bathroom is full of wee wicker baskets overflowing with soap. I'm playing with one shaped like an apple. Give it a sniff, and it's uncanny. Close my eyes, and I'd swear it was the real thing. I half think about taking a bite out of it, but then I'd have to finish it. I don't think I could explain a half-eaten soap.

I can't stay here. I think I've gone the limit with Donna's hospitality, might have even crossed the line with this one, especially considering she dumped me twenty-four hours ago. My clothes are being washed right now and once they're dry and I'm changed, I'll be out that door and back in the game. Maybe pay her or something. I don't know the etiquette. But I can't afford to stay around. My body might be relaxed in the water, but my head's all over the place. Every time I close my eyes I can feel the rain on my face.

Someone's going to get proper fucked for this one, but I have to get out of this bath first.

The aches aren't gone completely, and my back feels twisted out of shape. I don't realise how bad it is until I try to get up and I can't. Panic turns the water ice cold. I try to move my legs. They don't shift, not even a ripple.

Christ. I'm paralysed.

I grab at the side of the bath and try to pull myself out, but the strength has long gone and I drop back, splashing water onto the floor. I've seized up from the waist down. My fingers hurt from gripping the bath and my head starts thumping with a full-on panic attack.

Shit isn't the word.

There's a knock at the bathroom door. 'Cal?'

'Donna, I . . .' What the hell am I going to say?

'You okay in there?'

'I don't know,' I say. 'I can't move.' The door clicks. 'No, don't come in. I mean it.'

'Don't be daft.'

'Can you call someone? Just don't come in.'

She pushes open the door and I try to move under some bubbles. She stands there with a weird look on her face.

'Jesus, Donna, what'd I say?'

'It's my flat and you're being a fucking baby. Now can you really not move?'

My voice cracks. 'You think I'd make this up?'

She grabs a large blue towel from the rail and throws it into the bath. 'Cover yourself up. I'll help you out.'

It's a tough job; I'm a dead weight. But we manage, me holding the towel to my waist, her with her hands under my arms. It's the most she's ever touched me, and I feel like asking for dinner and dancing first, but neither look possible with my legs fucked. Thinking that makes my throat hurt and I have to fight back the urge to cry. It's not manly.

We make it to the couch and I drop and adjust myself. I'm still wet from the bath, the couch cover sticking to me. We both let out a long breath at the same time.

'You really can't move,' she says.

'I really can't move.'

She looks me up and down, then leaves the room. I can

hear her on the phone, her muffled voice urgent. Thank Christ this happened here. If it had happened on the road, I'd be dead right now.

When she comes back in, she goes into the kitchen and pours us both a stiff drink. She hands me the glass and says, 'Doctor should be here soon.'

I take a drink. 'Thanks, Donna.'

'He says it's probably just temporary, but he wants to take a look himself.'

'Christ . . .'

'Hey,' she says. 'How about you drink up? No sense in feeling sorry for yourself.'

'Look, Donna —'

'Save it,' she says. And takes her drink into another room.

The doctor looks like he should be on the front cover of a Mills & Boon novel, an honest-to-goodness clean-cut poster boy, Dr Kildare without the latent homosexuality. When he walks into the living room, he's in the middle of a conversation with Donna. He stops talking when he sees me sitting on her couch wearing nothing but a towel. I'm glad; this doctor has the plummy voice of another class way higher than mine. When he smiles, he shows the same American teeth Donna does, but they look false. A pair of expensive-looking specs sit on the end of his nose. It's an affectation, I'm sure.

'Callum, right?' he says.

'Yeah.'

'Richard.' He extends his hand. I shake it. He looks back at Donna.

'The waist down, Doctor,' she says.

'Ah.'

He's too gentle to be a bona fide doctor, but he talks like one. I need X-rays. I need to see a specialist. An MRI is mentioned. So are the words 'fracture', 'chiropractor' and 'back brace'. It's enough to put the fear of God, the Devil and all the Nolan sisters into me.

'I'm not saying all this will happen, but you'll need to get checked out thoroughly. We don't take chances with the spine. It could be that you're just bruised and your muscles have just seized up. Or it could be that you've suffered severe spinal damage and you might never walk again.'

'Oh, cheers.'

'I'm just saying "might", Cal. It's not paralysis, I don't think. Not yet. And I don't want to treat this lightly.'

'I don't want you to treat this lightly.'

'You'll need bed rest,' he says, then turns to Donna. She nods and sips her third drink since he walked through the door. 'But you'll also need to take some light exercise. Go for a walk. Don't overdo it.'

'Ah, right. Let me get my trainers on and I'll be out of here,' I say.

He writes a script and reads the drugs off as he's writing them. Ibuprofen, codeine if the pain gets worse. Diazepam. And he peers at me over his glasses as he writes the last one: 'And from what Donna's already told me, you'll need some antidepressants.'

'Cheers, Doc.'

'You'll be alright with him?' Dr Dick asks Donna.

'I'll be fine,' she says.

'Then I'll leave you to it.'

She follows the doctor out into the hall and there's more muffled conversation. At one point, I think I can hear her saying, 'I'll be fine, Richard, okay? Just let me handle this.'

The front door closes with a clatter. When Donna reappears in the doorway, her lips are tight.

'Sorry,' I say.

'You okay?' She drains her glass, sets it on the coffee table and avoids my eye.

'I'll be okay, yeah.'

'I'll pick up your scripts.'

Donna's gone for about an hour. I know, because I watch the clock on the video until she comes back. I've made this drink last because I've had to. The bottle on the coffee table cries out for me to up-end the bugger into my glass, but I can't reach it. Donna must have left it there on purpose.

Doctor Dick. Yeah, he wasn't a doctor. He looked like one, but he didn't act like one. I'm grateful for the prescriptions, but if he's NHS, I'll eat my socks. And Donna doesn't strike me as the kind of woman who'd have private healthcare. Nah, Dr Dick is a friend of the family, maybe more. The more I think about it, the more it burns me up. I need to get out of here, but I can't bloody move, and that burns me up even more.

I really want a drink. I try to move on the couch, but the towel starts slipping. The last thing I need is to be found face down on her carpet with my arse bared. No, I can wait.

I'm not paralysed. I've just seized up. But Doctor Dick can't be sure. Christ knows what I'd do if I end up paralysed. Yeah, it worked for Ironside, but I'm not Raymond Burr. I don't have his courage. And he could walk – he was just a lazy bastard.

Shut up, Innes.

I hear the front door open and hope that it's not a burglar. 'Donna?'

'Yeah,' she says. The clinking sound of bottles. She sounds tired. 'I got your prescription.'

'Just take the cash out of my wallet,' I say.

'Don't worry, I will. And I know you shouldn't drink with the pills, but I want one.'

'That's fine with me.'

I drink with the pills anyway. Donna doesn't stop me. After a couple, though, I'm ready to pass out. We make it to the bedroom before I lose consciousness. And just before I go, I'm sure I can feel her hand brush my forehead. My foot twitches as the bed sinks around me.

Maybe there's hope after all.

*

When I open my eyes, I have to blink against the daylight. I had bad dreams, violent, full of those screeching choirs and the heart-thumping fear of being recalled to Strangeways. If I slept, it was in thirty-minute stretches at most. A quick look around the room with blurred vision, and Donna's nowhere to be seen. I rub the crusted drool from the corner of my mouth and swing my legs out of bed before I realise what I've done.

Praise be and thank fuck for Doctor Richard. I'm shaky, but I can stand. Pain in my right leg, but I can limp. Which is better than wheeling myself around. I take a breather against the wardrobe, grab a dressing gown and slip it on.

'Jesus Christ.'

I look up and Donna's in the doorway. I smile at her. 'Nah, but aren't miracles grand?'

'You scared the shit out of me.'

'Sorry.'

'You want a drink?'

'What time is it?'

'Noon.'

Six hours' worth of waking up and dropping out. That's the closest I've come to a good night's sleep in a long time and I still feel like I've been dragged through a rusty fence. 'And the bar's open?'

'Early doors.'

She helps me through to the living room and I ease myself onto the couch. A mournful song on the CD player, a piano and an alcoholic's voice. Donna brings me a glass and fills it from a half-empty bottle on the table.

'I washed your clothes,' she says.

I sip my drink. Sweet with no burn, another single malt. 'Thanks. I thought I'd have to chuck them.'

'You still should. How you feeling?'

'I can walk, so that's a start. Doctor Dick did wonders. How do you know him? He can't be your GP, not with that kind of service.'

'He's a friend.'

'Uh-huh. Close by the sounds of it.'

'He's helped me in the past.'

'What with?'

'I don't want to talk about it.'

'Okay,' I say. Another drink and there's a dribble at the bottom of the glass. I swallow it and struggle to my feet. 'Thanks again, Donna. I should be going, though. Stuff to do.'

She doesn't answer me as I limp back into the bedroom. What am I supposed to do? I can't thank her again, and I don't know what else to say to her. It's like we're trying this on for size and it fits neither of us, this relationship hanging dead around our necks. And who am I kidding? What fucking relationship? I grab my jeans off an easy chair, slump into it as I pull them on.

Thanks for picking me up, thanks for getting the doctor, thanks for the booze and the bed. Thanks for clamming up. Thanks for making me feel like a shithead because I've got other more important things on my mind.

This isn't the time to get involved, even if it was possible. Even if she didn't put up this front every time I open my mouth. Every time she looks at me, she sees what? A drunk woman picking up rough trade in a pub?

I'm pulling on my shirt when I feel her presence in the room. The clink of ice cubes in her glass gives her away.

'You didn't tell me what happened,' she says.

'You wouldn't believe it.'

'I picked you up. You owe me.'

'I got knocked down by a car,' I say. 'And then they chucked me in the boot, drove me out to a lay-by and worked me over, left me for dead.'

'You know who it was?'

'Yeah.'

'So what're you going to do?'

'I'm going to fuck them up. What else can I do?'

'You could quit,' she says. 'Next time they might make sure you're dead before they leave you.'

'I'm not about to do that, Donna.'

'Why not?'

'Difficult to explain.'

'Try.'

I do. Start right at the beginning; fill her in so far. The job, the journey, George, Stokes, Alison, the fight, the supposed flight, the man in the black leather jacket. We take it back into the living room, and I spill the story over another couple of drinks. I let her know that these people, they're amateurs. I made plenty of mistakes, mind, and I admit that too. Trusting George, trusting Alison. Playing saviour when I should have been watching my own back.

'But I'll make up for it,' I say. 'They should have dug that fuckin' grave and dropped me in it.'

Donna sits in her chair, staring at me. Stella ambles into the room and hops up onto the arm of the chair. For a moment, I think Donna's eyes have glazed over and she's not listened to a word I said. Then she pipes up. 'So they'll have gone by now.'

'You what?'

'This Stokes guy, Alison. They'll have skipped town by now. If they know you're after them.'

'Yeah.'

'So what's the point in carrying on?' she says. 'You've got nowhere to go.'

'I've got George.'

'Give it up, Cal.'

'I can't.' I take another drink, ice knocking my teeth. 'I can't do it. I let this go now and they've won.'

'You let this go now and you get to live, Cal. Look at yourself. You're a bloody wreck. It's only the booze that's holding you together right now. You go out there and cause trouble, you're asking for a casket.'

I check my pockets, pull out a pack of Embassy and open it up. There's not one of them that hasn't been mangled beyond repair. So I say: 'What the fuck do you care?'

It slipped out before I got a chance to think.

Donna sits back in her chair and disgust flickers across her face. 'You know what, Cal? You're right. What the fuck do I care? What the fuck do I care if you go off and get yourself killed when I could have stopped it.'

'That's not what I —'

'If you'd just bloody listen to yourself, Cal, you'd know why I'd fuckin' care. You're a mess. You're in no state to think straight and you haven't been from the moment you came up to Newcastle, by the sounds of it. So you're looking to blame anyone you can get your hands on because you can't hack the truth of it.'

'I don't need this.'

'Nah, you probably don't. But you're not right in the head. A guy in a black leather jacket following you? You have any idea how mental that sounds?'

'He's following me,' I say. 'It's not Donkey, but it's some-one. Probably Stokes. I don't know.'

'You're paranoid,' she says. 'You're delusional.'

'And you don't know what the fuck you're talking about. You don't know the kind of world I live in.'

'Aw, stop the PI bullshit for just a second. I've seen kittens tougher than you. Just because you can take a beating, it doesn't make you a prizefighter. And I don't want to be the one who sees you hurt.'

'You won't have to. You made that clear,' I say.

'You don't get it, do you?'

'I get it. You're happy with me when you're pissed, but anything more than that and the doubts set in.'

'You know that's not true.'

'Why'd you pick me up in the first place, Donna? Doctor Dick knock you back and you were out for a pity fuck?'

Her blue eyes flash once, then go dead. She raises the glass to her lips, but it's empty. When she speaks, it's like someone shut off the electricity. 'Forget it, Cal. You do what you want to do. Go beat the crap out of the rest of the world if it makes you feel better. Just do me a favour and don't ring me the next time you're scared. I've got enough problems in my life without having to worry about yours.'

'I'm sure you do.' I head to the front door, cigarette still on the go. Then come back and grab the prescription pills off the table. 'Thanks for washing my trousers, Donna. I appreciate it.'

I leave the door open as I head out into the hallway. If I go to close it, I'll end up slamming the bastard in the frame. And once I get outside I realise I've no idea where I am. After an hour of painful hobbling, on and off, I find a Metro station, hop aboard a train and head into town.

And I'm burning up inside, but it's got nothing to do with Stokes.

FORTY-FOUR

I get off the Metro at the Monument stop. I've got a few errands to run before I pick up my car, and the city centre's the only place I can run them. I'm blinded by sunlight as I step out of the station onto Northumberland Street, and the moment my eyes adjust, my heart sinks.

Sunday afternoon, a shopping extravanganza. Like the Arndale Centre, but more people packed into a smaller space and pissed off about it. The street is jammed and most of the crowd have no peripheral vision. Pushchairs and screaming kids, old women who think they've got the right of way, young hoodlums and scally lasses hanging around with gimlet eyes and too much saliva in their mouths.

I visit a couple of sports shops, but they seem to be selling clothes and nothing else. It's summer, it's the height of the season, but I can't find what I'm looking for. A parade of children with name badges and attitude problems give me nothing but cock-eyed stares. I end up sweating through my shirt, my lips dry and my patience frayed.

I yawn, bone-shattered.

God bless the Index catalogue shop, that's what I say.

Air-conditioned, kept at a temperature somewhere between freezing and frostbite, it's like heaven compared to the hell outside. I wander up to one of the catalogues and leaf through it until I find what I'm looking for. Sporting goods. I can't smile because my face feels swollen, but inside I'm beaming.

That's the bastard right there.

I fill out a wee form with a chewed pen and take it up to the counter. Spend the next ten minutes waiting for my number to come up, gasping for a cigarette. My skin feels itchy, and I wish I hadn't talked to Donna like that. Fuck's sake, she was only looking out for me. But I'm in no mood to be civil. Things to do.

I have a plan, but it's blurred around the edges. I wouldn't go so far as to call it revenge, but it's a way of evening the score a little.

When my number fizzes up onto the screen, I go to the counter and pay. Then I tuck the package under my arm and brave the sun again. Only for a second, stocking up on cigarettes and Lucozade. I get short-changed, but I don't care. Outside, I light up, take a few puffs to get enough nicotine slammed into my brain, and then I'm back across the road and checking out the mobile phones.

I don't want anything too expensive. If Stokes shows up again, he might get as stamp-happy as he was the last time. So I scan the shelves for the cheapest phone there is. As I'm doing so, a guy built like a jockey's whip ambles over. He stands behind me, but I can catch a whiff of Cool Water.

'The new Motorola's a doozy,' he says.

'I'm after something cheap,' I say. I try to enunciate. It makes me sound like I have learning difficulties.

'Ah. You want contract or pay-as-you-go?'

'Whichever's cheapest.'

'And what extras were you thinking about?'

I finally turn round and get a decent look at him. The lad's riddled with acne, sports a tuft of blonde hair under his cracked bottom lip and looks like he'd fall over if I breathed too heavily. But then, he probably doesn't think I'm much of a looker, either.

'I want a fuckin' phone, mate,' I say. 'I don't care if it comes with a jacuzzi and a wet bar. I want something I can make a phone call on that isn't two soup cans and a piece of string. Something cheap, something durable and something that I can press a number on without having to use a fingernail, alright?'

His face tightens, looks like a pimple on his forehead is about to start weeping at the tension. 'Okay. Then I'll see what I can find for you, sir.'

Really hammering that 'sir'. Little prick. My head's started banging. I need to get back to the Micra, take some Nurofen, take a breather.

The sales kid shows me a phone. It's cheap. It looks cheaper.

I take it.

Outside, I grab the first taxi I can find, slump into the back seat and tell the driver where I'm going. He stares at me in the rear view mirror. So I tell him again. Once he pulls away, I catch him glancing at me like I'm some sort of free freak show. I feel like telling him to keep his eyes on the road, but I'm too tired. I crack the window to get a breeze going.

First things first, I need to get in touch with Uncle Morris. After a couple of wrong numbers courtesy of a directory enquiries service, I get the number for The Wheatsheaf. Three rings and the landlord answers.

'Brian, it's Cal Innes. I need to speak to Mr Tiernan.'

'What for?'

'It's personal.'

There's a pause. Then: 'He's not here.'

'If he wasn't there, Brian, you wouldn't have asked me what it was about. Now go fetch. I can wait.'

'I told you –'

'Don't fuck me about, Bri. I'm not in the mood.' I glare at the driver to make sure he gets the point too.

'Fine,' says Brian, and puts the phone onto the bar with a clatter. It's silent at the other end now. The Wheatsheaf is as dead as usual. It's nice to know some things don't change. A minute later, Brian comes back on the line. 'He says he'll call you back.'

'Then let me give you the number.'

'He's already got it.'

'Not this number he hasn't.' Jesus Christ.

Brian grumbles, rustles something. 'Okay. Fire away.'

I give him the new number and disconnect. The cab passes a girl with low-cut jeans and a hanging belly.

'Jesus, would you look at that,' says the driver.

I grunt, realise I'm hungry. My mobile starts bleating. After three shrill rings, I pick up. 'Mr Tiernan.'

'Mr Innes.' Morris doesn't sound too impressed. Either bored or homicidal; I can't work out which. 'You were supposed to phone Mo.'

'I would if I had his number,' I say.

'I gave you his number.'

'I lost it. I had an altercation with a couple of Stokes' boys.'

'They beat the shit out of you.'

'You can tell, huh?'

'You're mumbling,' he says. 'So you know where Stokes is.'

'He's about. But I don't know how long he'll hang around. He thinks I'm out of the picture.'

'Then I'll get Mo up there.'

'I want to find him first.'

'It's too late for that. I'll get Mo to call you from the road.' And he hangs up, leaving me with a dead line and an open mouth.

Well, that could have gone better.

I check my watch, try to work this out. Okay, give Mo a couple of hours to rally his bruisers, three hours on the road and he should be up here by tonight. Which doesn't give me nearly enough time. Donna's voice keeps telling me I should let this lie, but I can't do that. I don't relish the idea of Mo taking over. This is my job, and if he finds Stokes without my help, I'll still owe Tiernan. Which sends me right back to square one.

I can't have that. This is do or die.

When I glance at the cab driver, I see him staring at the package on my lap. His forehead is furrowed deep. I'm not surprised. A guy with a knocked-up head gets in his cab and starts talking about finding another guy, well, I can see how he'd leap to conclusions. I decide to play it friendly, give him a smile to show I'm harmless. He goes white.

'It's alright, mate,' I say, but my voice is too guttural.

He doesn't reply.

In fact, we don't exchange another word until he drops me off in Benton. Just to show there's no hard feelings, I tip him, but he's still out of there sharpish. I watch the taxi disappear before I light up and walk to my Micra, still where I left it.

There's no pleasing some people.

FORTY-FIVE

'Dad, I'm at home, where the fuck else would I be?'

'You weren't at home last night.'

'Nah, I were out with Rossie and Baz. Had some business to take care of.'

'You make much?' I didn't like the tone of Dad's voice. Summat wrong with it, either like he were trying to butter us up or he were taking the piss.

'Some,' I said.

'I got a call from Innes,' he said.

Me cheek reacted, but me voice didn't. 'What's up?'

'Nothing much. He's in Newcastle. Stokes is up there.'

'He got an address yet?'

'No. He knows where Stokes is, though. And he's going to need all the help he can get. A couple of Stokes' boys worked him over.'

'When were this?'

'I don't know. Just get whoever you need and get up to Newcastle. And give Innes a call from the road.' And then Dad gave us Innes' new number. I wrote it down. I broke the connection and sat there staring at Rossie and Baz. Baz caught me eye and I jerked me head. They could come back from fuckin' Coventry.

'What you grinning at?' said Rossie.

'Stokes and his lads did over Innes last night.'

'Fuckin' hell.'

'Saved us a job,' said Baz.

Yeah, I thought. Like you two would be any fuckin' use. 'So where's Stokes?'

'I dunno yet. But I want to go back to that flat, see if anyone's about, know what I mean? He were looking fuckin' proud of himself yesterday, so he got summat there. If he got a lead, we'll get a lead.'

'You don't know which flat it is,' said Rossie. Always the fuckin' nay-sayer.

'I'll sniff it out. If Alison were round there, I'll know it. Trust us.'

'Cause there were summat I had that Innes didn't. I knew me sister inside out. I knew what she were like and I knew the way her fuckin' mind worked.

Which meant that I'd get the bitch before Innes did.

*

'Y'alright, mate? I lost me keys.'

This lad with a beard and a belly didn't care, and he held the door open for us to prove it. I pushed through, Baz and Rossie behind us. 'Cheers, mate.'

Went up the stone steps, looked about the walkway.

'Well?' said Rossie. 'Where's she live?'

I didn't know. Shook me head. I could work summat out. Just had to think about it. Headed up one way, but it was all fuckin' pot plants and fancy number signs. Nah. Went back to the other end, and I knew we was in business. The door to thirty-five was open and the place stank like a burning poof. That were Alison. She loved all that fuckin' incense and shit. I looked at Rossie and Baz, jerked me head towards the door and pushed it wide open.

On the right, there was stairs. I told Rossie to go up them and check it out. Baz came with me. I didn't have nowt in the way of protection apart from me fists. But Baz and a wicked-keen Stanley. We went into the front room, all quiet. Ready to fuck someone over if they wanted to play ninja.

Nowt in here.

Looked like the place'd been fuckin' trashed an' all. I picked up a cushion and squeezed it like a stress ball. Me nose started running so I wiped it on the cushion and kept squeezing.

'You sure this is the right place, Mo?' said Baz.

I didn't answer him, went out into the hall and shouted up the stairs. 'Rossie, you found owt up there?'

Rossie appeared at the top of the stairs. 'You don't want to see this fuckin' bathroom, man.'

I tossed the cushion, took the stairs two at a time, pushed Rossie out the way. He were right – I didn't want to see the fuckin' bathroom. The smell were enough. Alison were a proper pig. That's why she used all that incense, hide the smell of her dirt. I said to Baz, 'Give us your Stanley.'

Baz dug deep into his trackies, handed it over. I clicked the blade out as far as it went and pushed open a door. The bedroom. Me eye itched so I scratched it. Went over to the mattress on the floor, still had the sheets on it, but nowt else in the room. They'd done a runner. That, or they lived like fuckin' squatters. On that mattress.

'Y'alright, Mo?' said Rossie.

I pushed the bedroom door shut, didn't take me eyes off the mattress. Lousy fuckin' cooze. If she wanted to come back, she'd have summat waiting for her. I got down on me knees and started slashing at the mattress, cut the fucker to ribbons. Tugged me way through the sheets and whistled while I worked, got me bladder pressed. When it were time, I pulled me cock out and pissed all over the remains.

Try fucking on that, Alison.

When I got out the bedroom, Rossie and Baz was waiting for us.

'What now?' said Baz. Rossie were staring at what was left of the mattress.

'Now we tear what's left of this shithole apart until we get a lead,' I said.

And I pulled Rossie away from the bedroom so's we could start on the downstairs.

FORTY-SIX

The GM Maxi Senior Cricket Bat.

It's a big bat in every way; handcrafting bows the blade into the drive area to produce the unique GM PowerArc *shape. A special pressing technique blended with a massive swell and strong edges gives the powerful players the bat of choice for awesome hitting.*

Awesome hitting. I like that. Nice ring to it. The Maxi's sitting across my lap right now. It feels too light to be of any use, but then what do I know? As long as it doesn't break into firewood on the first decent swing, I couldn't care less.

But then, the box doesn't say anything about using it on someone's legs.

Anger management. Controlling your emotion so it doesn't spill out and hurt yourself and other people. I know all about that. I did courses in jail about that. I had to. It made the authorities think you were serious about rehabilitation, and it passed the time.

'When you feel that urge, Deffenbacher suggests that you picture yourself as a god or goddess, a supreme ruler, striding alone and having your way in all situations while others defer to you. The more detail you can get into your imaginary scenes, the more chances you have to realise that maybe you are being unreasonable; you'll also realise how unimportant the things you're angry about really are.'

This from a young guy who crossed his legs too tightly and had a PhD in Patronising Prisoners. He was the leader of a group that encouraged enhanced thinking skills and anger management. We met twice a week in a cold room with green-and-white walls, sitting in a circle while this guy talked, his hands flapping like a couple of coked-up birds. He had his pet subjects, his pet theorists. He loved talking in a slow, soft and completely judgemental voice, telling us exactly why we were inside.

And we had to put up with it. Not that the group was compulsory. It was just that it looked better on your record if you attended. Which I did, because by that time, the last thing I wanted was to stay behind bars.

The group leader once told this brick-headed fucker called Hawkins that he needed to concentrate on his cognitive restructuring.

'You fuckin' what?'

'It means that when you're angry, your thinking can become *exaggerated*. Cognitive restructuring lets you understand how silly you're being.'

Silly? Hawkins looked like he wanted to batter the little prick. If he'd thrown a punch, I got the feeling the rest of us would join in.

'It's silly to lamp a cunt, is what you're saying,' said Hawkins.

'See, now –' The group leader raised one finger. '– you're using *humour*. That can be healthy, but there are problems with that. Can anyone tell me what they are?'

'Nobody laughs?'

His voice sounded like a sigh. 'There are two cautions in using humour, gentlemen.' The leader got to his feet and went to the white board. 'First, don't try to "laugh off" your problems.'

He wrote 'LAUGH OFF' and drew a line through it.

'Rather, use humour to help you to face your problems more *constructively*.'

'We should be more *constructive*,' said Hawkins.

'Second, don't give in to harsh, sarcastic humour; that's just another form of unhealthy anger expression.'

He wrote 'SARCASTIC' and 'UNHEALTHY'. Between the two words, he drew an equals sign.

Anger management. Manage my situation, you speccy fucker.

'All an angry person is saying, *really*, is: "Hey, things aren't going my way!"'

Fucking tell me about it.

I feel the weight of the bat and then lay it down again. Nah, it should be fine. I'm only going to use it the once. Before I got here, I was at the pub. Dutch courage, maybe Scotch and a pint or twelve of Belgian lager to make it a European dream. I called the casino, pretended I was George's brother, that his dad had had a stroke. When he got on the phone, I hung up. He's working tonight.

I did a slow recce of the casino carpark before I got settled in. George's car is a blue Fiat with a scuffed bonnet and dark spots on the boot. The bloke didn't have the foresight to scrub my blood off his car. Which means I'm not watching for him anymore, just anyone who goes near his motor. It's a good job, too. It's getting dark now, making it almost impossible for me to make out faces. I've already had my hand on the door a couple of times, ready to get out, heart thumping. But so far it's been nothing but false alarms.

I pop some Nurofen, notice I've got two left in the pack, and throw the box back into the glove compartment. Then one of each from the little brown bottles that Doctor Dick prescribed. I chase the pills down with a swig from the half bottle of vodka. Good job I bought that bastard, I think. The beer and whisky buzz is fading fast and I need something to keep me ticking over. Rage is a bitch to maintain.

Mo's coming. He'll be on his way right now. Sick bastard.

Gets his own sister pregnant. Alison, the wee whore. Stokes, the bullshit chip junkie.

And George. Borderline psycho. Workaholic. He'd rather do double shifts behind a bar than live his life. He's the only one with ties here. Stokes and Alison might have left the city, but George wasn't about to go anywhere.

He was stupid enough to think I wouldn't come after him. He's been sloppy and turned up for work, regular as. So my phone call might have spooked him a little, but he'd get over it the minute he gets a decent tip. The more I think about him, the less I care about Alison and Stokes. It isn't about them anymore. It's about that little prick who thrives on being an arsehole. Stokes had a reason to do me over but George got off on it. And that kind of violence, it's a drug. You know you're safe, you can play out your sadistic wee fantasies on whichever poor fucker you've got cornered.

Yeah, I've seen that happen enough times. Been on the receiving end more than I like to admit.

The power trip George was on, that rush of adrenaline, he should channel it elsewhere, because one day he'll throw it at the wrong bloke and it'll end up biting him in the arse.

I'm that wrong bloke. And better I bite him now than he ends up dead later on. At least I've got a conscience. Someone else, someone single-minded, someone greedy, fucked-up, twisted, some junkie, they might not be as nice to him.

What I'm doing here is teaching a bloke a lesson. And some lessons need a personal tutor. I'm doing him a favour.

It's all about anger management.

I notice I've started drumming my fingers on the blade of the bat. I stop, take another swig of vodka. All this waiting's killing me.

Donna loves me. Right. Donna doesn't want to see me hurt. Fuck her. She doesn't know me. Some drunk bitch wants a life mate, she should look somewhere other than bars. I mean, Christ, picking someone up in a pub. How desperate is that? It stinks of Brenda Lang. And look where that got me. On the fucking run.

I hope Paulo's alright.

Shake that thought from my head. No point in dwelling on that. Donkey's all talk. He wouldn't do anything to Paulo. He couldn't.

More vodka.

I watch a minicab pull into the carpark. A drunk punter comes staggering out of the casino. He holds onto the roof of the taxi and struggles with the door.

Some people just can't take their beer.

After the punter slides into the back seat, the cab pulls away. I watch it head past the casino and out of the carpark. Then look back at the side of the building. Two girls, two lads. My fingers tighten around the rubber grip of the bat.

It's George. The bar must be closed for the night. Telling a joke, a stupid story, he's doing everything he can to impress these two girls. They're not having any of it, but his mate is laughing his arse off. Overdoing it to make George look better. They stop in the light from reception and George points in the direction of his car.

Don't do it, girls. He's not worth it, really.

And you, George's mate, fuck off. I don't need an audience for this.

The group breaks apart, the girls heading for the main road, the two lads backing off towards George's car. George has his hands up and is shouting something at the girls.

Blown out. My heart bleeds.

George's mate is still with him.

Shit. I don't need this. I don't need witnesses. But needs must. Needs fucking must. As they reach the Fiat, I push open the car door, GM Maxi Senior in one clammy hand. My right leg is numb; I have to shake the blood back as I try to stride across the carpark. I zero in on George. Difficult to do, because there's sweat in my eyes.

He's still talking, the mouthy bastard. Concentrating on getting his key in the car door. I wouldn't be surprised if he's a little drunk. Tonight, we're all tipsy. It helps us do what a man's gotta do.

The lad with George is a mealy little bugger, skinny as a wicker man and twice as fragile. He sees me coming, but he can't get his brain around it. So he stares. He starts gold-fishing. As I get closer, I can hear tiny noises in the back of his throat, wee grunts and clicks. The fucker sounds like Flipper.

'They'll come running back,' says George. 'That Debbie loves me, Trev. I can smell it on her –'

I cut him short with a chop to his right knee.

'Howzat, you cunt.'

The bat makes a dull thump, not the ear-splitting crack I was hoping for, but George buckles, knocks his head off the roof of the car and crumples to the ground. His mate looks at me, wide-eyed and visibly shaking. There's a moment before George realises how much pain he's in. When he does, he starts screaming like someone poured acid in his eyes.

'Back off,' I say to Trev. 'Turn around and walk the other fuckin' way.'

George loses the breath to scream, falls into heavy sobbing. I want to take the bat to his head, but Trev's still here.

'Don't make me tell you twice, son. This is none of yours.'

I raise the bat. It's the picture he needed painting. Trev bolts straight for the casino and the bouncers. I need to hurry this thing along. I grab George by the shirt collar and drag him across the tarmac. He starts screaming again; no words, just noise. A quick glance at him and tears are streaking the blood on his face. He must have broken his nose on the way down.

Bonus.

For someone so bloody thin, he's a dead weight. I manage to get him to the Micra just as I look across at Trev. He's telling the bouncers what happened, pointing at me. I pull the driver's seat forward and say to George, 'After you, mate.'

He looks up at me. 'You broke my fuckin' *legs*!'

'Bollocks. I didn't break nowt.' I lift him under the arms and heave him into the back seat. One of the bouncers shouts. I look up and see one of the bruisers in full pelt towards me. The other one's disappeared. He must be calling the police. I slam the seat against George's fucked up leg and he yelps. Then I slide behind the wheel.

I start the engine and it catches no problem. There's a first time for everything. I gun it out of the carpark, light an Embassy as we pull onto the main road and away from the city centre.

George babbles in the back seat. 'Listen man, I'm sorry, alright? I got carried away, it happens. I'm sorry. I didn't mean to –'

'Save it, George.'

'Nah, I mean it. C'mon, you can't think I was really gonna kill you, do you? I'm all talk, you ask anyone. I'm a fuckin' *coward*, man. I'm a fuckin' *wreck*. Look, you just let us out here, I'll be fine, right?' He tries to move his leg and chokes. 'I'm gonna be sick.'

'Go ahead.'

'What d'you want, man? I'm not Rob, am I? You want cash, I got some on us, but if you want serious cash then you'll have to drop us off at a bank –'

I look at him in the rear view. 'What d'you think I want?'

He looks blank. The pain's made him slow. He'll get it soon enough, though.

Even if I have to break his other leg.

FORTY-SEVEN

Another night, another motorway.

I pull in, flick on the hazard lights and get out of the car. Cold out here, my breath misting up in front of my face. The drive here gave me a bastard behind the eyes. I didn't take anything for it, either. Let the pain dull the senses, stop me from thinking about what I'm about to do. The headache subsides for a second once I get some fresh air into my lungs, then I pull open the driver's door and flip the seat forward. George is still in the same position. He's frightened out of his mind, his eyes shining in the dark.

Good.

'Get out the car, George,' I say quietly.

'Howeh, you're not thinking straight.'

I grab his bad leg and pull hard. George splutters a shout as he tries to fight me off, but I give a good hard yank and he comes spilling onto the road, landing on his back with a thump. I give him a dig in the ribs. George tries to double up, winded. I drag him like the sack of shite he is over the lay-by and send him rolling down into a ditch. Then I reach into the car, heft the Maxi to my shoulder and stare at him until he manages to turn himself over.

'Fuck's the matter with you?' he says. His voice is strained, hoarse. Too much screaming, his fear boiled into anger now. I know that feeling all too well. Let him get wrapped up in darkness until it clamps around his lungs like two damp fists. Let him suffer those sudden jabs of light from passing cars.

Give him a taste of his own fucking medicine.

'Where is he, George?'

George shakes his head. 'Where's who?'

'Stokes.'

'I dunno where Rob is, man. He fucked off. He's gone.'

'I don't believe you.'

'I don't give a fuck. I'll have you locked up.'

Better give him something to grass up, then. I bring the sharp end of the Maxi down on his right shin, a swift hard stamp. He spasms on the ground, yelps like a scalded puppy. Bring the bat down again and twist the bastard against the bone. George tries to move his leg, but he hasn't got the strength. He keeps calling out for God. And I keep the pressure on.

'Where is he, George?'

'*I fuckin' told you where he is.*'

I twist the bat, feel bone stretch and crack under my weight. Then the bat's back up at my shoulder and over his yelling, I tell him, 'You told me nowt, mate.'

George curls up as best he can, snot all down his chin. He chokes on whatever he's trying to say because his whole body is racked with sobs. I toy with the idea of battering his teeth out, but then that would defeat the purpose. It's hard enough to understand what he's saying, thanks to a swollen top lip and a collapsed nose.

I grab the bottle of vodka from the car and take a swig until my lips feel dry and stinging. Then I screw the cap back onto the bottle and let the bat touch my leg. 'What's the matter with you, George? Stokes did fuck all for you, mate, except get you here.'

'He didn't tell me *nowt.*' It comes out as a scream, the indignant wail of a kid. A flash from passing headlights shows his red eyes, his bleeding mouth, the colour rising high in his cheeks. Like someone held a scarlet filter up to his face.

'He's a mate, though,' I say. 'You two are close. He must've told you *something*. I can't believe he didn't give you an inkling at least.'

'Rob's not a mate,' says George. 'He ain't fuckin' . . .' He shakes his head, gobs thick spittle from his burst mouth. 'Rob's an *idiot*, man.'

'So he's not a mate, so there's no loyalty.'

'That's not it. Fuckin' hell. You know what he did?'

'He stole money,' I say.

'He saw the chance for a big score and he went for it. And, y'know, I told him not to do it. I told him not to fuck himself over for her. Can't trust her as far as you can shit her.'

'This would be Alison.'

'Who else would it be? Aye, Alison.'

'And what's her big secret, eh?'

'It's not a secret, man. She's a fuckin' little cooze. A proper bitch and snide with it.'

'She call you a name behind your back?'

George blinks slowly, his eyes rolled to the whites. The lad'll pass out given half a chance. I slam the bat against the side of the Micra and the noise shakes him awake.

'Keep alert, George.'

'It was all her, man,' he says.

'It was Alison's idea.'

'Aye.'

'Not Rob.'

'Rob didn't have the balls to do it.'

'She robbed her own fuckin' father is what you're telling me,' I say. The vodka's kicked in, crackling the blood and throwing my brain around the inside of my skull. 'You're out of your mind.'

'And you're fuckin' blinkered, man.'

I stamp hard on his ankle. As I twist, something gives way

underfoot. George throws himself forward, scrabbling at my leg. I knock his hand away with the bat. As I step off, he tries to roll out of the way, ends up face-down in a puddle. 'How about you tell me the truth, George? How about that? Else I take this bat to your fuckin' skull.'

He breathes muddy bubbles in the puddle water, his face screwed up. When he talks, he sprays. 'I'm telling you the truth. I swear to *God* I'm telling you the fuckin' truth.'

Bringing God into it again. I test the weight of the cricket bat in my hand, aim my swing at his other ankle. It connects with a sharp crack. George buries his scream in the mud and when he tries to speak, it comes out with a throbbing staccato underscore: 'Whuh-huh-the *fuck* . . .'

'I don't like you, George. I thought I made that patently fuckin' obvious, mate. I don't like you because you were all set to top me and leave me in a bloody ditch, and I don't like you because you're lying to me.'

George shakes his head, pulls his body up with all the weight firmly on his forehead. A vein in his neck looks fit to burst. It's like watching a tape of myself from the other night. When he gets to his knees, he spits a mixture of blood and mud at me. 'And I told you the fuckin' truth, you *cunt*. You wanna do me in, go for it, fuckin' *do it*.'

I raise the bat quickly, ready to swing. Adjust my grip, make sure it's good and firm, take a second to wipe the sweat from my left palm. Draw a bead on the back of George's head – the fucker's cowering now – and narrow my eyes until he's a blur. Just the way it has to be. Holding up the Maxi, my fingers twitching against the rubber grip.

Go on. Do it. Swing the fucker. Knock some sense into him. Lying cunt, lying cunt, lying fuckin' bastard cunt.

Headlight flash behind me, grab George's shadow and throw it from left to right, headlights behind them punching the shadow into three. Time lapse. I open my eyes, feel the bile scratch at the back of my throat.

I can't do this.

Wimp. Pussy. Do it.

I can't fucking do it.

This is why you're constantly being fucked over, Cal. It comes to the crunch and you shit it, pal.

The bat trembles in my hands. I can't control it.

COWARD.

No.

'Fuck's sake.' The words come out in a rush. I lower the bat, massage the blood back into my hands. My leg hurts. My arms ache. My spine pinches at me. My heart is beating too fast, and I've broken out in a cold sweat. '*Fuck's* sake.'

George's back heaves in the dim light. It's the only movement he makes.

I have to lean against the car. I put the bat by my leg and light up.

I'd go for the vodka, but I can't move.

FORTY-EIGHT

Sitting on the tarmac, the arse of my jeans getting soaked right through to the skin, and I'd feel sorry for myself if it wasn't for George whimpering in the dark. Kind of puts my wet buttocks into perspective.

'If Alison set it up, then why did she agree to come back with me?' I say.

A loud, long breath escapes from George. I look up, and make him out lying on his back. A stiff breeze blows the smell of urine my way. 'She told us you'd be there. She wanted you taken care of,' he says.

'She does that, and someone else'll just come after her.'

'You think they're after her?'

I wipe the nose with the back of my hand. 'They're after Stokes. Fuck it, nah, I don't know who they're after anymore.'

'You had to find Rob,' he says.

'Yeah.'

'She set him up.'

'She had no reason to set him up,' I say.

'She doesn't give a shit.'

'Rob would beat her to death.'

'I need to go to the hospital.'

'Rob would hit her, mate. She's scared of him. I've seen her. She's taken a beating.'

'Mr Innes, Cal, I need to go to a hospital.'

I look up at George, find him staring at me. Pleading. I get to my feet, grab the cricket bat and throw it onto the back seat. 'I can't do that, George.'

'C'mon, it's the least you can do – you broke my fuckin' legs.'

'And you don't know how close I came to killing you, you ungrateful bastard. I wish I'd broken your mouth.'

'You've got to take me to the hospital.'

'I'm not taking you anywhere.'

'I told you everything.'

'You didn't tell me where he is.'

'I told you *everything*.'

'You think he's gone back to his flat?'

'I don't know.'

'What'd he say to you after you left me the other night?'

George's head twists like he's been through this and through this and he still can't get a handle on it. 'He said that it was over. He said that there'd be no more trouble from you, and Alison would be happy with that.'

'So he went back to his flat,' I say.

'I told you, I dunno.'

I move towards George and he flinches, tries to pull himself away. I grip his shirt collar and pull hard, drag him screaming to the back seat of the car. I throw the seat back and get behind the wheel, adjusting the rear view so I can get a better look at him. 'Tell you what, George – as soon as I find Stokes, I'll drop you off at A & E.'

He summons up a mouthful of spit and aims it at me. When it connects with my face, I feel fire in my cheeks. I lean over the seat and slap him open-handed. George recoils, his face growing red.

'Don't play gangster with me, son. Else I *will* finish you off.'

*

Driving back to Benton is a chore. My arms feel like lead weights, my vision blurred. Sick of the same streets, the same battered faces on the corner. I take a swig of the vodka to keep my blood going and have to tell George to shut up. He's moaning in the back seat that he's not comfortable. I tell him he's just going to have to make do. Life stinks, so hold your nose. At least I've had the decency to promise him a hospital. More than he ever did for me.

George says, 'Why me, man?'

'Why you what?'

'Why'd you come for me?' He stops himself. 'I know, for last night —'

'That's a good enough reason.'

'But it's not the only one, right? You're not just out to do me over.'

'You were the only one I knew I could find in a hurry.'

'Huh,' he says. 'You didn't have to bring the bat with you.'

I look at George in the rear view. 'What the hell else was I supposed to do? You deserved it.'

He falls silent. Tries to move, but falls back against the seat. Now he's propped up against the windows, staring up at the roof of the car. Mud on his face, blood hardening his top lip. He mops at his mouth with the back of his hand, then looks to see if he's still bleeding. Every now and then, he'll glance at something on the floor of the car.

I watch him. I know what he's thinking. If he could only get to the bat, he'd let loose with it on the back of my head. I catch his eye. 'I wouldn't bother, George. Think about it this way: you use that bat on me, I'll probably black out, right? I black out, I lose control of the car.' I press my foot on the accelerator; the engine roars, momentum pushing me back in my seat. 'I lose control of the car, we're just a twisted heap of metal and bone.'

'I wasn't –'

'Course you were. If I was in your position, I'd be thinking the same thing. Now picture this: I crash the car and, through some miracle, you haven't gone through the windscreen. Maybe you're so limp back there that you come out of it unmarked. We're in the middle of nowhere. How fast d'you think you can run on two broken legs?'

'Mr Innes –'

'Nah, hold up, let me speak. And don't go offering excuses, because you've got priors for making daft mistakes. So listen to me. You even *look* at that bat again, and I'll fishtail this car all over the sodding road, make things proper uncomfortable for you back there.'

George sighs. It sounds painful. He keeps his eyes on the passing scenery.

'We're going back to Rob's and you're going to sit quiet until I see him. Then when the cavalry's arrived, I'll take you to the fuckin' hospital, alright?'

'I don't even know if he's still there,' says George.

'Why wouldn't he be?'

George shakes his head, sucks his teeth. His eyes are shining. The guy's crying again.

'Look, I'm sorry to do this to you, but you brought it on yourself. You're a bloody idiot.'

'Don't I fuckin' know it,' he says.

I reach across and pull open the glove compartment. My head's throbbing, but I toss the Nurofen into the back seat. 'Here,' I say. 'Get them down you. Should dull the pain for a bit.'

He opens the pack. 'There's only two left.'

'I had a toothache.' I drain the vodka bottle and sling it into the open glove compartment, slam it closed. In the back, George dry-swallows the two pills as I pull the car into Manor Road.

The prescription pills rattle in my pocket, and part of me thinks about tossing a few his way. But then, they're mine. I could have given him something to wash the Nurofen down, but there's no way I'd let him get between me and my booze. I might be feeling slightly sorry for him, but there are limits.

I've already tested a few of my own tonight.

FORTY-NINE

Early morning silence gives you space to think, even if you don't want to. The vodka's slipping away fast, and I have the radio on. John Lee Hooker with a slow, mournful tune that I can't name or make out the lyrics to, reminding me of Donna. I switch the radio station. Another dishrag morning, another half-hearted shower of rain against the windscreen.

Reminds me of the last time I saw Kumar. We were out in the prison allotment, turning over manure which stank worse with the rain and the damp. I was keeping my head down and getting on with it, but Kumar had issues with it all. He should have known better than to act up. The screw watching us looked just like Gary Busey. That should have been a sign.

So Kumar said he wanted a cigarette. The screw said he wasn't allowed, that Kumar'd had his smoke break. Busey also said that if Kumar fancied himself a hard arse about it, he'd end up with that there spade in his spine.

Kumar didn't listen. Kumar ended up in the infirmary. When he got out, he mouthed off that he was going to file a complaint. It was inhumane, he said. He had a shit hot brief who'd make toast of Busey and the whole prison.

We stayed away from him. It was one thing to be a crusader; it was another to be a grass. Yeah, Busey was a guard, but he taught a valuable lesson.

You've got to know who's in charge. And sometimes it takes GBH to make a bloke learn.

I'm not proud of what I did to George. Now that the fuzz has disappeared from my brain, I'm getting snapshots of last night in every hangover-heightened detail. I could have killed him. And if I could have killed him in that state, it makes me wonder what else I've done when I'm drunk. Part of me wishes I could just be an arsehole when I'm pissed like everyone else. Why I get the fear is beyond me. But fuck it; I'll go to confession.

'What'll happen to Rob?' asks George.

He's been quiet since we parked. Now his voice seems back to normal. The Nurofen must have kicked in and he's had the chance to swallow enough spit to kill the rawness in his throat. He's been cadging cigarettes off me. He's got one in his gob right now, smoke wafting out through the front window.

'I don't care what happens to Rob,' I say.

'It's not his fault.'

'I don't care.'

George lets the smoke hiss out through his teeth. 'Fuck are you, anyway? I thought you was a private detective.'

'Investigator,' I say.

'Yeah, shit. Big fuckin' difference, eh? Private *investigators* beat the shit out of people with cricket bats?'

'They do if they're pissed off.'

George snorts. Coughs and spits something in the back of my car. 'Aye, you're a private investigator. You work for Morris Tiernan, you're not a PI. You're a bloody hatchet man.'

That's the third time I've been described like that. I didn't like it much the first time. Now it's starting to boil my piss.

'You done bird?' he says.

'I've been in prison.'

'So you're an ex-con.'

'You ought to be in the police, you're that fuckin' smart. What's your point?'

'You got a licence?'

'They don't license.'

'So you're just playing the part,' he says.

I don't like where this is going. I glare at him in the rear view.

'You're not a PI,' he says. And he laughs. Loud. 'Fuckin' hell, you're no more a private investigator than I'm James Bond, man.'

'Shut your mouth, George.'

'You honestly think you're doing good here?'

'I don't have to do good. I just have to do a job.'

'You talked to Alison, man. No, wait, I got it. You got chivalrous because she was sporting a shiner, right?'

'Your mate Rob's a piece of shit,' I say.

'Oh, come *on*, man. You saw him the other night. She gave as good as she got. And if I know her like I think I know her, she was the one that threw the first punch, and I bet it was nowhere near being over the fuckin' belt, either.'

'That's not true. I was there.'

'And what did you see?'

'I saw a fight.'

'Who started it?'

'I know what I saw.'

'Fuck that, you saw what you wanted to see. And how pissed were you then?'

I twist around in my seat. 'You going to shut up, George?'

He takes another drag on the cadged Embassy and smiles with a swollen lip. It's an ugly sight. 'I'm trying to tell you what's going on here, man. You see what you want to see, you don't realise that you're playing for the wrong team. C'mon, the Tiernans are the good guys? Give your fuckin' head a shake, man.'

'I didn't have a choice.'

'Way I see it, you're responsible for what happens to Rob.'

'Am I fuck.'

'You've as good as set him up. You tell the Tiernans where he is, you're as good as killing him yourself. How's that sit on your conscience?'

'It's none of my business.'

'Course it is,' he says. 'You're as bad as the rest of them. A charva fuckin' gangster playing PI because you're too scared to stand up for yourself.'

My elbow finds his teeth before I know what I've done. George flies back in his seat, hand up over his mouth, swearing in blood bubbles. I turn back around in my seat and stare through the windscreen, my skin itching. Behind me, George is mumbling through broken teeth.

'I didn't have a choice,' I say.

And I'm out of the car before George can say anything else.

FIFTY

George. Dickhead. Fucking *dickhead*. Where does he get off playing the morality card with me? Where the hell does a guy who wanted to kill me and leave me by the side of the road in a ditch find the balls to put his boot in the stirrup and get up on that high horse? Fucking hypocrite.

And there he goes, muddying my thoughts with this bullshit conspiracy theory. Alison Tiernan behind it all, which makes Rob Stokes a scapegoat and dead man walking. She's unhappy with her life and her bastard kid, so she decides to steal from her dad and go on the run. It fits with what she said, but it's the guilt I'm having trouble with.

I've seen battered wives and girlfriends before. I know what they look like and there was something defiant about Alison that didn't fit. Like she was willing me to start in on her. At the time, I thought it was just her way of coping. And thinking of Stokes now, I'm not sure if he was sporting any new wounds. I thought I saw something, but the state I was in, it could have been a trick of the light.

But if Alison's behind it, then I've been fucking up since day one. And Rob Stokes is going to pay for it. Maybe he's just like the rest of us, caught up and in too deep to swim.

I light a cigarette even though I don't want one. The sky's the same colour as the smoke that drifts from my mouth. Somewhere I can hear birds chirping and when I check my watch, it's five in the morning. I wonder where the night went, can't remember the last time I had a good night's sleep. My back's all knotted up and jabbing at me. A yawn builds until my ears pop.

Too much to think about right now. I check my mobile for messages. There's a half-dozen from Mo. He's staying at the airport Travelodge, wants me to call him as soon as, or else. A message from Morris, basically the same thing. Where the fuck am I?

I'm right here, boys. No need to get shitty with me.

So what now? Time's running out. Soon it won't be just Rob Stokes Mo's after, it'll be me. And why would that be? Because he wants to hand over some personal justice for the guy nicking his girl and me, I'm the guy his dad said would be able to find Stokes. Even though Mo probably wanted the job himself, which would explain a lot.

I look in the car and George seems to have fallen asleep. A loud, rattling snore fills the Micra with noise, drowns out the radio. I prod his leg hard. He snaps awake, yelling.

'Stokes has a mobile,' I say.

'Fuck're you talking about?' George blinks rapidly, his eyes narrowed against daylight.

'Stokes has a mobile, right? Give me the number.'

'He doesn't have a mobile.'

'I don't have time to fuck about, George. Stokes has a mobile, you have a mobile, we've all got fuckin' mobiles. You want the truth, I'm going to help him out.'

'Fuck off.'

'Fuck off? That's nice, but if I don't call him, he's dead.'

George looks at me, wipes some crust from his eye. He's still not convinced.

'I'm not lying to you, George.'

His jaw pulses, then he shuffles in the seat so he can reach inside his jacket. 'If you're fucking about –'

'Then I already know you can contact him, don't I? And if

that's the case, I can use the bat if you don't fork out the number.'

He pales. 'You're kidding.'

'Give me the number and we'll see.'

George pauses, then pulls out his mobile phone. I snatch it off him and slam the car door shut. I lean against the window so he can't see what I'm doing. Scrolling though his contact list, I notice there's only one ROB.

This idea taking root, it's probably daft. But the way I see it, I haven't got many cards left to play, and this might just get me out of feeling guilty. It might go some way to making a bad situation better, or it could make it a hell of a lot worse. But it's about the only thing I can do right now that makes sense.

I call Stokes. He's kept his mobile switched on, because it hasn't gone straight through to voicemail. Which means he's either too lazy to switch it off, or he's waiting on a call. When he picks up, he speaks with a voice full of early morning phlegm.

'Rob, it's Cal Innes.'

'How'd you get this number?' Sounding more awake by the second. Fear, otherwise known as the body's own caffeine.

'I want to make you a deal,' I say.

'Who'd you get this number off?'

'Doesn't matter. Is Alison there?'

There's a pause, as if he's thinking. Then: 'No, she's not.'

'Then we can talk.'

'Fuck do I want to talk to you about?'

'I have a proposition for you.'

'Fuck your proposition.'

'I'm outside, Rob.'

'The fuck you are,' he says.

'You're a grumpy bastard in the mornings, aren't you? Look, my deal is you keep the money you stole —'

'I didn't steal —'

'Listen to me. You keep the money you took, you keep the lot. But you get out of Newcastle right now. Go somewhere nobody knows you. Change your name, do whatever it takes. Don't fuck it up like you did the last time. Stay out of the casinos, stay out of the bookies, curb that particular enthusiasm, you get me?'

Stokes grunts. If he was here, I'd slap some sense into him. Anger management might as well bite me. It went out the window the day I started this job, and I've been growing angrier by the second. Funny how easy it is to fall into the old ways given half a chance.

'Don't piss about, Rob. I'm offering you a way out here. All you need to do is keep your trap shut and get out of town. And you need to tell me where Alison is.'

'Alison?'

'That's right. She's going home. That's all they wanted. And if it wasn't, then it's what they're going to have make do with.'

Stokes starts to stammer. 'Wait a second.'

'No waiting. The offer stands for the next ten seconds. After that, I collar your man George here and I go to work on his fuckin' arms. Then I'll call Mo and tell him where to find you.'

'Hold on, George is there?'

'Kind of. And you're running out of time.'

'Look, can we meet up and talk about this?'

'I already fell for that one.'

Stokes sighs into the phone; it rasps in my ear.

'Use your brain, mate,' I say.

Another sigh. Then he starts talking. He gives me an address, rattles it out and it's not far from here. I disconnect, open the car door and chuck George's mobile back at him as I get in. He catches the phone. 'What's going on?'

'You're going to the hospital, George.'

'What about Rob?'

'He's not as stupid as he looks.'

FIFTY-ONE

'If we'd stayed at the airport, we'd be fuckin' comfortable at least,' said Baz.

'Shut up,' I said. Me mobile started ringing. I didn't know the number. It weren't Innes, and I'd been trying to call the fuck all night. But nah, he had it on voicemail. Which meant he were up to no bloody good.

'He's right, Mo. Let's just call it a fuckin' day, alright?'

'What'd I tell you?' I answered me mobile. 'Fuck's this?'

'Mo,' she said.

Well, look who it weren't.

Baz started saying summat again, but I knocked him in the mouth so he kept quiet. Instead, he sat there holding his gob and glaring at us.

'Y'alright, Sis?' I said.

'No. No, I'm not.' She started on with the heavy breathing. Crying, but trying to keep it quiet, like. 'I can't do this, Mo. I can't do this anymore.'

'Tell us where you are,' I said.

'He's sneaking about. I think he's gonna grass me up.'

'We'll sort that out.'

'Mo, I'm scared.'

You fuckin' should be, I wanted to say. But I said, 'Tell us where you are.'

'No,' she said. 'I can't. You –'

'We'll find you anyway, Alison. You might as well make this easier on yourself.'

'I don't want you to hurt Rob.'

'I promise, I won't hurt him.'

'I can't go back, Mo.'

'You'll come back with me. It'll be alright, Sis. I promise.'

There were silence at the other end. Then she said, 'There's still some money.'

'Good.'

'We could maybe use it.'

'Maybe.' Like fuck. Think I'd mess around with you again, Sis? You're out your fuckin' gourd, love. Give us your address and we'll come round.'

'We?'

'I got Rossie and Baz with us. We been looking for you.'

'He already called you, then,' she said. 'I knew he would. He's a fuckin' liar. Rob's been talking to him. I'm sure it's him. Rob hasn't been talking to you, has he?'

'Nah. I don't know the lad.'

'What about Dad?' she said.

'He misses you. He wants you to come home.'

'I'll give him a ring.'

'Nah, that's alright. You just hang tight and tell us where you are, and we'll come over and you can ring Dad from the road, okay?'

She didn't say nowt for a bit. Then she whispered the address to us over the phone. And I felt like I'd just cleared me bowels after a year of constipation.

'Stay where you are, Sis. We'll be right round.'

I hung up, lit a ciggie and fuckin' savoured that first drag.

'What's up?' said Rossie.

'We're going home,' I said. 'But we got to go round and pick up Alison first.'

'Well, thank fuck for that,' said Baz.

FIFTY-TWO

Newcastle General, Accident & Emergency. I help George out of the car and walk him wincing towards the entrance. The ramp leading up to the automatic doors is a struggle, but he makes it into the reception area without being dropped. I ease him into a chair and he stretches his legs as far as the pain allows. I crouch by George and slip two hundred and fifty notes into his jacket pocket. 'Came through in the end. Thanks, George.'

His face cracks into a sarcastic grin. 'Don't mention it, *mate.*'

'You going to be okay?'

'I'll be fine.'

Then I'm out of the building, bump into a wheezy old guy with hair as white as his face, dragging down the last of a filterless cigarette. He tries to swear at me, but he can't find the breath. I get behind the wheel of the Micra and spark a cigarette of my own. The car smells like stale sweat and urine. I make a mental note to get it cleaned when this is over.

The address Stokes gave me, it's in Heaton. I have to consult the A–Z, and when I finally roll into the right street, the place is deserted, just a white van down the road. This is student country, could be anywhere in Britain. Lots of terraced houses with overgrown gardens and tapestries for curtains. I park up the street, keep an eye on the front door. He's been given a last-minute reprieve. I just hope he has the sense to grab it with both hands. When I spoke to him, there was that tremble to his voice that meant I'd put the fear of God into him. Putting the fear of Mo would have been good enough. But the bottom line is that Alison's in there, probably asleep, and she's got no idea that she's been rumbled.

I close my eyes for a moment. The seat seems to sink and I feel myself slipping away, so I have to snap awake.

Let's get this over with. I grab my mobile, call Mo. Takes him a few rings to pick up. He sounds like he's having a whale of a time, like he's actually smiling down the phone at me. 'Innes! The *fuck* are you?'

'Morning,' I say.

'Where are you?'

'I'm in Heaton.'

'What's the address?'

I take a moment to flick ash from the end of the Embassy. 'I hear you got your sister pregnant, Mo.'

Silence at the other end. Then, for a moment, I hear what sounds like a man's voice in the background. He's not at the Travelodge anymore, that's for sure. Mo makes a sucking sound then says, 'You talked to Alison.'

'Is it true?'

'When'd you talk to Alison?'

'I'll take that as a yes, then. So what happens when your dad finds out you've been rolling your own?'

'She's me half-sister.'

'Semantics, mate. She's sixteen, barely fuckin' legal.'

'What's the matter with you? You have a run-in with the law or something?'

'I had a run-in with the hairy side of someone's hand, repeatedly. Then some boots. All this after a nasty wee meeting with the front of a speeding car. And you know what? It makes a bloke think different, gives life a new spin. Because this was never about me finding Rob Stokes, was it?

This was about bringing Alison back home, and some lanky streak of paedo piss bricking it in case I tell his father.'

'Where are you?' he says quietly. 'Tell me where you are.'

I give him the address. Then: 'I lost Stokes. I lost the money. Alison's here. You might catch her. See, the thing is with me, I'm so knocked up I can't think straight. I've been lied to that fuckin' much, I don't even know if I'm at the right house, know what I mean?' A laugh breaks out of me; it sounds like someone else. 'Tell me something, Mo. Did your dad hold you back from this? Is that why you had to have me followed?'

'Fuck are you talking about?'

'Your man in the black leather jacket. Didn't occur to me until now, really. The guy who took a knife to the tyres of my car, updated the paint job with a spray can. The fucker who replaced that scally who tried to tail me in Manchester.'

Mo hangs up. Something I said? And it's the only confirmation I need. There was a moment there when I thought I was going nuts, but it's all falling into place now. Morris tells Mo he can't take care of this – either because the lad's a psycho or a fuck-up or because deep down Morris knows that Mo's been keeping it in the family – and Mo, being the tenacious cunt he is, he decides to have me followed. When it looks like I'm straying from the job, looking for Alison, he gets his thug to slice up my car.

And perhaps that would have scared me off before. But the past couple of days have made me stupid, hard. I look at myself in the rear view. Well, not *that* hard – my face is still black and blue. I stretch out in my seat, pull it back a few notches and stick Johnny Cash in the tape deck. One of the later songs, when it sounded like he'd been gargling with gravel. A man going round, taking names.

My muscles start to relax, my back isn't pinching me like it has been. A couple of clicks in the knee, and my tongue roams the empty socket where my tooth used to be. Thanks for that, Rob. I owe you one.

I'll stay here until Mo turns up. It's that last loose end I need to tie up. I need to see Alison taken home. I don't want to leave and have to come back up here again. This city's given me enough gyp the past couple of days and I don't want any reason to come back here. I'm a Manchester lad through and through. There's something about Newcastle that stinks of failure and mental deficiency. Case in point, the last good band to come out of Newcastle was The Animals, and that was over forty fucking years ago. It didn't get any better than that.

Donna's still up here, though. And she's been in the back of my head since I met her. Part of me wants to call her now, but it's too early. That same part wants to make amends for the way we left things. But then, that part of me is too romantic for its own good. I'm told she looked at me in a different way, like she didn't care I was an ex-con, like she actually cared about what happened to me, like I was actually one of the good guys.

But that's all speculation. It's all reading between the lines, two and two making five.

I might call her, I might not. We'll see how it goes. There are things about me I haven't told her, and those things aren't the easiest to bring up in polite conversation. I don't even know if I can talk about them yet. When I got out, word had already spread. Declan looked at me differently, like I was the type to give up his dignity. Like I was the type to take anything as long as it led to an easy life. This coming from a junkie grass. You know you've hit rock bottom when they start looking at you like you're something they stepped in.

But Declan knew that if it hadn't been me, it would've been him. And he wouldn't have lasted five seconds. Dec was a bigger coward than me back then, which is saying something.

When my dad took his hand to the pair of us, Declan was the first to bolt from the house. When he moved to Manchester, he left me to fend for myself and didn't think twice about it.

He once said to me, 'Cal, I couldn't take it, man. One more day and I would've topped myself.'

My dad's voice was full of thick spit. He sounded like he had a cold when he drank and he drank most of the time. Once the strike of '84 was over with, he refused to work. The unions were gone, he said, and there was no such thing as an honest wage anymore. Everything was poisoned, but it didn't stop him sending me and my brother out to work. He'd pour that cash down his neck and take the back of a hairbrush to our faces if we brought it up. Mam knew, but she didn't show it. She couldn't do anything to stop my dad, so what was the point of dwelling on something she couldn't change? She just pretended it never happened.

Then Dad got stupid. His vision blurred one too many times. He didn't realise I was bigger than him.

'Innes.'

So I knocked the fucker out. My first punch thrown in anger. Hit him hard with my left, broke two fingers doing it. And that pain, that burning, grinding pain of shattered bone on bone, it was fucking worth it.

'*Innes.*'

I watched him hit the floor. Watched the blood spill out from his mouth. Watched his eyes roll up into the back of head and thought, *Oh fuck, I just killed my dad.*

A smack on the window jars me awake. My eyes snap open, a whole world of light going through me like electricity. The tape's stopped. I don't know where I am.

Another smack on the window. 'Innes!'

It's Mo.

And through the haze, I think I can make out Alison Tiernan screaming.

FIFTY-THREE

So this were how it panned out, right?

We got there, street were fuckin' deserted. I got out the van and left Baz in there to keep the engine ticking over in case Alison'd fuckin' done us over and sent us to the wrong place. I wouldn't put it past her. She were a sneaky fuckin' bitch. So me and Rossie, we went up to the front door like we was normal lads, just out to pay an early morning visit on a mate of ours and we pressed the doorbell and waited.

There were all this thumping from inside. Someone coming down the stairs. I gave Rossie a look what said, you get your fuckin' blade out now, big boy.

The door opened and I grinned at me sister. She were standing there in her nightie, looking all sexy-like, even if she did have a black eye. I jerked me head at Rossie and said to Alison, 'Where is he?'

'Upstairs,' she said. She had red eyes like she'd been crying.

'Cool.' I grabbed her arm and pulled her in the house with us. Rossie were already up the stairs. I closed the door behind us and followed him up. 'Rob, mate? You wanna come out?'

Silence. Rossie were looking at us to do summat and I looked at Alison. 'Fuck is he?'

'I dunno,' she said.

'He done a bunk?'

'I dunno.'

'You keep an eye on him?'

'He didn't know you were coming,' said me sister.

'Fuck that. Where is he?'

We went in the bedroom and there were the cash in a bag on the bed. Rossie said, 'Fuckin' hell.'

'Yeah,' I said, then to Alison, 'Where is he?'

She were almost in hysterics now – started crying again and her breathing were all over the fuckin' shop. 'I dunno. He was here. I swear, Mo, he was here.'

I let go of her and zipped up the bag just in case Rossie got any funny ideas.

'We got the money, Mo. You got Alison. Let's go,' said Rossie.

'You fuckin' what? Yeah, we got the money and the girl, but where's the cunt what nicked both?'

'Mo –' she said. And I wanted to belt her right then, but she caught it and shut the fuck up.

I went round the bedroom like the proper predator, sniffing about. Looked under the bed, but he weren't there. 'He never left this room is what you're telling us,' I said to Alison.

'I dunno, Mo. I really don't. He was here the last time I checked.'

'You don't know much, do you? So he didn't leave the room. So the fuck's in here somewhere.' I stopped in front of the wardrobe and looked at Rossie. Rossie shook his head. But what Rossie didn't know were that when fuckers are frightened, they do pretty stupid shit.

When I opened the wardrobe doors, two things happened.

First were that I came face to fuckin' face with Rob Stokes. Second were that me mobile went off.

'Y'alright, you daft cunt?' I said to Stokes. He were standing there in his boxers and a T-shirt with 'Kiss Her Goodbye' written on it in all swirly writing. Aye, mate. Kiss Her The Fuck Goodbye, because Mo owns your arse now.

I answered me mobile. It were Innes. I grinned. 'Innes! The *fuck* are you?'

'Morning,' he said. The cunt sounded pleased with himself.

'Where are you?'

'I'm in Heaton.'

'What's the address?' Like the fucker knew where we was. Rossie looked at us, his arms out.

'I hear you got your sister pregnant, Mo,' said Innes.

'What the fuck are we gonna do with him, Mo?' said Rossie.

I waved me hand at Rossie, looked at me sister. I sucked me teeth and watched her eyes start to overflow again. 'You talked to Alison.'

'Is it true?'

'When'd you talk to Alison?'

'I'll take that as a yes, then. So what happens when your dad finds out you've been rolling your own?'

'She's me half-sister.'

'Semantics, mate. She's sixteen, barely fuckin' legal.'

'What's the matter with you? You have a run-in with the law or something?'

And he started whinging on about how some daft fuck knocked him down or summat. I weren't really listening. It all sounded like: *Blah blah fuckin' blah.*

'Where are you? Tell me where you are.'

Rossie beckoned me over to the window. I followed, pulled back the nets and looked down at the road. There he fuckin' were. In that scabby Micra with me paint job all over it. I felt like waving at him. He were leaned back in his seat, staring out the windscreen and gabbing away in me ear.

I was gonna do the cunt, first chance I got. But there were another cunt what needed doing first. Innes laughed in me ear. Lad were going nuts.

'Fuck are you talking about?' I said.

And he went on about how he had it all figured out, like he knew it were Rossie following him an' all that. Oh aye, he were the big fuckin' private dick. Sorry cunt, more like. And I'd had enough of his fuckin' rambling, so I cut him off, turned round and Stokes were gone from the wardrobe.

I ran downstairs, caught the fucker in the hall messing with the door. Punched him in the back of the head and bent me finger-splint doing it. Pain roared through me hand as Rossie came down and pulled Stokes up the hall. His feet went all over the place and I kicked him in the bollocks on the way to the kitchen. Alison at the top of the stairs, crying again. I went up and grabbed her, pulled her down and into the kitchen. Rossie had grabbed a chair, sat Stokes up in it and leathered the cunt hard in the face. Stokes made a noise like a fuckin' pig and I pulled Alison right in so's she could get a better look.

'See that?' I said. 'That's your boyfriend right there.'

She closed her eyes and shook her head. Looked like it were gonna come flying off her fuckin' shoulders. I grabbed her face and pulled it about until she opened them eyes. 'You look, Alison. That's your fuckin' boyfriend. He did a runner. And you're gonna find out what happens to people who try to fuckin' run from me.'

'You said you wouldn't hurt him,' she said. 'You said you wouldn't do owt to him.'

'I lied.' Said to Rossie, 'Give us your butterfly.'

'Mo –'

'*Give us your fuckin' knife.*'

Rossie handed it over. I flipped the blade out and held it up to Alison. 'You keep them eyes open, Sis, or I'll cut your fuckin' eyelids off.'

FIFTY-FOUR

Can't focus, but my hand finds the door and I force it open, stand on trembling legs and Mo's right in my face. He doesn't back off, just looks at me with dull eyes. As my vision comes back, I can see his nostrils flared, the colour in his sunken cheeks.

Then he butts me sharply just above the nose.

A white flash and someone pulls the ground from under me. I go down hard on my arse, my forehead crackling with pain, my mouth hanging open like the stupid bastard I am. I fumble for the side of the car, try to pull myself up, but my head spins too fast. Dizzy as fuck, I can't quite make it. Mo plants a boot in my stomach and I keel forward onto my hands and knees. Before I know it, my gut clenches hard and I spew on the road. Talk about déjà vu.

'I owe you that one, Innes,' he says.

I try to blink through the tears, contain the throbbing in my gut long enough to make out what's going on. Across the street, a fat guy has Alison Tiernan by the wrist. She's in her nightie, barefoot and stumbling, screaming with the cracked voice of someone who's been dragged from her sleep. The fat guy hauls open the passenger door of a white Bedford and pushes her in. She kicks and swears, but once that door slams shut, she contents herself with spitting at the window.

'She had a bag packed,' says Mo.

I cough; it hurts. I spit the bad taste in my mouth at the tarmac.

'Stokes is inside,' he says.

It's difficult to focus, but Mo seems relaxed now he got the head butt out of his system. I pull myself to my feet and slump against the Micra, hold my head back to stem the blood from my nose. 'You found him,' I say.

'He were in there,' he says. 'They're dealing with him right now.'

My mouth doesn't work. It's like I'm drunk again, and it's not a good buzz. Rob can't have been that bloody daft to go over to Alison's and warn her Mo was coming. He's not that thick, surely. For all his faults, I never took the guy to be suicidal.

'He got away. I lost him. He's not in there. You're fuckin' lying.'

Mo draws closer, smiling. His hand snakes up to the back of my neck, grips hard and before I know it, I'm being frogmarched across the road. And this bloke, I've taken him before, I could do it again. But the thing with a head butt is that it messes with your motor functions, throws your balance and perspective out of the window. He lets go as we near the front door, standing to one side. I sway, trying to centre; I look at the ground and focus on his twitching feet.

'Well?' he says.

The house smells damp. The odour's enough to make my gut twitch. 'Well, what?'

The left side of Mo's face ticks into a half-smile. For a moment, I see Morris Tiernan there. 'Go on, Innes. You know you want to.' He places a hand on my shoulder. I want to shake it off, but my head's spinning and I need the support.

'I'll leave you to it,' I say.

'Don't be daft. The party's just started.'

'I think I lost my invitation.'

'You're on the guest list, mate.'

Mo pushes the front door, guides me into the hallway. Too

gloomy to see anything, like a house long deserted. I want to turn back, but I don't have the energy. Somewhere out of sight, I can hear the sound of muffled sobs. As I get to the end of the hall, I make out a door, closed. The sobbing gets louder as Mo pushes it open. Then the sound cuts short.

And in the dim morning light, I see Rob Stokes. Tied to a wooden kitchen chair that was white before someone started beating him, his pants round his ankles, his face a battered mess. He's been sick down the front of his T-shirt which is ripped open at the navel. His head is down; it looks like he's staring at the reddish brown stain between his legs. A stiff breeze blows through the open window, billowing nets and wafting the stench of shit and vomit my way. I cover my nose with one hand.

'Reeks, don't he?' says the fat guy. He walks over to Stokes and pats him on the head. Stokes jerks to one side, a low painful sound escaping his lips. 'Not surprising, like. He had an accident.'

'More than one,' says another guy from the shadows. I can see the shine of black leather. He's holding a butterfly knife in his right hand, absently working the blade in and out of the twin handles.

'Cal, this is Baz and that's Rossie.'

'Kind of a name's Rossie?' I say. Trying to be hard as. Trying to make aggro conversation when there's ice in my veins.

The guy in the black leather jacket says, 'Kind of a name's Cal?'

Stokes raises his head at the sound of my voice. I catch a glint where I think there's an eye, but the rest is obscured by shadow and blood.

'He was here when you arrived,' I say.

'Yeah, we found him upstairs,' says Mo. 'He were hiding in the fuckin' *wardrobe*.'

The stupid things you do when you're scared. Acting like Robin Askwith in a *Confessions* film. Running to your girlfriend when you know she's the reason you're getting fucked in the first place. Taking a job you know is going to end in tears because you're afraid of what'll happen if you don't. Acting the prick with a woman who cares about you, because it's easier than contemplating an honest relationship. Spinning yourself a cunt's yarn to hide the truth.

'Way Sis tells it, he were here all the time,' says Mo. I look across at him. Yeah, he knows. He takes a step towards me. 'The way Sis tells it, he got a phone call and woke her up, started acting all weird.'

Stokes mumbles something. Saliva drips onto his chest, glistening red.

'He went for the cash.' Then Mo turns and shares a giggle with Rossie and Baz. 'And it were sitting there on the fuckin' bed, can you believe it?'

'Priceless,' says Rossie, letting out this laugh that sounds like a horny pig. Baz joins in, laughing through his teeth like someone throttling a snake. It's a proper zoo in here.

I try to smile but my face hurts too much.

'But what I don't get is, who called Rob?'

'Fucked if I know,' I say, but I blurt it out.

Mo pauses, then looks at Stokes. 'Yeah, well, we'll find out, won't we, Rob?'

Stokes doesn't answer but his legs tremble. He shifts position in the chair, sniffs hard.

'I think you better get back to Manchester,' says Mo.

'You think so.'

'Yeah.' His lips are thin. 'Yeah, I think you should go home. You look like you need a good night's sleep, mate.'

Mo slaps me hard on the back and a bolt of pain runs up to the nape of my neck. I flinch, but other than that, I'm rock steady. Too busy staring at Stokes, wondering why he would stick around so long, wondering why he didn't tell me that Alison was in bed next to him and trying not to look too hard at the answers because it would hurt too much.

Yeah. Stokes was there with Alison. And they were getting ready to go when Mo came knocking. Which meant Stokes was delayed somehow. Alison, maybe, digging her heels in, stalling him until Mo came round.

'I want to speak to Alison,' I say. 'I've still got some questions for her.'

'Nah, y'alright, Cal. You're done up here. You're finished. Well done. Nowt more to do.'

'*Rien à faire*,' says Baz.

'Bazza's part French,' says Rossie.

'Yeah, the part that don't wash,' says Mo.

I turn and walk out of the room as the laughter hits its peak, Stokes left half-dead in the middle of it all. Through the hallway, out onto the street. I light an Embassy and draw the smoke deep into my lungs as the speed freak pushes his way into the house. In the passenger seat of the van, Alison watches me with lazy eyes. I watch her straight back.

If she had any sense, she'd be running down the street right now, but she stays put. But then, why should she run? It's worked out exactly the way she planned it.

Alison realised it didn't matter what she did, she was going to get caught. And when Stokes got my phone call, made for the money, that was the kicker. She couldn't trust him to be a willing patsy anymore, so she decided on damage limitation. Mo was coming, she might as well be here when he does, crying rape and making Stokes out to be the bad guy. Any chance I had of saving the dealer was scuppered the moment he went for the money.

Always the gambler.

I stand in the middle of the street and blow smoke at the van. She turns her head, looks at herself in the wing mirror. I walk back to my Micra, glance at the cricket bat, dotted with dried blood.

What the fuck.

I reach in for the Maxi and limp across to the van as fast as my aching legs allow. Build up speed, breeze against my face, and swing that bat straight into the windscreen, Alison screams in fright; I find a roar tear its way out of me. The windscreen spider-webs, then the bat breaks through, glances off the dashboard. I pull the Maxi free, aim at the left wing mirror and take it off with one swing. It bounces off the tarmac. Then the right mirror. Then I change hands and stab out the headlights. Once, twice, glass spilling onto the road. Pain burning my limbs as I batter the front of the van with all my strength. I knock the rest of the windscreen into the cab, Alison screeching behind her hands.

I can't touch her. If I lay this Maxi across her, I won't stop until she's dead.

Somewhere above the thumping in my ears, I can hear the sound of a car. Out the corner of my eye, I can see it too. A police car. Fucking sneaked up on me. One uniform already getting out now.

Good.

I'm about to open my mouth to say something when the copper speaks. 'You put down the bat, alright, pal?'

'I'm alright, I'm okay. You've got to go in there.' I point at the house with the bat. And I can't talk properly, feels like my lungs are on fire. Too much exertion, too little time to recuperate. 'You go in that house, man. You go in there now.'

'You just put the bat down, son.'

Behind him, the other uniform is trying to calm Alison down with a voice like anal sex. He's a squat bastard, loving every moment of it. I flare. 'Don't fuckin' talk to her, mate. She's a *liar*.'

'It's okay,' says the uniform. 'It's alright. You just put that bat down and we'll sort this out.'

'You want to sort it out, you go in that fuckin' house and you see what they did.'

'I will,' he says. Drawing closer now, his hands out. 'Just drop the bat.'

'Fuck's sake, man.' I toss the bat to one side. It clatters onto the tarmac.

Then he's on me, faster than my brain can work. My hands slapped behind my back, the cold bite of metal on wrist. I catch a whiff of cheap deodorant. It makes me jerk in his grip, shout, 'You want to find out what's going on, you go in that fuckin' house, you go in there right the fuck now, you bunch of daft fuckin' cunts.'

The copper's elbow knocks me in the side of the head, throws me off. And he did it on purpose.

'I got him, Chris. Get the girl.'

'You're making a mistake, man.'

'We'll see.' His hand on my shoulder, one on my wrists, guiding me towards the car. 'You been drinking?'

I can't speak. My tongue feels thick in the back of my throat.

'I'm going to ask you to take a breathalyser. Do you understand what I'm saying?'

'I understand what you're fuckin' saying, but you've got *no* idea what's going on here.'

He presses my head down as I slip into the back of the police car. My wrists feel bloodless, every muscle in my back raging tense and painful. All the injuries from the last couple of days – every knock, crack, punch and kick – come rushing through my system like a bad trip. The breath rips out of me, and it tastes like smoke.

I gaze heavy-lidded at the dashboard of the police car.

Then I see Alison being interviewed by the two uniforms. She's shaking her head, looking at the ground. Her cheeks are streaked with tears and dirt. Mo emerges from the house in the middle of a stride. When he sees the two coppers, he looks my way and a smile makes his mouth jump for a second. Then he slips an arm around Alison's shoulders and looks concerned as the diplomatic uniform asks him questions. Some nodding and Alison looks up at Mo. I feel like throwing up; she's playing this to the hilt.

Rossie comes out of the house, quickly pocketing the butterfly knife when he sees the police. Then his face cracks open when he sees the van. The thing must be his pride and joy; it looks like someone punched him in the throat. I savour that face he's pulling. I got some revenge there, I think. Teach him to mess with my car.

The squat copper gets in the driver's side and watches me in the rear view.

'What you smiling at?'

'Nowt.'

'Cause you got nowt to smile about, man. You want to pray he doesn't press charges.'

The diplomatic copper approaches the car, gets in. 'Domestic.'

'Christ, how old is she? You want to watch you don't get sent down for kiddie-fiddling,' the squat copper says to me.

'What about him?' I say.

'None of my business.'

'Well, if you were after ruining the guy's van, you got the wrong one,' says the diplomat.

The squat copper brays out a laugh. 'Not your day, is it?'

'Nah,' I say. 'I got the right van. I definitely got the right fuckin' van.'

It's about the only thing I've done right so far.

FIFTY-FIVE

'Here, officer, I want to thank you an' that. This were a bad lot, all this, 'specially this early in the morning. Lad must've had a few too many.'

There were me, like, showing plenty teeth and playing the good citizen. Hey, it were fun to be the good guy for once. And Christ knew, I'd been put out by that fucker Innes from the get-go. Time he got-gone.

'Don't mention it,' said this busy behind the desk. 'I take it you're not pressing charges?'

'Nah, I told the lads before. Let's face it, a bloke has too much to drink, he gets to feeling lonely and aching downstairs, he wants his old lass back. But then, she ain't exactly old, know what I mean?'

'Well, we'd like to ask her a few questions, if that's alright.'

'Nah, don't worry about it.'

'There's the statutory rape charge —'

'Mate, she's sixteen, she's legal.'

'Yes, but we've got to follow up.'

'Here, listen, button it a sec and listen to us. I don't know what this lad Innes and her got up to when they was going out together, and it's really none of my business, you get me? But the point is she's safe now. We'll sort it out when we get back to Manchester.'

'You're going to Manchester?'

'It's where we live, innit, Sis?'

Alison nodded like a good girl.

'We'll need an address,' said the copper.

'Not a problem.' I gave him an address. It were a wank shack off Lime Street. Let 'em come looking. Like they didn't have enough crime up here, they'd come after me and Alison for nowt. 'Listen, we got to be going and everything. Thanks again, mate. Nice to see you're keeping Newcastle's streets clean an' that.'

The copper looked at us like I were being funny. And I weren't, not really. I were glad his lot were about. Else I probably would've murdered Innes with me bare hands, splint or no fuckin' splint.

Me and Alison left the station. Rossie were standing by the van, his face all screwed up. 'How'm I gonna explain this to Jimmy?' he said.

'Tell him the truth.'

'He'll kill us.'

'Then get it fixed.'

'With what, man? I was skint when I came up here. I didn't make no money in the meantime, did I?'

'Course you did,' I said. 'There's a bag of it in the van.'

Got Alison in the van, and with me and Baz and Rossie in there, it were a bit of a squeeze. I told Baz to get driving, we was going back to the house for Alison's clothes. When we was on the road, I fished around for me mobile, called The Wheatsheaf. 'Brian, put Dad on.'

'Who's this?' said Brian.

'I called him Dad, who the fuck else would it be? Now get running, fat lad. I need to talk to him now.'

Took a couple minutes. Then me dad came on the phone. 'Where are you?'

'On our way back, Dad. I got the girl.'

'You get the money?'

'Some of it. Stokes spent a couple stacks.'

'Where's Innes?'

Always asking after that cunt. 'He's with the busies.'

'You what?'

'He went nuts, smashed up Rossie's van. Got nicked.'

'Right. Which station?'

I gave him the address. 'Why d'you want to know?'

'I'll get Clayton up there.'

'For fuck's –'

'Where's Stokes?' said Dad.

'He's out of the picture.'

'You kill him?'

'Nah.'

'Don't kill him. Leave him. Just bring Alison back and we'll have a talk.'

'Dad –'

'Leave Stokes alone. And get your arse back to Manchester.'

Dad hung up. I put me mobile back in me pocket. Aye, he were losing it. Time were, he'd have a fucker like Stokes buried in five seconds flat. He'd have me cut him to ribbons and scatter what were left to the fuckin' wind. What I'd said to Rossie and Baz in the pub, I meant it. One day, somebody'd come up to us and ask us was I interested in going into business with a professional outfit? And I'd say yeah, but then they'd say, you wanna join up, you gotta do your dad.

And I'd wait in The Wheatsheaf, watch me dad drink his black and smoke his Rothmans, keep meself pumped with whizz and wait until he went to the bogs and then I'd sneak up on the cunt with a claw hammer and batter him until his brains made it hard to swing. And then I'd go out in the bar, hammer at me side and I'd yell at the crowd to come and have a fuckin' go, the king were dead, and I were large and in charge.

But that'd have to wait.

First I had to clean up me sister's fuckin' mess.

FIFTY-SIX

A holding cell and a mattress that cuts you if you don't lay on it right. The smell of antiseptic and whatever they use to kill the fleas the late night drunks bring in. Someone's written SHIT FUCK CUNT on the wall, and I can't help but notice they've taken time to chisel it into the brickwork. You'd have thought they'd come up with something profound.

The police arrived thanks to a conscientious Neighbourhood Watcher, drawn to the nets by the commotion in the street so early in the morning. Apparently a guy going apeshit with a cricket bat isn't a normal occurrence in Heaton, and this grass thought the police should sort it out.

I've gone through it enough since they left me in here. The breathalyser didn't help matters; it showed me way over the limit. Which I probably am. I can't remember the last time I drank something that wasn't alcoholic. So the police get this idea in their heads, here's a guy with a cricket bat demolishing a van with a girl inside, they think it's a domestic. It's probably the way it was reported and I doubt Alison and Mo did anything to dissuade them from that, especially considering there was a bloke choking his last in the house.

If they'd just checked it out. If they'd just seen beyond what was in front of them. If they'd just fucking believed me instead of being the bull-headed pricks they were . . .

My Nan said, 'If "ifs" and "buts" were berries and nuts, then squirrels would never go hungry.'

And she'd know all about nuts.

Ach, it's probably for the best. If I'd stayed there, I don't know what would have happened. From the look on Baz's face, I'd be cut up and bleeding to death right about now. So there's something to be thankful for. It's his face that's kept me smiling all the time I've been in here. I'd know exactly, but they took my watch.

I wonder how long they're going to keep me in here. I've had no contact for a while now, and fear's started to prick at the back of my mind. They keep me in here much longer, then they think they have something on me. Something's cropped up.

Christ, I hope George hasn't spilled his guts.

I get off the bunk and stop in the middle of the cell. No idea what to do, where to go. Being back in a cage is sending my memory into overdrive. I can't go back to prison. I gave George a bundle to keep his mouth shut.

But then, he's a rat and he's got a survival instinct. And how do I know he didn't lie to me last night?

Because you were beating the shit out of him with a cricket bat, Cal.

Ah, Jesus. That Maxi. Still got blood on it. If George was doped up, or if he was just plain sick of the pain, he'd talk. He talked to me. And I get picked up for a domestic with a cricket bat in the same twenty-four hours; it doesn't take a genius to put it together.

You'd think I'd know better by now.

I haven't been charged, though. They're probably letting me sweat it out in here, get myself worked up so I'll tell them anything rather than go back inside. Once they find out I've got form, they'll throw that in my face. They'll make me feel guilty, they'll bring up Paulo, how I disappointed him. They'll go easy on me if I just cooperate.

'We know you're not to blame here, Cal. You just tell us how you got into this and we'll see what we can do.'

See what we can do. Working for Morris Tiernan, it's like the mark of Cain. Invisible to everyone but the police and fellow criminals. The criminals keep the respect coming, the fear flashing behind their eyes. The police look at it as a beautiful opportunity, a way to make their names. This is one of Tiernan's, this is the one that might roll over. The fucking busies pray for people like me, the ones so scared they'll say anything to keep out of prison, the ones that have that wee snippet of information that'll put the big bosses behind bars. They look at me the way Ness looked at Capone's accountant.

I can't keep thinking about this. It's what they want me to do. I'm innocent until proven otherwise. Everything I did, it was because I had to. I didn't have any other choice. I sit back on the bunk and stare at the cell door.

Donna doesn't want to see me hurt. As if self-preservation wasn't important enough, there's a part of me that doesn't want to disappoint her. Even though I'll probably never see her again.

If the probation services find out about this, I'm recalled. Back inside. And it doesn't matter if I'm guilty or not. Just the appearance of an illegal act is enough to get their knee to jerk.

Hanging out with known criminals, those that put me inside in the first place.

Not cooperating with the Manchester Met on a manslaughter case in which I'm the prime suspect.

GBH with a GM Maxi cricket bat.

Criminal damage to a van and attempted kidnap.

And all this with a bloodstream that's a hundred per cent proof.

They won't prove half of it, but I deserve my old cell back.

I haven't been able to call anyone yet, and I don't know

who I'd call if I got the chance. I don't have a lawyer anymore, and I doubt Paulo would help. Not now. I'm left alone here with no idea what's going on.

Someone's coming up the corridor. The kind of boots a copper wears, the steady, officious sound of someone who knows those footsteps put the shits up people. They stop in front of my cell door. The clatter of the hatch coming down, then keys in the lock.

'Your brief's here,' says a uniform who's built like a cathedral and has the face of a priest.

'I don't have a brief.'

The uniform looks startled for a moment. Then he says, 'Well, he's here.'

'You got the wrong cell, officer.'

'You're Innes.'

'Uh-huh.'

'Then your brief's here.'

I get to my feet, brush myself down and follow the copper to a waiting interview room.

FIFTY-SEVEN

Stokes were out of it when we got back to the house. I told Baz to go and grab Alison's things from upstairs and I went into the kitchen, stood in front of Stokes and lit a ciggie. Smoked it halfway down and watched the bastard squirm in his seat. His head came back and he tried to look at us with his one good eye.

'You're a lucky cunt, Rob,' I said.

His neck couldn't keep his head up. It dropped down. His shoulders started heaving, like he were crying. Poof.

'I'm gonna let you live. You remember that. Anyone asks, you tell 'em Mo Tiernan let you live. I'm fair.'

Stokes said nowt, opened his mouth. Closed it again. I went up to him, untied his hands and gave him me ciggie. He coughed it out onto the floor. I didn't pick it up. Had all this spittle and shite on it. Fuck it, let it burn the place down.

'Get yourself cleaned up, Rob. Else you won't be able to pull any more fuckin' teenyboppers, know what I mean?'

Went out into the hall, and there were Baz with an Asda bag overflowing with Alison's stuff.

'Anything she wanted in particular?' said Baz.

'Give your head a shake, Baz.'

When I got back in the van, Alison were staring at us. I chucked the bag at her. 'There you go.'

'Did you kill him?' she said.

'Nah, I spared him.'

'*Spared* him. Fuck's sake, Mo, you think you're a proper hard arse, don't you?'

'I can go in and finish the job, you want me to.'

'He'd done nowt to you.'

'He'd done plenty to us. He'd fucked me sister, stole me money.'

'It wasn't your money. You think this is about that? You could've left him alone, Mo. But nah, you have to go proving you're the hard arse.'

'Dad knows what I am.'

'Dad reckons you're a fuck-up,' she said. Her eyes was blazing now. 'Dad said to me that he reckons you're a fuck-up.'

'When'd you talk to Dad?'

'After I called you, you daft bastard. When I told him you were up here. Told him what you said an' all. Told him everything. Told him it was you what got me pregnant in the first place, told him the whole fuckin' story.'

I scratched me cheek. Sat in silence for a bit. Then I said, 'What'd he say?'

'He said that you were a fuck-up and he'd deal with you when you got back.'

'He said that?'

'Yeah.'

'He said that.'

'You fuckin' deaf? Yeah, he said that.'

I grabbed her by the hair and bounced her fuckin' head off the dashboard. When I pulled her back up, her face were all bloody. She breathed red bubbles. She gabbed on. I twatted her against the dash again, harder this time. Wanted to keep going, but when I pulled her back, she'd shut her fuckin' yap. Let go of her hair and smoothed it down, looked out the windscreen.

'You show me some fuckin' respect,' I said.

She were weeping. I looked at Rossie. He were staring at me like I'd just broke her neck right in front of him.

'She's me sister, Rossie. Call it sibling rivalry. Now stick her in the back of the van before she fucks us off even more.'

FIFTY-EIGHT

I know this guy. I've seen him before. He's a shitheel with all morals of a sewer rat, but with the bonus of personal hygiene thrown in. He's an old-school gang lawyer, the kind of local lad who had his tuition paid and his accent softened in order to represent the best interests of his criminal clientele. I know him, because I was offered him once before when I was looking at a stretch inside. The stretch I ended up doing because I turned him down flat.

Derek Clayton, LLB and wannabe QC. If it wasn't for Morris Tiernan, Clayton would be practising personal injury and advertising on Living TV in a battered ill-fitting suit. As it turns out, he's wearing something tailored and expensive, the kind of suit that doesn't wear its label on its sleeve. The kind of suit I'll never be able to afford. He cries out for the legit gig, but working for Morris Tiernan has aborted that baby, so he contents himself with the cash.

Clayton extends a hand to me as I enter the interview room and I take it. A handshake means nothing to a lawyer and his hands are too dry. We're alone in here, a pre-interview briefing. Which doesn't bode well.

It doesn't mean I'm happy to see him, though.

'Sorry it took me so long to get up here,' he says.

'I didn't expect to see you.'

'Mr Tiernan asked me to come up and see what I could do.'

'Good, then you can leave right now.'

'You're in serious trouble, Cal.'

'A domestic isn't serious trouble.'

'I'm not talking about that.'

'Then what the fuck are you talking about?'

Clayton pushes his specs up to his eyes and raises his eyebrows all at the same time. It's like a stiff breeze blew his face up. 'The hospital has a duty to report incidents involving young men being dumped in A & E with broken legs. You're lucky the police here haven't added it up. You using the same cricket bat on Baz's van hasn't done much to help you out, though.'

'Ah, fuck off. You're making this up.' All bluster and bullshit.

'If I'm making this up, I'm doing a bloody good job,' he says.

'So what've they got me on? GBH? Vandalism?'

'Nothing at the moment. But if George wants to press charges, yes, you could end up back inside.'

'What about Rossie? He want to press charges? What about Alison?'

'Alison's back home now.'

'Yeah, I thought as much. And I bet she didn't say a fuckin' word about her boyfriend in the kitchen, did she?'

'The question is, what are you going to say?'

'You don't want to know.'

'I do.'

'Then the answer's fuck off. How's that?'

He taps the end of his pen against the notepad in front of him. Looks down at the paper, then up at me. 'You shouldn't talk to me like that, Cal. I'm here to help.'

'You're here to make sure I keep my mouth shut.'

'It's not just Newcastle, you know. There's a copper in Manchester baying for your blood.'

'Let him fuckin' bay. I didn't do it. And it's got nothing to do with what's happened up here. I don't need you, Mr Clayton. I don't need Morris Tiernan checking up on me, either. I'll tell the police whatever the fuck I want to. Because someone's got to pay for this.'

'And you're willing to go back inside for nothing?'

'I'll end up back inside anyway, Mr Clayton. Donkey's sure I did Dennis Lang.'

'Dennis Lang was stabbed, Cal. From what I know, it was a short blade. I'm sure DS Donkin could be pointed in the right direction.'

My junkie client. 'He came back?'

'A man like that, he wouldn't like leaving his weapon behind.'

I sit down, try to get my head round this. Because if Dennis Lang was killed by that smackhead, then I could have saved myself a load of grief. I could have gotten Donkey off my back no bother whatsoever, I could have solved a case instead of making the situation ten times worse. It wouldn't have saved a life, but it would have made me feel better. And at the end of the day, right now, that's all I care about. Surviving as the good guy. Which Derek Clayton is insisting won't happen without his help.

'You know Donkin's been making your mate's life hell down in Salford,' says Clayton.

'He's just stirring shit.' I lean forward, my elbows on the table.

'Sometimes that's all the council needs. Just a scent. You know that.'

'You threatening me?'

'I'm telling you what the situation is, Callum. As your lawyer, I'd suggest you listen to me.'

'As my lawyer? I didn't ask you to come here.'

'Mr Tiernan did.'

'Would that be big Morris or his screw-up son?'

Clayton sighs and drops the pen on the pile of paper in front of him. He leans back in his chair and regards me. 'If you've got much more of this, I suggest you let it all out now, Cal. As much as I don't like being your therapist, if it gets you to a point where you understand that there is no way out without my help and the help of Morris Tiernan, it's worth it.'

I have plenty of clever things to say, but none of them come out of my mouth: 'Fuck off.'

He sucks his teeth, runs the spit around the inside of his mouth and picks up his pen, slots it into an inside pocket. 'You don't want my help, that's fine. I'll say you've changed your mind. But if these lads decide to dig beyond the topsoil, Cal, you're in the shit. And if you decide to spill your guts about what's been going on, I can't vouch for your safety. You're still on probation, aren't you?'

Again, zingers all over the place, but the one that sticks is the one I say. 'Fuck off.'

'You're liable to recall, you know that. They don't have to give you a reason,' he says. Clayton stands, grabs the papers on the table and tucks them under one arm. 'You're the tough guy. We'll see how tough you are after a second stretch.'

Clayton looks at me like he looks at every case he gets from Tiernan. I'm judged before I get a chance to plead not guilty. He sees me as Tiernan's hatchet man. Just like everyone else. The way I treated Donna, so fucking selfish when I want. The way George cried out and I gave him more of a beating. Christ, that wasn't the way I was supposed to be. That wasn't the way I thought I'd act.

And yeah, if my PO gets wind of this, he could recommend a recall, and I'd be even further up shit creek. I could be hard about it, demand prison as a right and a respite, turn over the Tiernans.

But what could I tell the police? There's nothing to tie Rob Stokes to Morris Tiernan, just Mo. And that wouldn't be enough to buy me safety. Mo would end up getting off because he'd have Wonderboy Clayton here representing him. Morris would have an airtight alibi all worked out for his son, no matter how sick the lanky bastard was. The family that lays together stays together.

So then what? I would end up back on the spur with a price on my head. I wouldn't last day one. Someone would carve me up like Dennis Lang, and I'd end up with a pauper's grave, hired mourners at the service.

Clayton's about to knock on the door to leave when I stand up.

Because a deal with the devil is better than no deal at all.

ACKNOWLEDGEMENTS

In chronological order, thanks go to Victoria Esposito-Shea, Jim Blue, G. Miki Hayden, Megan Powell, Kevin Burton Smith, Gerald So and Anthony Neil Smith for letting Cal Innes kip on the floors of Handheld Crime, Hardluck Stories, Shred Of Evidence, Thrilling Detective and Plots With Guns respectively. To Ken Bruen and Craig Macdonald for believing in Mo when few did. Also the dual threats of Dave White and Jim Winter for keeping me on my toes, Allan Guthrie for being a perfect first editor and constant source of inspiration, friendship and support, Alison Rae (chain-smoking cosmetics expert extraordinaire) and Neville Moir at Polygon for having dubious taste in fiction, Marc Gerald for pushing me to write that 'bigger book' and for putting up with my insecurities. And most of all, thanks to my wife, who keeps my ego in check and gives me much more than I'll ever admit.